Fire and Rain

LAUREN DANE

ELLORA'S CAVE
ROMANTICA®
WWW.ELLORASCAVE.COM

An Ellora's Cave Publication

www.ellorascave.com

Fire and Rain

ISBN 9781419964503
ALL RIGHTS RESERVED.
Fire and Rain Copyright © 2007 Lauren Dane
Edited by Ann Leveille.
Cover art by Syneca.

Electronic book publication September 2007
Trade paperback publication 2011

FIRE AND RAIN

🙰

Dedication

&

*As always, no book would be possible without the love
and support of my fabulous, long-suffering and ever
patient husband. Thank you, Ray, for being the best
husband a girl could ask for.*

*Thank you to Ann Leveille, my wonderful editor, whom
I've been fortunate enough to have been with since the
very beginning!*

*Assorted thanks go to my beta readers one and all, my
readers and friends who are on this wonderful journey
with me and to Laura Bradford, who loved this series and
this Pack from the start.*

Trademarks Acknowledgement

&

The author acknowledges the trademarked status and
trademark owners of the following wordmarks mentioned in
this work of fiction:

Canucks: Vancouver Hockey Club Ltd

Chutes and Ladders: Hasbro, Inc.

Doritos: Frito-Lay North America, Inc

Embassy Suites: Hilton Hospitality, Inc

Goldfish: PF Brands, Inc

Maple Leafs: Maple Leaf Sports & Entertainment LTD

Chapter One

ℬ

Rain smiled as she bustled from the kitchen to the dining room holding several plates. It had been a good morning at The Black Cat Café and Coffee House. When she added the tips she'd earned to what she'd made over the last week she'd be able to buy those sable brushes she'd been drooling over.

She dropped off her plates at their designated tables, topped off coffee and water where it needed it and looked up to catch one of her regulars come in and take a seat. She waved as she approached his table.

"Morning, Shane. How are you today?"

"Hey, Rain. I'm good. And what's up in your neighborhood today?"

"Not much, the usual breakfast crowd." Looking down at him, she cocked her head. "Hmmm. Let's see, two slices of whole grain, three egg scramble, latte with honey and soy bacon?" It wasn't like she was performing a great feat of precognition or anything, he ate the same exact thing every time he came in.

He laughed. "Sounds good! Hey, I wanted to tell you that The Holt Gallery down in Pioneer Square is looking for up-and-comers for a series of shows they want to do to highlight new artists. You should take your portfolio down there."

Her eyes widened and hope burst through her. "Seriously? Oh wow, thanks for the heads-up."

"You're really good. I'd hate to see you lose a chance like this. You're exactly the kind of artist they're looking for. This could be a great opportunity for you and for The Holt."

She squeezed his shoulder. "Thanks, it means a lot. It really does." Before she got teary she took a deep breath and focused on her job. "Let me go and get this started." She held up the ticket. "Although I'm sure Alex saw you when you came in and is making your breakfast as we speak." Winking, she tossed her braid back and headed toward the kitchen where, yes, Alex, the cook and owner, was already scrambling the eggs and the bread was toasting. She loved the small café, it was warm and friendly and her customers felt more like friends and family than clientele.

Rain Foster had landed in Seattle the year before having walked — *run* — away from a life of restrictions. A life where she was destined to be one thing and one thing only, a pretty accessory on a man's arm.

Her father had already made the choice for her, the son of a "business associate" who was also destined to be in the family business. Of course while some had family businesses where they repaired watches, she'd known most of her life that her father was a major boss in a crime syndicate.

There was no way she would have been allowed to be an artist. Heck, her father only let her go to college because that's what the daughters of all of his cronies did. Before they got married off to each others' sons, that is. Then they'd sit at the club all day and drink, oh and occasionally play golf or tennis — *wouldn't pay to let yourself get out of shape*. In between they'd have children to continue the cycle. The boys to take over for their fathers and the girls to marry and continue to have more children.

Thank god her mother cared about her wishes and dreams. Thank god her mother had helped her by squirreling away money over the course of the last few years Rain, who used to be Julia, lived there. That money got Rain as far away from her father and his life as possible and she had her own life for the first time. Her mother's love bought her that freedom.

Though dangerous, her mother waited for Rain's call at a pay phone near her regular beauty salon back home. Still, Rain hadn't told her mother where she was for both their sakes. She did know from her mother that her father had been livid, still was as a matter of fact, but apparently felt that she'd come back when she got poor.

Her father was wrong because she wasn't going back at all. Not ever. Poor was one thing—it did suck—but she still had some money from her mother squirreled away and knowing she had something to fall back on in an emergency helped.

She was determined to make her painting a success. For now she shared a large warehouse space in Queen Anne with two other people and she had lots of free time to paint and enough money from her waitressing job to buy canvas and paint and to pay the bills.

Shaking herself out of her reverie with a sigh, she grabbed Shane's order and his latte to take to his table. The lively chimes over the door sounded right as she turned. Smiling, she looked to see who'd come in.

Instead of one of her usual customers, she found herself looking at two of the largest men she'd ever seen and *my goodness weren't they just the alpha male specimens?* Her mouth dried up and her heart leapt into her throat.

Her eyes slowly made the circuit up one and down the other. They were a visual feast. One of them had shoulder-length hair the color of wheat, sleepy, sexy amber eyes and was, for want of a more eloquent term, a muscle-bound hunk.

The other though was the kind of man to make any woman melt into a puddle. Dark and mysterious. Brooding even. His nearly waist-length black hair was tied with a leather thong at the nape of his neck. And her fingers itched to touch it. Eyes so brown they looked obsidian took in the room warily. His skin was hard and smooth with an olive tone much like Rain's own. His nose was just a bit crooked, as if it had been broken more than once, and a small scar bisected his left eyebrow. But those small imperfections only seemed to heighten his wild, dangerous beauty. He was tall, although not quite as tall as the blond, but he was muscular and his blue jeans hugged those long legs and tight butt like they were painted on. She wanted to lean against one of the tables and fan herself as she had a nice, long, naughty and possibly illegal in a few states fantasy about him. Whoo boy.

Instead she took a deep breath and approached them before the other servers saw and jumped in. "Good morning. How are you two today? Would you like to sit in here or on the deck?" Her heart skipped a beat when they both gave her their complete attention. But when the dark one smiled slowly at her the hair on the back of her neck stood on end and goose bumps rose along her arms. Holy cow she wanted to lick him.

"The deck please," the blond one said, his voice low and rumbling.

Trying not to gulp like a cartoon character, she grabbed two menus and led them outside to the deck. She motioned to a table in her section. "Why don't you two take a look at the menu?" Electric heat sparked up her arm as the dark one brushed his fingers against her arm when he took the piece of paper from her. "Uh?" She blinked until she remembered what the hell she'd been doing. "Can I start you off with juice or coffee or espresso?"

"Two large orange juices, an Americano with room and a mocha please," the dark one said, never taking his eyes from hers. She felt caught, like she was standing surrounded in warm honey and he was a very big spider. His voice was low and melodic.

"Great," she squeaked out and cleared her throat. "Be right back with those." Before she gave in to the absurd urge to lick him she tore herself away to go grab the drinks.

Laurent Cole stared at the retreating woman and a smile slowly erupted across his face. He watched her long legs, the sway of her ass, the glimpses of the band of flesh between her shirt and jeans. Her long hair reached her waist and was inky black. He wondered what it would feel like wrapped around his fist as he fucked her mouth. His cock hardened to the point of pain at the thought of her mouth, hot and wet, surrounding him, licking and sucking. He moaned softly.

"Laurent?" Andreas asked, amusement clear in his voice.

Laurent turned slowly and faced Andreas, his Alpha and best friend. "It's her, Andreas. She's the one."

"Her? The one?" Andreas repeated, confused for a moment until realization dawned across his face. "You don't mean... She's your Mate?"

"I can feel it. When I first saw her it was as if every cell in my body sang out. Her scent...she just smells perfect. It's like every other female in the world suddenly doesn't count, hell, doesn't even exist. The world just narrowed down to her."

Andreas smiled slowly. "Ah. That's how I felt the first time I saw Kari. It's about time you found her. But you know human women are different." He sighed and Laurent knew he was thinking of his own petite and very pesky wife.

Laurent laughed then and he and Andreas watched as the waitress froze in place and looked their way. "You deserve this. You've served me and the Pack for sixteen years. Kari is going to be as thrilled as I am. Hellie may not be that eager to share but I'm sure you can talk her around."

"I cringe to think about what it will be like—conquering this woman if she's anything like Kari. I'd better take my vitamins," Laurent said, never taking his eyes from the woman in question.

She smiled their way and brought the tray of juice and coffee drinks to them with effortless grace. "Here you go. Juices, fresh squeezed. An Americano with room—here's cream for it, we also have soy milk, rice milk or nonfat milk if you'd prefer—and the mocha. Honey and sugar are right there." She straightened and looked back to their faces. "Do you know what you want?"

"Yes," Laurent said simply.

She waited but he didn't say anything else and she laughed. "Okay, care to share it with me? Hi, your waitress?" Pausing, she caught something out of the corner of her eye and scowled. "I'm sorry, I need to deal with this. I'll be right back," she said, stalking off to where a man lounged, lighting a cigarette dramatically. Laurent and Andreas watched her.

"Leon, why do you do this? Put it out now," she said, hands on her hips.

The short, balding man took a deep drag on the cigarette and then blew the smoke in her face. Her eyebrows shot up in outrage. Wanting to kill the obnoxious man for daring to insult his woman, Laurent stood up, but Andreas put a staying hand on his shoulder. In any case, before he could do anything his woman was a blur of action. She grabbed the asshole, who tried to shove her off. Using the force of his movement, she twisted his arm, pushing it high up behind his back and shoving him out the door. She even managed to pull on his ear as she got him outside.

"You are a very maladjusted individual. Did your mother raise you that way? I bet she didn't. Get out, Leon, and don't come back. You're barred. If I see you in here again I'll kick your scrawny ass from here to Portland." With a satisfied hmpf she closed the door in his face.

The whole place erupted in applause and she took a comical bow. "Back to your food now, nothing to see here, folks." Laughing, she went back out to the deck where Laurent still stood, his admiration and the need to protect her warring inside him.

"Sorry about that. He's been a problem for a few weeks. So do you know what you want?"

"Are you all right?" Laurent asked, concerned and furious.

She smiled. "Oh of course."

"Yes, you did look like you could handle yourself quite ably." Andreas tugged on Laurent, pulling him back to his chair. "Give me the western omelet with two slices of sourdough."

She looked to Laurent who cleared his throat. Seeing her in action made him drunk with her. She was magnificent. "What do you recommend?"

"Well what do you like? Are you a vegetarian or vegan? Do you like eggs? Big meat eater?"

"Yes I like eggs and yes I eat meat."

"The omelets are very good, Alex is a whiz. I had some of the smoked ham this morning before we opened and it was yummy. You can have the ham and eggs. Comes with two eggs done any style you like, toast and three pancakes. Or you can have the western omelet. The waffles are really good too. My personal favorite are the strawberry waffles with bacon — there's just something heavenly about the way bacon tastes when it touches maple syrup or strawberries but I'm weird so don't mind me." Her eyes danced with amusement but there was a sadness there too, it touched him deeply.

"I'll have the strawberry waffles with bacon then. Six slices though, I'm very hungry."

She took the menus from them. "You got it."

When she'd gone back inside Andreas began to laugh quietly.

"What?" Laurent growled, feeling a bit more like himself.

"You, my brother, are smitten."

"Yes," he said, smiling again. "I do believe I am."

"It's good to see. It's time to have someone of your own, someone to love and cherish. You've spent four years protecting my Mate and my children. Sixteen years protecting me. I haven't seen you interested in a woman like this. Not ever. It's time to start your own family."

Laurent simply nodded. He loved Andreas, Kari and their children very much. But Andreas was right, it was time to have it for himself.

"Rain, who are the hunks out on the deck? I'll trade you tables," another server, Alice, said as she watched them dreamily.

Rain snorted. "Don't think so! The blond one is wearing a wedding ring and the dark one is, well, mine. At least while they're here," she added with a laugh.

She checked back on her other tables, refilling coffee and juice, and Shane left, leaving a large tip behind. "Don't forget about The Holt. Call me if you need any help choosing pieces to put in your portfolio."

"Oh really? I'd appreciate that a lot."

Shane was just taking off in his career. He was a painter and also did large sculpture and multimedia works. He knew how hard it was to get a career off the ground and he'd been really supportive of Rain. They'd flirted a lot and up until tall, dark and sexy walked in she'd always been sad Shane had a girlfriend.

"It's no problem. I mean it. You know my number. Call me if you need help." He smiled.

She hugged him and kissed his cheek. "Thanks so much!"

He laughed and waved as he left and she headed to the kitchen to pick up the orders for her handsome men on the deck.

"Did you see that? He touched my woman!" Laurent growled.

"She's not your woman yet."

"She is, she just doesn't know it," Laurent said smugly.

She brought out their food and placed it before them. "Enjoy. Can I get you anything else?"

"Yes, as a matter of fact. Would it be possible for me to have your phone number?" Laurent said, feeling awkward all of a sudden. He wasn't used to this sort of thing. Women usually approached him. More than that, he couldn't say he'd cared one way or another about any particular woman before. What this one felt and did was important to him.

"How do I know you aren't an ax murderer or something?" she asked teasingly.

"I give you my word that I am not an ax murderer," Laurent said smiling, making an "x" across his heart. "Anyway, I bet ax murderers don't eat strawberry waffles."

Rain laughed at that, hesitating as she thought. Laurent willed her to agree. "Well. I don't usually do this but since you did try the strawberry waffles on my recommendation you do show some taste." She wrote her phone number down on a sheet in her order pad and tore it off, handing it to him. "I'm Rain Foster."

Laurent stood, towering over her, and took her hand, kissing her knuckles softly. Her scent sang through his senses, tightening his gut, making him dizzy with need for her. "Rain? That's a very pretty name. I'm Laurent, Laurent Cole. I'm pleased to meet you."

She raised an eyebrow at that and he sat back down. Andreas cleared this throat. Without looking at his friend, Laurent just waved a hand in his direction. "Oh and this is Andreas Phinney. He's married." Andreas threw back his head and laughed at that.

"Nice to meet you both. I've got to get back to work. Enjoy your breakfast. I'll be by in a bit to see if you need anything else." With a small wave she headed back inside, the long rope of her dark hair swinging from side to side down her back.

"Lackwit! Why did you laugh?" Laurent grumbled but his bad mood was softened when he tasted the waffles. She'd been right, they were indeed quite delicious and the bacon with the sweetness of the waffles and fruit was perfect, as she'd promised.

"You'll have to woo her now. You can't have a situation like mine. It was hell to have Kari so angry at me when Michael bit her. Don't rush her. Human women need time. It's not like they meet werewolves every day."

Laurent snorted. "Yes well, I can certainly learn from all of your errors, can't I?"

Andreas punched his arm with a teasing growl. "At least you won't be fawning over Kari anymore."

Laurent snorted but his eyes never left Rain. "Your little mate is such a pleasure to look at. I can't say I plan to stop. But while I will continue to enjoy her putting you through your paces, I've got my own bundle of feminine trouble now."

Andreas grunted as he ate his breakfast. "I can't wait to see her knock you down a few pegs."

She came back out a few times to clear away plates and to check if they needed anything. When they were done Laurent left a twenty for a tip. "What kind of change back do you need for that?" she said, digging into the apron she wore tied at her waist.

"None, it was a wonderful meal and your service was exceptional."

"Laurent, your bill wasn't even twenty bucks."

He shrugged. "But it was such a pleasure to have you serve it. I'll be calling you, it was a pleasure to meet you, Rain Foster," he said, kissing her hand once more.

* * * * *

When Rain's shift ended at noon she rode her bike back home and eagerly began to examine the photographs of her paintings. She needed to decide which ones she wanted to put in her portfolio to show to The Holt people. She knew how important the choices were and it made her nervous and excited at the same time. If this worked out she'd have her big break.

"Hey, Rain, what's happening?"

Rain looked over at her roommate and pseudo big brother Harrison as he entered the room.

"Shane came in today and told me The Holt is looking for submissions for shows. I'm as nervous as a cat because I'm trying to decide which paintings to show them," she said, looking back through the pictures.

Harrison moved to stand behind her, looking over her shoulder at the pictures arrayed on the table in front of her. "Hmm. Well, you'd be a fool not to submit *Meteor Shower* and *Whirlpool*. I think those two are exactly what the folks who buy from The Holt like to see." He tapped his chin thoughtfully as he looked at the photographs on the table and then walked over to the wall where the canvases leaned. He looked through them for a while before turning back to her. "Add in *Picasso's Dream* and *Crazy Diamond* and for the last *King's Men* will add a nice variety of style. I'd say those five are your strongest pieces by far. Add in some of your other stuff, don't overfill the portfolio though. Not more than ten photographs, don't overwhelm, let your work suck them in."

Rain sighed with relief. "That's what Shane said. I called him twenty minutes ago in a panic. He's going to look over the portfolio before I submit it to The Holt."

Rain's work was awash with color and texture. It was abstract but at the same time it gave a feel, an impression of what she was trying to convey. She liked big natural events and historical figures. She'd just finished *Crazy Diamond* two days prior. It was big, much bigger than her usual stuff, the colors were bold, reds and silvers and blues and blacks. She had a good feeling about it.

"Shane's a good guy. He can be a lot of help to you in the Northwest especially," Harrison said. "And if I'm not mistaken he's got a bit of a crush on you."

Harrison Watts was a photographer and a damned good one. He'd spent fifteen years freelancing for the AP wire doing work in war zones. His girlfriend of eight years had been shot and killed while on assignment in Bosnia and it had gutted him. It had taken him two years to pick up the camera again and now he chose to stick stateside. His work, though, was still compelling. He'd just finished a photo essay for the *Seattle Times* featuring the residents of a homeless encampment that ran along and underneath the 5 freeway. He owned the space she and their other roommate Andrew shared with him. Harrison didn't need renters, he had money, he just liked sharing his space with other artists.

"Shane has a girlfriend. He's a flirt, not a cad. Anyway, I met a guy today, Harrison."

"Yeah? What's he like and how could he possibly be good enough for you?" Harrison asked, kissing the top of her head and yanking on her braid.

"He's dark and mysterious and has a voice like honey. Big, at least six four, and muscled. Not my usual type at all. He's got hair nearly as long as mine. He chatted me up at The Cat this morning. Asked for my number." She shrugged, fighting a blush and feigning nonchalance. Laurent was way more man than she could possibly handle but she couldn't quite bring herself to talk herself out of him.

Harrison made a sound of disapproval. "Rain, you don't know this guy from Adam and you gave him your number? Honey."

"I don't usually! Really. But yeah I did. I don't know, there's just something about him. He probably won't even call but if he does I'll be careful. I'll meet him in a public place with loads of people around."

Harrison scowled. "Be sure you do. There are loads of freaks in the world who prey on pretty, sweet women like you. I should meet him just to be sure."

"I have a father and he's an asshole, I don't need another one. And I'm not naïve you know. I can handle myself."

Harrison laughed. "Okay, just please be careful."

18

* * * * *

Back at the lodge, Laurent had told everyone about meeting his Mate. He and Andreas had discussed different strategies to bring Rain into the Pack carefully and in ways that wouldn't scare her. He wanted very much for her to *want* to be part of his family. It would be hard enough on her life to have to move and make the conversion, the thought of it being scary for her made him want to take it at her pace, even when his natural instincts were to grab her and run.

"So tell me about her," Kari demanded as they sat around the dinner table after a late lunch.

The entire family crammed around the table. Andreas' brothers Sean and Devon were there with their wives Emma and Perri. Pack Fifth in command Skye smirked as Ryan, another member of the Inner Circle, smiled, looking pleased for his friend. The children had finished eating and Kari's bodyguard Phillip busily chased them around the yard with their uncle Jack.

Laurent smiled as he thought about Rain. "She's amazing, Kari. Beautiful. Tall for a human woman, about five nine or so. Long black hair, like mine, she wore it in a braid this morning. Long legs, heart-shaped ass." He paused and thought about what she'd looked like that morning, braid swinging like a living thing, her bottom swaying as she walked.

"Earth to Laurent?" Perri said and they all laughed.

"Her voice is beautiful, soft, throaty. She's very strong, we saw her kick a man out of the place who was giving her trouble."

"What, you didn't run over and try to save her?" Kari asked sarcastically, knowing what male werewolves were like when their Mates were threatened.

"I wanted to. I stood to help her but she took care of it on her own and Andreas had a hold of my arm anyway." He took a sip of his wine and continued. "Her eyes are a greenish brown, more brown than green, with a gold ring around the iris. She has thick black lashes. Lovely mouth, carnal almost. Bottom lip so full that it was like a cupid's bow. Dimples. Gorgeous smile."

"What about the rest of her?" Skye asked, wagging his eyebrows suggestively.

"Pig." Emma laughed.

"Do tell though," Ryan added.

"She's curvy. One of those classic long-line backs. That slope right above her ass was exquisite. Nice hips, she's got flesh there, her thighs were rounded. Plenty for a man to hold onto in bed. And her skin was soft as velvet when I took her hand to kiss it."

"Keep going." Skye winked.

"I'll tell you about her breasts but if I think for a moment you're imagining them when you see her I'm going to hurt you. I'd say she was a C cup, nice and high breasts. Her nipples were hard every time she spoke to me." His cock throbbed at the memory, his mouth watered as he'd thought of her taste, the shape and color her nipples might be.

"Her hands were beautiful. Long fingers, but I noticed she had paint under her nails and I smelled turpentine, maybe she's an artist." Laurent leaned back and closed his eyes, thinking of her again.

"Oh my, you're as bad as Andreas was when he came home that day after he'd seen Kari the first time," Anna said.

"Laurent, I'm so glad you've found her. She'd better be good enough for you." Kari smiled. "I love you like you're my brother. And I have to admit it'll be nice to have another woman around here who was born human. Perhaps I can help ease her way as well."

"Thank you, *reine*. You'll be her Alpha of course but she'll need friends as well. For now I need to call her, to ask her to dinner. Do some wining and dining. Get to know her more and hopefully she'll be amenable to coming up to visit the lodge soon. For the immediate future, Andreas, Skye said that he'd trade with me so that he can be on duty whatever night I go out with her."

Laurent was the Pack's Lieutenant and Andreas' personal bodyguard. He'd been so for sixteen years. He was the chief law enforcement for the Pack. It meant though that he had to be at Andreas' side or at least in the same place at all times.

"Laurent, we'll need to talk about this more in-depth. Once you're Mated it won't be possible for you to be my bodyguard anymore. You'll still be Lieutenant but my bodyguard needs to be an unmated wolf. No one would be as good as you or have my total trust the way you do but what do you think of Alek as your replacement? He's strong, loyal and young enough but not too young."

Laurent shrugged. "Who'd have thought that Alex and his brother would turn out to be such strong Pack members?" For a time they'd been suspicious that Alek's brother Alex was responsible for the attempts on Kari's life, sadly it turned out to be their own cousin Michael. "I hate to leave you hanging, Andreas."

"Laurent, it's the way of things. It's time for you to move on from a job you did so well your shoes will be impossible to fill, but I'm happy for you. Seeing you in love makes my heart glad." Andreas reached over and clapped his shoulder.

Kari reached out and took Andreas' hand and he kissed her fingers. "This makes me think about our first months together. Except for being changed in a murder attempt and all the other drama." She laughed and he touched her face. Laurent used to ache when he saw their connection, wanting it for himself. And now he had it. His whole life opened before his eyes, so much waiting to be experienced.

"Go and call the woman! Don't leave her waiting, Laurent. What if another man is interested?" Skye grinned.

"There *are* no other men for her. She'll know that now that she's met me," Laurent said smugly and Andreas roared with laughter.

"My little wolf taught me a great many things about human women, Laurent. Don't expect Rain to fall into your lap so easily." Andreas smirked.

Laurent sniffed indignantly, waving it away. "Please. There is no other for her. I'm hers, she is mine. Of this there is no doubt." He stood up. "I need to call the records office tomorrow to follow up. Her DNA was on the paper she wrote her number on, I saw her lick her finger to separate the page from the others. I couriered it over before we left Seattle. They're running it to see who she is and what lines she has."

Werewolves had a very sophisticated records registry. Because not all werewolf females could reproduce and even then, most of the children born were male, it became necessary over time to find human women who were compatible for mating. Usually this meant that the woman had another relative who had crossed over and mated with a shifter in the past. Kari, for instance, had three relatives in her past who were changed, one was even an Alpha so she'd had a natural wolf in her family too.

The records office used to search by name but now they had a DNA registry that made everything even easier. The humans had no idea such things were possible — werewolves or that there was data that tracked their genetic histories through human records. Technology had saved their species many times.

"If you'll all excuse me, I'm off to call my woman." With a low bow Laurent left to head to his room to call Rain.

Chapter Two

ဆ

The sound of the ringing phone roused Rain from her late afternoon nap.

"Hello?"

"Rain?"

"Mmmm," she said, stretching. "You got her."

"It's Laurent Cole. I'm sorry, did I wake you?"

She smiled then, warming that he'd called. "Why hello, Laurent. Don't apologize, I was just napping and needed to be up soon anyway. Hang on a sec, let me sit and wake up a bit." Sitting up, she arranged her pillows behind her back and smoothed the comforter over her legs. "Now then, that's better. I have to be at work at five a.m. so I usually try to sneak in a nap around four in the afternoon to refresh my day. How are you, Laurent Cole?"

"Better now, hearing your voice does wonders for me." The rumble of his voice, even over the phone, made her want to crawl through the receiver and into his arms.

"Oh aren't you the flatterer!" She laughed, glad he couldn't see her blush.

"You bring it out in me. What are you doing tomorrow night?"

"I have plans. I'm sorry. One of my roommates has an audition for the Seattle Symphony and we're going out for drinks afterward."

"Okay. And what about Sunday night?"

"I'd planned to attend a gallery show for one of my friends." She hesitated. "Would you like to join me? It'd only be an hour or so out of the evening, after that we'd be free."

"I'd like that. I haven't been to a gallery show in years. Can I take you to dinner afterward?"

"Sure." *Sure*, hell, she wanted to jump up and down and wondered why in the heck she was so excited. He was nice-looking and all, well, gorgeous actually, but it wasn't like her to get all giddy over a man. Gorgeous, sexy, testosterone-laden, yummy and warm. Like a slice of pie with ice cream melting over it.

He must have heard her whimper. "Are you all right?"

Good lord, she was such a dork. "Uh yeah, fine."

"Okay, what time shall I pick you up?"

"Why don't you meet me at the gallery at eight? We can hang out for a while and then leave for dinner. "

"I'll meet you there then."

She gave him the name and address of the gallery and hung up after he'd told her good night and wished her sweet dreams. She was sure they'd be of him anyway. At least now she wouldn't be so nervous about taking her portfolio to The Holt and with dropping the portfolio off she wouldn't be as nervous about the date either. Instead she'd just be a general bundle of stress.

Laughing to herself, she got out of bed and headed off to the shower.

* * * * *

The next night, just as she was on her way out the door to meet her friends he called again.

"Did I catch you at a bad time? I know you're busy tonight but I just wanted to hear your voice today and I didn't want to wake you up this time."

A grin split her face as she melted inside. "Hi, Laurent. You didn't wake me up. I do have to leave shortly but I have enough time to chat a bit." She sank to the floor next to the hall table.

braid it to wrap it at the base of the ponytail. Rain, you're going to look very beautiful."

"All of this fashion knowledge is totally wasted on a straight man," Andrew said with a wistful sigh as he walked into the room. "Duckie, we're going to make you up so lovely that this Laurent won't know what hit him." He smiled and looked at the dress admiringly. "Good choice. Now let's get working, Cinderella."

* * * * *

"Laurent, are you leaving already?" Kari asked as Hellie came over and jumped into his arms. It was early in the day but he wanted to head out to Seattle to be sure he got there in time for his date with Rain that night.

He couldn't believe how nervous he was. Not seeing her for a few days, knowing she existed, was driving him crazy. He ached to touch her, to hold her. Talking with her on the phone had been nice but thinking of her out there with no car, taking the bus at night, had made it difficult to sleep.

"Handsome! Am I still your best girl?" the four-year-old who thought he was the center of her world—that is, after her papa—asked as she looked up at him.

"Helene, my love, you'll always have my heart." Laurent dropped a kiss onto the top of her head and sat her down.

"Nana says that maybe you'll make some boys with your new Mate and maybe they'll be our Mates someday. Is that true?"

Laurent held back his laughter and looked over at Kari, whose eyes twinkled with amusement. "Your grandmother sure has a lot to say." Kari winked at Laurent. "Okay, Hellie, Laurent needs to go now to get into the city. He needs to actually go out on a date with Rain first. And then they'll get married and say the Mate bond and it'll be a while before there'll be any children."

Laurent chuckled. "I'll keep all that in mind." He leaned down to kiss Hellie again. "Good night, *reine*, Hellie. Skye, take care of Andreas. I'll see you all tomorrow." He turned to go. Since he was going to be out late he planned to stay in the apartment that Andreas and Kari owned downtown. He hoped that he'd get a chance to wake up next to Rain.

He needed her. He wanted her to need him as well.

Once he got to town he made sure the apartment was well stocked with food for breakfast, champagne and chocolate and plenty of candles in his room. He wanted to spoil her. He got the feeling she didn't get much of that in her day-to-day life.

He dropped by Drew's small shop while he was in the neighborhood. Drew was a clothing designer as well as a member of the Pack and a good friend.

Drew's face lit up when he saw Laurent come in. "Hey, Laurent! It's nice to see you. I hear you've met your Mate. When can Janine and I meet her?" Janine was Drew's Mate and another designer.

"News travels fast." Laurent chuckled. "I'm here in town to see her actually. I'm going to a gallery show and dinner with her in a few hours. I'm just out doing a bit of shopping and wanted to stop in and say hello. She doesn't know yet about me. About Cherchez. I'll save it for when we know each other better. You'll like her though."

"Of course I will, she's your Mate. Tell me about her. I'd be honored to design her conversion robe."

Laurent paused a moment, thinking of what the night when she made her first change into a wolf would be like, what she'd look like, feel like running at his side. Smiling, he described her to Drew.

"She sounds beautiful, Laurent. Wait a moment." Drew bustled around the shop, pulling things from hangers and off shelves, and brought them back to where Laurent waited. "Do you think she'd be offended if I sent over a few things?"

Laurent knew Drew loved to give people things he made and designed and it touched him that he'd want to include Rain. "She's shy but I think if I explained it she'd be touched. As I am. Thank you, Drew."

"I think the jeans should fit given your description of her size and shape. Be sure to bring her by when you're ready. I'm happy for you. Finding your Mate is a truly wonderful thing."

Laurent embraced his friend and took the bag of clothing with him when he headed back to the apartment to get ready.

It was funny, the need he had to take care of her, nurture her. He wanted to be her family as well as create one with her. She gave off a sort of vulnerability and it called to his heart.

* * * * *

Nervously, Rain looked at herself in the mirror. "Wow," she murmured. She had to admit she looked classy and sexy and a bit sassy. Her hair cascaded down her back from a high ponytail. The way it was pulled back tightly from her face only accentuated her large eyes and lips that shimmered candy apple red. The slingbacks she told Harrison about worked perfectly and she was sure she'd hate them in a few hours but for the time being they were gorgeous. Thank goodness Laurent was so tall because in the heels she stood at six feet. Andrew brought her a powder that had a gold shimmer in it and it gave off a subtle glimmer as she moved.

"Holy cow, cupcake, you need to know if I was straight I'd snap you up in a minute. Your boobies look marvelous." Andrew winked.

"Uh, thanks, Andrew." She laughed at his teasing. "My boobies appreciate the compliment. Jeez they feel so high, like I'm serving them or something." Nervousness ate at her stomach. She hadn't felt so pretty in a very long time. Certainly she'd never worn anything revealing before. She twirled in front of the mirror, loving the way the skirt flared

29

and the pretty crinolines showed. Still, she did have a slight jiggle when she walked. "Are you sure I don't look obscene?"

"Rain, you look heavenly. Seriously," Harrison said.

She took a deep breath and grabbed her wrap and her bag. "Okay. I'm off then. Thanks for your help. I don't know what I would have done without you tonight." She hugged Harrison and she and Andrew headed for the door. He'd offered to drop her at the gallery.

"It's going to be fine, Rain. Really. You have my cell and Harrison's just in case there's an emergency. You know how to dial 9-1-1. Don't let him pressure you into anything you don't want to do. Do you want me to stick around?" Andrew asked as he pulled up in front of the gallery.

Rain squeezed his hand. "You're so sweet to me. No, I'm fine. I'll be fine. And I won't let him get past second base." She winked and he laughed.

"Who knows? But just in case, do you have condoms?"

"Yes, Dad, I have some in my bag. Harrison checked earlier too. I'll see you later. Thanks for the ride." She leaned over and kissed his cheek.

Laurent looked in the mirror one last time before leaving. At the last minute he'd left his hair down. He wanted to show off a bit for her. Yes he had a human side but he was a werewolf, dominance displays and showing off the beauty of one's pelt and other features was part of the male mating process. He wanted her to desire him and find him attractive. Heaven knew he thought she was the most breathtaking woman to ever walk the planet.

When he parked and walked over to the gallery, Laurent was drawn immediately to her. He swallowed hard as he took her in through the windows. She towered over most everyone else like an Amazon goddess. Her black hair shimmered nearly blue under the lights, the dress encased her torso, the skirt and a pair of ridiculously sexy high heels made her legs look miles long.

His cock ached and he had to wrestle back the urge to stalk in, grab her and stalk out to fuck her against the nearest surface. Oh how he wanted to mark her as his own and he hadn't even seen her face yet. He quickened his step and entered the gallery.

Laurent took a deep breath as she turned around. It was as if she knew he was there and turned to greet him. Her skin glowed, looking sun-kissed, but he knew it was her natural tone. Her breasts heaved enticingly from the top of the cowl neck of the dress. He wanted to walk over there and put his face to her cleavage and breathe in her scent, to feel the soft skin of her breasts, to follow the curves with his lips. Her hair was pulled back from her face and it made her artfully made-up eyes look gigantic. And the lips— if he'd thought they looked carnal before, wearing that sheen of red glossy lipstick they looked downright X-rated. A wisp of her scent reached him and his system went into overload as he felt his wolf react.

Rain smiled then and he returned it as he moved toward her. "You look beautiful, Rain. I really like the dress."

"Oh this old thing?" She laughed. "Thank you, you look pretty good yourself." She reached up and touched his hair and electricity ran through him on contact. "Your hair is so beautiful, I'm glad you left it down."

"I'm glad it pleases you, I had it back earlier and decided to free it." He wanted to strut around the room at the compliment.

"Would you like a glass of wine or something?" she asked as he took her hand and tucked it into his arm and they walked through the gallery. He heard the undercurrent of nervousness in her voice and wanted her at ease.

"No not now, I'll have some with dinner. We have reservations at Matt's On the Market for nine if that's all right. He's got a great wine list."

"I've never been there but I've heard great things." Heard and not experienced because it was totally out of her price range.

"You're in for a treat. It's very small and they cook right in front of you. The food is amazing. Fresh local ingredients. It doesn't look fancy, it's the food and wine where all of the effort goes."

"I like that. Food as art. Sounds heavenly."

"So is this your friend's work then?" He motioned to the walls.

"Yes. I met Sully when I first came to town and started painting. He's been a huge help to me. He's very good, this is his third show so far this year."

It was good but Laurent had a feeling her work would be better. "So you mentioned taking your portfolio to a gallery, I take it you're an artist too?"

"Yes, I paint. The portfolio is to be considered for a series of gallery shows The Holt is going to host over the next months, all showcasing up-and-coming artists. It would be a big break for me to get a show." He saw the passion for her work on her face.

"What kind of work do you do then? Modern, classical, abstract?"

"Modern. It's eclectic. Not so abstract that you can't see what I'm trying to convey. I draw upon themes from nature — mountains, rocks, the ocean, rivers, streams, the sky, stars, planets, big historical themes and events. I don't know how to explain it really, things that tug at the fabric of our existence."

"I'd love to see it sometime and I hope you get a show." As a matter of fact, he knew that Andreas owned a part interest in The Holt. He might mention it to Kari and see if she thought it was something to bring up to Andreas. Kari was someone he could trust to give an opinion about what Rain would like. He wanted to help Rain but not to take over and make her feel she couldn't do it on her own.

They enjoyed the showing and he drove over to the Market for dinner.

"This place is just as great as you said it would be," she enthused over her trout with wasabi crust. "The Gruyère leek tart was so good. I haven't eaten this well in a very long time."

He sensed that she'd grown up around some kind of money, she knew her wines very well and had spoken in French with a man on the corner selling roses. It wasn't the kind of French you learn in high school, it was the kind of French that you learned while in France. Laurent should know, he'd spent time there growing up before he'd come to live with the Phinney family.

"So where are you from originally? Do you have family here?"

She shifted in her chair and looked out the window a moment. "What about you? I take it you and Andreas are close. Are you related to him? How'd you come to work for him?"

Laurent narrowed his eyes at her, smelling her evasion, seeing her body tense and her hands shake for just a moment when he'd asked. She was hiding something. What he didn't know but he'd find out, help her through whatever it was that made her afraid. For the time being he'd let her evade.

"Andreas and I have been best friends since I was eleven and he was thirteen. His family took me in and raised me."

"Why? That is, if you don't mind talking about it."

"My mother died and my father didn't feel he could raise me on my own. My mother and Andreas' mother were like sisters so my father brought me to them, to be raised in a family setting. And that's what they did. Andreas' mother and father took me in and raised me like one of their own children. My working for Andreas sort of grew from that. Back to you though. Do you have any family?"

"Um, yes. I'm, um, estranged from them. I still speak to my mother on occasion but I haven't spoken to my father in a year."

"Why?"

"He wanted me to be something that I couldn't be. I...we couldn't come to any agreement about my life so..." She shrugged but he saw the shimmer of unshed tears in her eyes.

Still, family was so important. He couldn't understand how any man could turn away from his own child. "Have you tried to work it out? How does your mother feel about it all?"

She sighed. "My mother feels however she's told to feel. No, that's unfair really. She's a loving woman but the world she lives in isn't made for women who are strong and opinionated. She helped me es...er, leave home last year. She has to keep my contact with her a secret. My father of course thinks I'll come back when I need money. And that's really all I want to talk about that subject."

Laurent wished she'd lighten her burden and share with him but he understood that he'd have to earn her trust first.

"Would you like to come back to my apartment and watch the ferries on the water?" The apartment was in the Harbor Steps complex and overlooked Puget Sound.

She hesitated a moment, clearly thinking. "Sure. That would be nice." Her voice was soft but free of doubt. He relaxed a bit.

They walked back to the car and Laurent moved it the few blocks to the building and took her up. Among the little touches he'd made earlier that day had been to put new sheets on his bed. They were silky soft with a bit of flannel for warmth. He sincerely hoped she'd let him make love to her that night. Between Mates, the first time making love would create binding ties between them—he wanted to brand her in some way.

"This is a beautiful place," she murmured as she looked around, her hands trailing over the spines of books, the curves of vases. "Do you mind if I take these heels off? They're beginning to kill me."

He shook his head no and watched as she sat and pulled off the pumps, exposing coral-colored toenails.

"That feels so much better. Of course now I'll never have the courage to put them back on because it will hurt even more." And frankly, the way he looked at her made her weak in the knees and she had to sit down before they buckled. The whole evening had set her off balance. She'd never been so attracted and attuned to anyone in her life. It felt so natural to be with him that it freaked her out.

"I'll carry you to your door if you wish it," he whispered and came to kneel in front of her.

"What is it about you, Laurent Cole? I feel like I've known you my whole life," she whispered as he ran a finger around the curve of her bottom lip. Little zings of electricity sparked in the wake of his touch. Her breath hitched as her heart kicked in her chest. She'd been wet and achy since she walked into the gallery earlier that evening and her skin felt so alive and sensitive, like it begged for his touch. His very presence was totally overwhelming, it scared her even as she loved it.

"It does feel that way, doesn't it?"

"Are you going to kiss me?" If he didn't soon she'd swoon from want.

He chuckled as a grin hitched the corner of his mouth up. "You're impatient."

"Yes, where you're concerned apparently." Greedy, impatient, needy.

"Okay then, you must know that I'll make any sacrifice to please you."

A long moment passed in delicious tension before he leaned into her body and touched his lips to hers. Freed and able to act, avaricious hands sought the muscled wall of his chest over the smooth material of his expensive dress shirt. The heat of his body nearly scalded her even through the fabric. The muscles of his chest jumped at her touch as she moved upward, seeking the silk of that long dark hair.

A low sound broke from her throat and he echoed it before grabbing her waist and pulling her to his body tightly as he walked on his knees to get closer. Her thighs widened to give him room and her skirt rode up, exposing the tops of the stockings she wore.

Laurent felt the heat from her pussy as he moved to her and it drove him wild. He scented the honey there, nestled in the folds, and his mouth watered to taste her. "God you feel good," he murmured against her mouth and she sighed, opening to him, pressing her breasts into his chest, arching her back.

Need rode him and he groaned into her mouth as his tongue followed the sound. Her taste was more intoxicating than her scent. She tasted of cherries and dessert wine and her lips were firm and lush under his. He tried to hold back the fantasy of what that mouth would feel like wrapped around his cock but failed, instead moaning at the carnal images.

When her tongue flicked over his, past his into his mouth, the sinuous dance of their kiss seduced him. She was open to him, gloriously inviting him to taste her, but he could also sense that she was inexperienced and that thrilled him. The idea that his Mate wasn't someone who'd been with a lot of men in the past made his male ego swell. *He'd* be the one to show her erotic delights, *he'd* learn every inch of her body, *he'd* know spots that no one else had touched. Wanting to burn his name into her being thrilled him to his toes.

The rest of her body called to him. Tamping down on his desire to take her hard and fast, he slowly moved his mouth from her lips and skimmed down to her neck. The heat of her skin warmed her scent, called to his wolf. The edge of his teeth abraded the tender skin just below her ear and the flat of his tongue followed to lave the sting and take in her taste.

Rain's lips tingled at the loss of his mouth and she whimpered until he laved her neck with his tongue. Shivers of delight broke over her and she grabbed his head, holding him in place. He chuckled in response, low and wicked, and she smiled. He made her feel so sexy, so...something she couldn't even find words for.

Every muscle in her body tensed sharply and then totally relaxed when he gently bit down over the jumping pulse in her neck. It was like something slammed into her, filling her up and easing her as he held the tendons and muscle between his teeth. Her head lolled back, her breathing shallow. She nearly came just from that one action, nothing had ever, ever felt so pleasurable.

Her response to the bite brought Laurent's balls tight against his body. He scented the slickness of her pussy, felt her nipples tighten against his chest. Unable to stop himself from touching her more, he slid his hands around her waist and just under the swell of her breasts. But when she yanked the hem of his shirt out of his pants and skimmed her hands over the bare skin of his lower back he gasped at the pleasure. She felt so right against him then. Like she was made for him and him alone, and of course she was. So this was what it felt like with the right person, the *right* person. No wonder Kari and Andreas fucked like bunnies.

He gave in finally and did what he'd been wanting to do all night, he pressed his lips to the curves of her breasts, to the creamy skin that heaved with her breathing. She hummed in satisfaction and he stood up then, bringing her with him. She put her face into his neck then and he felt her body tighten in response. Silently he begged her to do what he'd done.

"Oh my god!" Laurent groaned out as she bit down, her teeth grasping the tendon, her tongue flicking out to taste his pulse. She had no idea but it was a show of sexual dominance for a wolf to bite the neck of another. His cock stiffened even more and his arms trembled. He rolled his hips without even thinking, seeking her cunt, needing to join with her.

She pulled back and looked at him, her eyes glazed over with lust. "Why? Why did that feel so right?" she whispered, sounding a bit dazed.

"You're mine, my heart. We're made to be with one another, my cells sing to yours," he said softly.

"What? How? I just met you yesterday."

"You know what I say is the truth. You can feel it in your heart, can't you? When you placed your face in my neck and breathed me in—have you ever done that with another?"

"No." She shook her head, still dazed.

"But you did with me. Why?" He wanted to tell her everything but it was too soon.

"It just felt like the right thing to do. You did it to me."

"I did, *mon amour*. I did because I knew, just as you know."

"I don't know *anything*. I'm just a girl who wants to paint, heck, I haven't had sex in nearly a year. I've only been with two people in that way before. I feel like I'm in way over my head here. It scares me."

He took a step back, still on his knees before her. "Sweetness, we'll go slow. I'll show you that you and I are meant to be together. You need never be afraid of me. I'd die before I harmed you or ever allowed harm to come to you. I won't lie, Rain, I want very much to make love to you tonight. But if you're not ready I'll wait until you are."

"Who are you? You're too good to be true. I keep thinking I'm going to wake up and you'll have been a dream."

"I am yours," he answered simply. "Will you stay the night, Rain? Or shall I take you home now? It's your choice. Either way I'll be here tomorrow. All of your tomorrows." He stood and waited for her answer.

The honey of his voice drew a shiver from her. Licking her lips nervously, she looked up into his face. She wanted him more than she'd ever wanted anything in her entire life and that scared her. All her life she'd had one passion and that had been painting. She didn't know what to do with two. Didn't know if they'd both fit in her life. "I don't know," she whispered.

"Oh love." He pulled her into his arms tightly. She pressed her face to his chest, finding herself calmed by the beat of his heart, the warmth and smell of him. His hair swept forward and lay across her bare shoulders like silk. He stroked gentle fingers down her back. "How old are you, Rain?"

"Twenty-six. And you?"

"Forty-four." The juxtaposition of the siren in his arms with her youth and relative inexperience fascinated him. There was a wisdom in her eyes that belied her physical age. She'd seen a lot. "Sweetness, have you ever felt so strongly toward a man before?"

"Never. I've dated but I've never really been into the men I was with. I've had close friendships with men—both of my roommates are men—but I haven't ever felt on fire for any of them. I do for you."

He shuddered at her words. He didn't want to scare her away but he wanted to let her know how she affected him. "I've been with other women in the past but I've never wanted any of them with such a deep longing. You make me feel on levels that I hadn't imagined before."

Rain felt total sincerity from him. She had no reason to trust him, she didn't know him. And yet she did. She trusted him with her very heart. Taking a deep breath, she made her decision. "I want to stay," she said softly.

It was all Laurent could do not to sweep her up and run toward his room but he knew she was hesitant and he needed to take his time. Loosening his hold on her, he stepped back, holding his hand out to her.

When she took it he smiled, sent out a prayer to do all the right things for his woman and slowly walked with her into his bedroom, shutting the door behind them. Immediately it felt like the space was a safe haven for the two of them, a world where it was just Laurent and Rain.

She stood there, looking expectant and nervous, and it squeezed his heart. Pulling gently on the hand he still held, he brought her to his body and kissed her softly, sweetly. It was a kiss that sealed his fate. He was hers and he was giving himself to her freely. After a slight hesitation on her part she encircled his neck with her arms and he felt the tension fall away from her.

They stood there kissing for several minutes as he devastated her with his mouth. Her bones turned to mush as Laurent's hands swept over her body in gentle exploration. Down the curve of her back, over the curve of her ass, pulling her snug against him. She gasped when the notch of her pussy met the hard line of his cock, thrilling at the electricity between them. He rolled his hips and the blunt head of his cock brushed over her swollen clit and light burst behind her eyelids.

It became natural then to just give herself to him, to trust that he could treat her gently and kindly, that this was meant to be.

Laurent ground himself into her for a moment, teeth on edge at the contact of hard meeting soft. Her gasp of delight when he did it spurred him on. She wanted him as badly as he wanted her. Even better, he felt the moment when she gave herself to him.

Humming his satisfaction at her abandon, he found the zipper pull on her dress and the metal sound of the dress parting filled the room and rode his spine. When he stepped back the dress fell at her feet and he simply stared, openmouthed, at the body it revealed. She stood there, golden-skinned, high full breasts freed, nipples hard and tight, in a pair of red lace boyshort panties with garters attached to nude stockings.

"Do...do you like them?" she asked shyly, blushing.

Blinking several times, he had to concentrate to remember how to speak. Reaching out, he brought her hand to his cock. "Can't you tell?" he answered hoarsely. He was surprised when she brought the other hand over to rub the length of him before undoing his button. The sound of his zipper slowly descending brought his breath short. Before long his pants slid down his legs and he toed off his loafers and kicked out of them and the pants.

Gently, he picked her up and moved her out of the pool of the dress at her feet before bending to pick up her dress and his pants and tossing them over a nearby chair. He pulled off his socks and she came back to him, unbuttoning his shirt, sliding it back over his shoulders. His skin tingled in the aftermath of her touch on his bare chest.

Her hands, still shy but determined, were back, stroking over his cock through the material of his boxers. "I like your boxers but they need to go," she whispered and he nodded mutely, shucking them off.

"My goodness. Laurent, I've never seen a body as beautiful as yours." She ran her hands over his chest and down the flat planes of his stomach, down through the thatch of hair at his groin and at long last she took his cock into her hands. He gritted his teeth, willing himself to give her time to explore. It felt damned good, her hands all over his body. He'd thought of little else since he'd seen her the first time just days before. The reality was far better than the fantasies and her hands on his cock were far more satisfying than his own.

As stereotypical as it was, Rain found herself pretty damned impressed with the length and girth of Laurent's cock. She had sex toys, she liked them thick, but he beat silicone hands down. Her pussy spasmed with greed as she thought of him inside her.

Her last attempt at sex hadn't been overly satisfying. Not as horrible as it had been with Anthony — mister unzip, leave the pants on, no foreplay, three dry thrusts and come. But certainly lacking any real fire or finesse. She'd never had the

41

inclination to simply look her fill at her partner's body. No man made her clit throb in time with her nipples. No man made her pussy so wet she felt the heat on her thighs either. Sex with Laurent, she had a feeling, would be a far different animal. Something she was quite eager to experience.

Laurent smiled at her, eyes alight with passion. "It makes me so happy to see you react to me this way. And it isn't me who is beautiful but you." He brought his hands to her breasts and held their weight in his hands. "Look at these. I've never seen such pretty pink nipples before." He ran his thumbs up and across their pebbled surface over and over and her hips hitched forward in response. "You're built like a goddess — lush, curvy and soft."

"I believe the word you're looking for is chubby," she said with a wry grin.

He pulled himself back, looking angry. "Never. Rain, you're lush and womanly. Your body is curvy and delightful. You make me so incredibly turned on," he said, bending his head down to a nipple, taking it into his mouth. She gasped and arched her back, her fingers digging into the muscle of his shoulders. "I plan to show you just how turned on when I kiss every inch of you." He took a step back. "Are you ready, Rain? Still with me?"

It touched her that he cared to ask and be sure. She nodded and he gently laid her back on the bed behind her.

"These sheets are fabulous, Laurent. The room smells like you, I feel like I'm surrounded by your essence in here," she said, running her nails lightly down his back as he settled just on top of her.

"I wouldn't want you sleeping on anything that wasn't as soft as you are. Now lie back and relax and let me love you slowly. Thoroughly." He pulled her arms up and over her head. "Leave them here," he said, kissing her lips, this time with heat and passion. His hair swept down and surrounded them both in a jet black curtain. The scent of it, the heat of him, made her dizzy.

He kissed his way over to her ear and down her neck and throat to one breast and nipple then the other. It was all she could do to look down at him, the dark hair trailing over her naked skin, his mouth, teeth and nimble fingers at work on her nipples. No one had ever paid much attention to her nipples, she hadn't known anyone could make them feel like this. Could make *her* feel like this just from playing with them.

It had been nice enough but the hand not rolling and tugging her nipple moved down her belly, stroking over her fevered skin until it stopped at the waistband of her panties.

"As much as I like these, and I do, they've got to go so I can get to your sweet pussy," he murmured against her nipple as he pulled her panties and stockings off, tossing them off the bed.

He sat back on his haunches, between her thighs. "Now then." He gently petted the close-cropped hair at the top of her pussy for a few moments. She watched him, rapt. The heat of his palms on her inner thighs nearly scalded her as he pushed them wide apart. She should have felt embarrassed to be exposed to him in such a way but watching him devour her with his eyes was fascinating. "So pretty and cocoa pink."

His gaze locked on her pussy, his fingers made a slow, slick circuit through the folds there, carefully avoiding too much contact with her sensitized clit.

"That feels so good," she murmured. Another truth was that she'd never had an orgasm that she hadn't given herself. She was so close just from his nearness, the kissing and his worship of her breasts, that when his thumb came up and flicked across her clitoris while another finger slowly slid inside of her she climaxed, arching into his hand, trembling and seeing stars. She whispered his name hoarsely.

Laurent shook as she climaxed so beautifully it took his breath. He hadn't expected her to come so quickly and he smiled at how responsive she was to his touch. He also needed her so powerfully it made his teeth hurt. "That was only the first one," he said, lowering himself to lie between her thighs, head at the space where leg met body, gazing up at her. Her scent gripped him and he didn't resist swirling a finger through those swollen, wet, pink folds and bringing it to his mouth, tasting her honey.

They both gasped. Her taste shocked through him, rocked his senses and dizzied him a moment. He had to have more.

She tried to close her legs, blushing. "No, baby, never. You are so beautiful, let me see you." He opened her with his thumbs and ran a tongue along her wet, hot skin. Her body was a freaking symphony, lighting up his every cell.

"I've never, OH!"

"Never? Oh love, let me show you then. Please. I swear to you that it's worth it." He lowered his head again. How could any man have resisted this sweet pussy? Slowly, thoroughly, he used teeth and tongue, lips and mouth to explore every fold, every dip and curve. She was hot, hot and juicy and he wanted more. His tongue slipped into her body and she arched her back. Moving back up, he circled her clit with the tip of his tongue. Over and over until her entire body vibrated. More, god he wanted more. It was all Laurent could do not to surge up and shove himself inside her, she was so exquisite, so perfect.

How could she have lived without this all these years? Rain's breath came out in short pants, wave after wave of intense pleasure rocked her, building and building. "I want oh...that feels so...oh god...please, Laurent," she breathed out, her hesitance at being pleasured that way giving over to the need for him to make her come.

Without thinking she put her hands on his head, threading her fingers through his hair, holding him to her. When he reached up and pinched one of her nipples she jerked off the mattress with a cry. His moan of approval sent vibrations up through her clit. It was so good it just bordered on too much. Her head thrashed from side to side as she moaned softly, hips churning against his mouth.

Just when she began to beg, he sucked her clit into his mouth, his teeth lightly sliding over her, his tongue flicking underneath the hood softly but insistently, orgasm slammed into her body. She bit her lip so hard she tasted the metal of her own blood as she came and came. With a long satisfied sigh her thighs fell open and she let her hands fall to the bed as she gasped for breath.

It took several minutes for her to come back to herself, all the while Laurent lay with his head on her thigh, petting her softly. She pulled him up to lie beside her. "That was... Wow, thank you."

He kissed her gently. "Don't thank me. You have no idea how much pleasure that just brought me."

She pushed him back against the mattress, laughing. "Not as much as it brought me, I'd wager. Now I'm not a virgin or anything but I've never done this before. I'll probably be horrible but I'd like to taste you too. Can you help me? Tell me if I'm doing something wrong?"

He smiled then, his hair spread out around his head. "You'll be fine. Just watch the teeth," he said with a chuckle. He caressed her thighs and she wanted to rub herself all over him.

All she wanted at that moment was to make him feel as good as he'd made her feel. Focusing her energy and attention on him, she studied his body intently. Running her hands down the wall of his chest, she didn't fail to notice his nipples. Although they were flat they were hard. She wondered if they were responsive like hers. Bending down, she licked one, swirling her tongue around it, and he gasped. *Apparently so.* She grazed one with her teeth and he groaned.

"*Yes.*"

Abrading her nails lightly over them, she moved on, slowly kissing her way down his chest and stomach. He smelled so good, tasted warm and masculine. Kneeling between his thighs, she reached up and undid her ponytail, letting her hair down to curl around her face and cascade down her back.

Leaning down, she ran her tongue around the edge of his navel, catching the skin between her teeth. His hands gripped the sheets and the power of making him react that way roared through her.

Moving lower still, she dragged her hair lightly over his belly and thighs and he sighed, writhing. At last, the good stuff. Grinning, she grabbed his cock gently, examining it. Soft, velvety smooth but hard too. Skin hot to the touch. She ran a fingertip down the tightened skin of his balls and he groaned, arching up into her touch. *You learn something new every day,* she thought with a smile.

Time to get down to real business. She moved, bending to run her cheek along the length of his cock, stopping to kiss the head. Pre-cum beaded at the slit and she dragged her tongue across it, the salty taste of him sliding through her senses.

"Holy...yeah, that's it," Laurent hissed as she licked along the crown.

Good gracious she hoped she didn't injure him. It seemed like a huge act of trust to let all those teeth so near something so precious and tender.

She took him into her mouth slowly, incrementally, waiting and watching him for cues about what he did and didn't like. She took him back as far as she could and pulled back, trying different things with her mouth and tongue. There was no way she'd get all of him in her mouth so she concentrated on what she could reach without embarrassing herself and gagging.

"Rain, you are so beautiful. Yes, yes, baby, like that. Oh." He groaned, his hands drawing through her hair and over her shoulders.

Suddenly he pulled her up off him.

"What? Did I do it wrong?" she asked, confused and slightly embarrassed.

"No," he said, laughing. "You did it too well. I'm going to come if you keep that up and I'd rather be inside of you when that happens." He kissed her and laid her down on her back. Her pulse thundered and nervousness made her slightly queasy, warring with her intense desire to have him inside her that very moment.

Reaching across her, he pulled a condom out of the side table drawer and she wondered just how many women he brought here to do this with.

As if he read her mind he said, "I just bought these today, for you. I've never had a woman in this bed before." She felt better until he sheathed himself and settled back, between her thighs. The head of his cock nudged against her gate and it occurred to her that he seemed awfully big and it had been a long time since anything other than her vibrator had been in there.

"We'll go slow," he said, pushing inside of her and stopping immediately. "Oh Rain, you're so tight." Beads of sweat popped out along his forehead and she felt the strain in his muscles.

"It's been nearly a year," she said and he groaned. "I'm sorry."

"No, baby, don't apologize. You feel so damned good that I have to take it slow or I'll come before I even get all the way inside of you. I don't want to hurt you either," he said and slid in a bit more.

She felt full, it burned a bit. He slid in a bit more and she began to feel pleasure singing along the nerve endings being stroked by him. She moaned and he moaned along with her. "This feels so good. Please, Laurent." God, she had to have more of him.

"Honey, I need to go slow or..."

She couldn't wait, she arched her pelvis the next time he moved to get inside of her a bit more and he ended up sheathing himself fully in that one stroke. Tears sprang to her eyes — *that was a bit painful* — she felt full, stretched, but damned good.

"Am I hurting you? You should have waited. I'm sorry, sweetheart," he said, desperately trying not to move. She was so tight and hot that he was a second from exploding. Having her beneath him, naked, her cunt gripping his cock in a tight embrace, was so much more than he'd imagined.

"No, it's passing. Please please, I need you to move," she begged and he obliged her. He knew she was feeling better as her face lost the strain and loosened and she rolled her hips. He saw the desire in her eyes, saw her pupils enlarge and her lips part. Her moan was laced with pleasure and it shot straight to his balls. "Omigod. Laurent, that's so good," she whispered and he smiled and began to move, setting a rhythm. Shortly he changed his angle to drag across her sweet spot and give her friction across her clit.

She was incredible, so beautiful as her head moved from side to side. *He* made her feel that way. Pride and possessiveness rang through him.

"What do you need, Rain? What can I do for you?"

"I need, oh, I don't know. I want to, oh, it feels so good." Her voice was hoarse and he was suddenly right on the edge listening to her, knowing that no one had ever made her feel that way before. He reached down and began to stroke across her clit with his thumb and she went over right at that moment, the muscles deep inside her rippling and spasming around his cock, pushing him into climax as well. Her name broke from his mouth as she pulled her knees back, encircling his waist with her calves. Her cunt pulled his cock back inside each time he stroked out.

Her moans had gotten louder, more intense, as their climaxes united and drew out. He then understood why Kari and Andreas were so loud — making love with a Mate was simply beyond comparison to any sex he'd ever had. It was like comparing scratching an elbow to a mind-numbing orgasm.

Finally, long moments later, he pulled out, pulling her into his arms after he'd disposed of the condom. He kissed her temple gently and sighed, totally satisfied for the first time in his life. "That was so beautiful. Thank you for trusting me, Rain."

"Thank you for making love to me. Or was it fucking? I don't know, I mean, I'm not up on all of this relationship stuff. Like I said, it's been a year and even then it was only three times and before that it was twice with my ex and let me tell you, he's got nothing on you, Laurent Cole. I've never had an orgasm, well, not that I didn't give myself anyway and god, did I say that out loud? Now I'm babbling, which happens when I'm nervous and mmmmfp!" Laurent put two fingers over her lips to stop her, trying not to laugh.

"It was making love, Rain. I could take you, hard and fast, up against a wall or a door but it would still be making love, always that between us," he growled. "Thank you for the compliment but it isn't about experience, it's about the combination of you and me."

"Oh," she said softly, smiling at him. "You don't look a day over thirty by the way."

"Thank you, the men in my family age well." It wasn't time to tell her yet, werewolves lived well into their second century.

"Um, so..." She twisted the sheets in her hands nervously.

"You can always talk to me, Rain." He took her hands, kissing each one.

"Well, two things really. One, I should call my roommates and tell them I'm not coming home so they won't worry. And two, I'd really like to do it again."

Her guilelessness charmed him. "The phone is right there, sweetness, and yes, I'd very much like to make love to you again."

"Are you sure?"

49

Chuckling, he brought her hand to his already reviving cock. "What do you think?"

She grabbed the phone and sat up against the headboard, the sheet pooled at her waist, her breasts bare. He lay there and looked up at her, entranced by her beauty. "Harrison, hey. Listen, I won't be home tonight, I just wanted to call you to tell you so you wouldn't worry."

She paused, listening. "No, he's fine. Yes. *Yes*, I know. We did use a condom. The Harbor Steps, I swear to you he's not a creep or a weirdo. Yes, good night and I'll see you tomorrow. Bye."

She hung up and sighed, snuggling back down and into his body.

"Who is this guy?" He frowned.

"Who? Harrison?"

"The man you just spoke to, yes."

"He's my roommate. Harrison Watts. He's like a kindly big brother. He worries about me. You're a stranger, he wants me to be safe."

"Harrison Watts the photographer?"

"Yes. Do you know his work?"

"Yes, Andreas has several of his photographs in his office. He's got an incredible eye."

"I'll tell him you said that. He's hurting."

"He stopped doing war journalism, didn't he?"

"Yes. In Bosnia he and his girlfriend were caught with a group of journalists and pinned down. She was shot in the neck right in front of him, she died instantly. He didn't pick up a camera for two years. But recently he did a photo essay on the homeless tent city beneath the freeway. It's some of the most breathtaking stuff I've ever seen. Evocative, angry, sad. It stirred something inside him and he's working again."

"You have feelings for him? He obviously cares for you," Laurent bit out. He wasn't used to feeling jealous, he didn't like it.

She laughed then and caressed his face. "Laurent, he's celibate. Has been ever since Emily died. More than that, he's just a good friend, he cares about me and since I am not in contact with my family anymore, he's like an older brother to me."

"And your other roommate, you said you lived with two men?" Did he actually sound jealous?

"Andrew, he's a cellist, he's also as gay as the day is long," she said and he looked relieved. "Laurent, um, well I mean to say, we just met, are we dating or just going out?"

"The distinction being?"

"Well um, is this an exclusive thing or will you see other people and sleep with them too?"

"There is no one but you, Rain. There will never be anyone else but you. I don't think what happened between us tonight is something casual, do you?"

"Laurent, didn't I tell you several times that I haven't had sex in a year? Jeez, of course it isn't casual. Not to me anyway but like I said, I don't date really and I don't know what the rules are."

"The rules are that I exist to make you happy," he said, hugging her tightly.

She smiled and reached down and found him hard. "Look at you, working so hard to obey the rules."

He laughed and proceeded to show her how well he could obey, three more times.

Chapter Three

છ

Rain woke up naked and pressed up against something very warm and very firm. She opened her eyes slowly. *Oh yeah,* she thought with a smile. Laurent. He lay there sleeping, one arm lying across her stomach, the other up above her head. One of his thighs was thrown over hers. Their hair spread out, entwined across the pillows. The sun came through the windows and she extricated herself from him to go and look out over Puget Sound at the glittering water and the ferries dotting the horizon.

The night before had been more than just good sex, it had shattered her tiny life and set it on its ear. Being with Laurent felt so good, so right — it scared the hell out of her. He was this sophisticated older man and she was already on her way to falling in love. She felt like a rube but at the same time it was wonderful to be so damned happy. She just didn't want to be in some lopsided relationship with a guy who buzzed into town for dinner and a quick fuck every once in a while.

"I've never opened my eyes in the morning to a more beautiful sight," Laurent said sleepily. "Come back to bed, I'm lonely without you."

She turned and saw him there, her heart leapt into her throat. "You've never seen a more beautiful sight? Laurent Cole, you're an exemplary specimen of manhood, all broad and muscled, that glorious hair spread out around you. You're like sex on legs."

She crawled back into bed with him, into the refuge of his arms.

"Mmm, you feel good and you inflate my ego as well as my cock. I think I'll keep you." He winked and moved in for a kiss.

She ducked back. "Don't kiss me, I have morning breath. Sheesh, I'm a novice at this spending the night thing, I don't even have a change of clothes or a toothbrush."

He kissed her forehead. "I have an extra toothbrush for you and I hope you don't mind but I took the liberty of buying you a few things. Some clothes for you to have here should you wish to stay over more often. I'm not in Seattle every day. My job keeps me up at the lodge most of the time but I'd like to come out as often as I can to see you. And I'd love for you to come up to the lodge. You'd love my family and they'll love you too. It's beautiful up there."

"You have this whole life so far away from here." God, she could get really hurt by this man if she gave him her heart and he didn't want to change his life.

"Love, my life is with you. Yes I live a few hours' drive from here but I make it often enough for business I can surely do it to see you."

"This is moving pretty fast. I mean, you just met me two days ago and now you're saying I'm your life?" She felt so calm about it, she knew she should be wary but it all seemed so right, so normal. Still, she didn't just fall off the potato truck and instant true love did not happen.

"Listen, aren't there things in your life that you just knew to be so?"

"I suppose, a few."

"Well then. Rain, from the moment I saw you in The Black Cat the other morning I knew that I wanted to be with you. Trust me, trust yourself. When do you have your next days off?"

"I do four days a week and then three days off. I'm off today, tomorrow and Sunday."

"Come with me to the lodge then. Just for the afternoon. It's a long drive, yes, but I'd like you to meet the people I consider to be my family. If you like you can stay over. I'd like that. But baby steps first. Come and see it and I'll bring you back tonight. We can stay in a hotel if we get too tired."

"I don't know. I do a lot of painting on my days off."

"Bring your supplies with you, paint there. The light is beautiful, it's clean and clear. The lodge sits on Star Lake. You'll love Kari and Emma, their kids are wonderful. In fact, my number two girl, right after you, lives there."

She raised an eyebrow at that. "Oh is that so?"

He laughed, thrilled that she was jealous. "Her name is Helene and she's four. She's Andreas and Kari's daughter, the oldest. She and her siblings are like my own children I've been so involved in their upbringing." He kissed her nose. "So? What do you say? You can give my mobile number and the number at the lodge to Harrison so he won't worry about you." He wanted to show her his life, where her life would be.

She inhaled and blew the air out. "I really want to agree, Laurent, but I just met you. This is just too fast. I'm sorry."

He sighed but shook his head. "Don't apologize. Of course I want you to come and visit but you know, we can take it at your speed. I know this seems fast and scary, all I can do is tell you my intentions and back them up with my actions. We can do the trip to the lodge another time. You just say when and we'll do it. For now why don't I make you breakfast?"

"You're not mad?"

He sat up and pulled her to sitting beside him. "Rain, I respect you. I realize this seems very fast to you. I am not angry that you're taking things slow. How could I be mad at you for that?" He kissed her nose and suddenly she knew her choice.

"Okay. Let's do it. I've lived here a year and haven't been to the Cascades at all yet."

"Are you sure? I don't want you to feel pressured or rushed. I want you to feel comfortable and enjoy yourself. Like I said, I'd love for you to stay over for a few days but I'll bring you back tonight. It's all totally up to you."

If she'd had any remaining doubts about going his reaction cleared them up. He didn't try to pressure her. Still she knew it was insanity, going up to the mountains with a man she'd just met. Harrison would freak. She could not explain it but it felt right and safe and she'd lived for so long making the careful choice, never doing anything impulsive or even fun, that she wanted to be just a bit wild.

"Yes. I'm sure. Since I've been here I've worked and painted and that's about it. Going up to the mountains sounds like fun."

"You lead an awfully serious life for someone so young. Listen, why don't you shower? I'll call up to the lodge and tell them to expect you. Your toothbrush is the red one. If you're comfortable with it there are clothes hanging in the closet that should fit you. My friend, sort of a brother to me, he and his wife are clothing designers. They own a shop just up the street. Anyway I was passing through and said hello and he sent some stuff home with me. He loves to give people clothes. The lingerie is something I happened across and thought of you."

She blushed. "Well, wow, um, thanks. And tell your friend I said thank you as well, it's very nice of him." She got up, he lay on his back and smiled as he watched her walk into the bathroom, shutting the door behind her.

He leaned over to grab the phone and call the lodge.

"Anna, this is Laurent, is Andreas around?"

"Yes, hang on a second."

A few moments passed, he could hear the water in the bathroom and the sound of Rain brushing her teeth. The domesticity of the moment spread with warmth through his chest.

"Laurent, how did your date with Rain go?" Andreas asked and Laurent heard the smile in his friend's voice.

"It went very well indeed. Listen, I've invited her up to the lodge for the afternoon and possibly a few days. Can you keep the *activity* away from the house please?"

"Ah, of course. It's just the regulars this weekend. Devon and Perri are going to the coast with Andy so they won't be here. It should be calmer with just us. I'll make sure that Anna takes care of your room and plans a nice welcome dinner for her tonight. Kari will be over the moon about this."

"She's a painter so she's bringing her supplies. I told her she could paint wherever she wanted. And she's only agreed to come up for the day. I'd like her to stay over of course but I want to leave it up to her. So tell your lovely wife to keep it mellow."

Andreas laughed. "Easier said than done, my friend. But she's better at this stuff than any of us are anyway. Rain can paint wherever she likes of course. By the way, I've asked Alek to take your place as my bodyguard and he's accepted. He won't be able to get here until next week so Skye has volunteered to take over while you're with Rain. Sealing your mate bond is the most important thing right now."

"Excellent, Andreas. I'm glad to hear it. I'll see you all later."

Laurent got up and walked to the bathroom door and knocked. "Rain, care to learn just how wonderful a shower can be?"

"Do tell," Rain called out and he went into the steam of the shower to show her yet another reason to love him.

* * * * *

He smiled as she walked into the room wearing the jeans Drew had given her.

"Laurent, these are…well, you're very thoughtful. I can't believe you guessed my size so well."

"Like I said, it's Drew. I just described you to him and he chose all the stuff. I do prefer your choice of shirt though." He smiled. She wore one of his dress shirts with no bra, tied at the waist, the sweet swell of her stomach peeking out.

"I hope you don't mind. It just smelled like you." Her blush was so endearing. She had no idea of her effect on him at all.

Moving to her, he put his arms around her. "If you keep on saying things like that we'll never leave." He gave her a sexy smile. "You'll have to wear just it later. I have a fantasy about you wearing nothing more than one of my dress shirts."

"Oh my," she stammered a bit. "I don't have any shoes other than the pumps so I suppose I'll wear them."

Laurent looked down and then back up. She looked like sex on legs and the fact that she had no idea made her even sexier. Her breasts were high and round against the front of the shirt. It was white and when he concentrated very hard he could see the pink of her nipples through the fabric. Nipples that tightened under his gaze. Her hair was wet and curled around her face and down her back, leaving damp spots where it lay. The jeans were slung low but long so the heels just accentuated the length of her legs. He sighed wistfully, she was so damned beautiful.

"What?" she asked, looking amused. So she had a slight idea of how she affected him at least. She sidled up to him, swaying, her breasts moving as she walked. When she stopped the tips of her nipples just touched his chest. "So shouldn't we go now?" she said with her lips against his neck.

"You are a very naughty girl." He smiled, tapping the tip of his index finger on the end of her nose, liking this saucy side of her.

"Hmmm. Really? Will you punish me for it?" she asked, taking his finger and sucking it into her mouth, swirling her tongue around it until he groaned.

"Most assuredly, with interest for the raging hard-on you've caused."

She smiled sweetly and looked down, excited. "Really? Wow, this siren stuff is cool!"

He threw back his head and laughed then. The shift from sexy minx back to sweet innocent was wonderful, playful. He put an arm around her shoulder. "Shall we go, miss trouble?"

"Okay. I'm looking forward to today, you know."

"I'm glad. I think you should pack a bag just in case. Like I said, I'll bring you back tonight but if you want to stay you'll have clothes, or if we decide to stop at a hotel. You know, like if I can't keep my hands off you another moment." He locked up behind her and they headed to her house.

When they entered her house Harrison and Andrew were at the table eating breakfast. Both men looked up and did a double take, clearly stunned at her and Laurent's appearance.

"Hi, guys," Rain said as she came into the room. "Laurent Cole, this is Harrison Watts and Andrew Keller. FYI, I'm going to the mountains for the day with Laurent. While I toss some clothes in a bag Laurent is going to give you the number at his house and his mobile too, call me if you need me." She flounced into her room with Laurent in her wake.

Laurent looked around her bedroom as she threw on some tennis shoes and then packed a few things into a duffel bag.

"Where's your art?"

"Oh it's in the studio. Hang on and I'll take you through. I need to grab some supplies anyway," she told him, her head still in the closet.

"Music and books are also a passion I see," he said when she turned around, indicating the stacks of books and CDs that littered the room.

"Yes, I spend too much money on both." She reached down and picked up her mp3 player, adding it to the bag. "I like to listen to music when I paint," she explained.

He took her bag and followed her out. The phone rang and Harrison called out that it was for her.

"Excuse me a second," she said to Laurent and moved to the phone in the hallway. "Hello?"

"Rain Foster?"

"Yep, that's me. What can I do for you?"

"This is Diane Holt of The Holt Gallery. We're looking at your portfolio right now. Ms. Foster, your work is exceptional and we'd love to see more than just photographs. Would it be possible for you to bring down *Whirlpool* and *Crazy Diamond* to the gallery? If they're as good as they look in the photos we'd like to offer you a show."

"Are you serious? You...I just turned in the portfolio yesterday. Oh my god I can't believe it. Yes, yes, I can bring them down. When do you want to see them?"

"Today if possible. If not it'll have to wait until Monday because I'm going out of town for the weekend."

"Can you hold on for just a moment? I need to see if I can make arrangements." Heart racing, blood pounding, she still managed to sound reasonably calm.

"Yes of course."

"Thank you." She punched the *hold* button.

Rain turned to face Harrison, Andrew and Laurent, who all looked at her expectantly. "Oh. My. God. That's Diane Holt from The Holt Gallery. They love my stuff. They want to see two pieces in person. She said if they're as good as the photos they want to offer me a show!" She started jumping up and down and Harrison began to laugh while Andrew clapped and Laurent just smiled and took her in. Rain stopped and took a deep breath. "Okay, enough of that, she's holding. Laurent, I know you want to get back home but I need to get these paintings down to Pioneer Square. Can you wait for me or can we do this another day? I'm sorry."

"Sorry for what? Rain, this is incredible. I'll take the paintings over there right now. My truck is most definitely large enough. I'd never be unhappy that you have a great chance like this."

"Thank you!" She hugged him and got back on the phone. "Ms. Holt, I can be there with them in about half an hour, will that be all right?"

"Yes. I promise you that they will be safe here, of course. I'll see you in half an hour then."

Rain hung up and let out a whoop of joy. "This is crazy! I just gave her that portfolio yesterday. Thank god I put a bra on," she mumbled and started out into the studio.

Laurent looked back at Harrison and Andrew as they went past him into the studio with Rain. They both hugged her, kissing her cheek.

"Congrats, babe. You deserve this. They love your stuff because you're good. Now be careful this weekend. Laurent, we don't know you but we love Rain very much and if you harm her in any way it will be very unfortunate for you," Harrison said sternly and Andrew nodded.

Laurent held out his hand to shake theirs. "I make my solemn vow that I would never hurt Rain. Ever. I'm glad she has you two around."

At that moment Laurent saw her paintings and he stilled. She was incredibly talented. Her work was stacked all around the room and he took it all in slowly, awed.

"This one is *Whirlpool*," she said, pointing at a painting that was all blues and grays. Something about it drew him in, compelled him to look more. "And this one," she said, pointing to a larger canvas of silvers, reds, blues and blacks, "is my newest, *Crazy Diamond*. Diane said they wanted to see these two so let's load them up. Let me get them wrapped for the ride over. Oh and Harrison, can you please bundle up my paints and brushes and throw in two pads? I am going to work while I'm at Laurent's. Thanks!"

She put corner protectors on the two canvases destined for The Holt and threw an insulating cover over them to protect them from light and the elements. Laurent grabbed one and she got the other while Andrew and Harrison grabbed her duffel and other art supplies.

She hugged them both once again and assured them she'd be fine and then she and Laurent headed toward Pioneer Square.

"Rain, I need to tell you something. It's really not a big deal and it has nothing to do with anything but I'd hate for you to find out and think I was hiding it from you."

"Okay." She looked at him pensively.

"Andreas owns half of The Holt Gallery. I was considering telling him about your work but I never even got the chance. He doesn't know anything of it and has nothing to do with the process of selecting artists that they do shows for. I just didn't want you to hear on some off chance that Andreas has a share of The Holt and think that I had anything to do with your selection. It's all you. You're really good. Your work blows me away."

"I can't tell you what it means to me that you understand that I'd want to do this on my own merits. Not that this business isn't about who you know, it is. But knowing this was me and my work means a lot. So thank you for thinking of my feelings. Thanks also for liking my work, it's so important to me and, well, I'm glad you like it."

He helped her carry the canvases into The Holt where Diane Holt was waiting for them. "You must be Rain Foster. I'm Diane Holt, pleased to meet you." She smiled and shook Rain's hand and then looked to the canvases. "Leave them near the windows. I want to see them in the natural light. Go on then, show me what you've got."

Laurent stood near the doors, letting Rain run her own show. Rain went over to the smaller canvas and pulled off the corner guards first and finally the insulating cover. Taking a bracing breath, she stood back and hoped like hell her painting did the talking.

Diane walked forward and put a finger to her lips as she examined the painting slowly, methodically. She studied it for about ten minutes, not saying a word the entire time.

"The other one now please."

Rain did the same thing and stood back. She clenched her fists behind her back, digging into her palms to keep calm.

Diane let out a long sigh and looked at Rain silently, head cocked to one side. Suddenly a smile broke out over her face. "Young woman, you have a hell of a lot of talent. You have a bright future ahead of you, especially if I have anything to say about it."

Relief rushed through her. "Really? Oh my god! Thank you. You don't know how much your opinion means to me."

"And you have no idea how much exposure a show here and another at my smaller gallery in Portland can give you. I'd like to offer you a show in six weeks. Your own show. We can work out the details next week. I need to get going and Patrick, my husband, will want to see these canvases for himself. We'll store them for you, unless you want them back right away?"

"No no, go ahead and take the time you need with them."

"John, please move these to Patrick's office, he'll be in on Sunday to look at them," she told the man standing near the front doors and then looked back toward them. "Rain, I'll be calling you next week to work out the details. As for Portland, I was thinking of doing a show in about six months, which will give you time to produce more work because, my girl, I tell you, I know you'll sell every single painting you show."

"Thank you so much for this opportunity." Unable to hold back a huge grin, Rain shook the other woman's hand.

* * * * *

"I'm really proud of you, Rain. Two shows, incredible. She clearly believes you to have talent and she's got quite a bit of power to break new artists from what I understand."

Laurent held her hand as he headed east toward the lodge. His woman was totally amazing.

"Thank you, Laurent. I'm stunned and thrilled. I can't quite believe it just yet."

"We sort of left off the topic last night, Rain. Tell me more about your family. I sense that you haven't told me the whole story."

"It's not that exciting. Nothing I want to talk about."

"What are you hiding? You sound afraid when you talk about them. Are you afraid, Rain?"

"Let's just drop it."

"Rain, I've been a professional bodyguard for sixteen years, I am entirely capable of protecting you and me both."

"Laurent, I said I didn't want to talk about it and I don't. Drop it please," she said sharply.

"You're being stubborn! Why won't you trust me?"

"*Because.* Jesus, I've known you for a few days. I can't talk about it. I don't want to talk about it. Stop pushing me. Are you telling me that in the few days you've known me you've told me everything about your life?"

She had him there. He sighed deeply. "Rain, I care about you deeply. I want to protect you. You can trust me to do that."

She turned and faced him then. "Laurent Cole, if you ask me about this one more time I will make you turn this truck around and take me back to Seattle. I. SAID. I. DON'T. WANT. TO. TALK. ABOUT. IT!"

"I'm sorry, I won't ask about it anymore. For now." He scowled.

It was tense for the next hour while she stared out the window, sketching on her pad, leaving him to his mood. Stubborn woman. Laurent's mobile rang and he picked it up, putting the receiver bit over his ear so he could talk without his hands but still have whatever was said to him remain private. "Laurent," he bit out.

"Laurent, it's Phillip. Her DNA came back but her name isn't Rain Foster, it's Julia Margoles. She's got wolves in the family tree though, many of them. She's compatible. I did wonder why the name change so I checked her out. Laurent, her father is a mob boss. She went on the run a year ago. No one knows where she ended up but according to some of my sources the father has started to look for her recently."

"Shit." Laurent cut his eyes to her briefly, she turned to him, alarm on her face.

"Yeah. Are you okay?" Phillip asked.

"As long as she is, yes."

"She's right there?"

"Yes."

"We can talk later. Do you think the first part is good news?"

"Of course, that hasn't changed. Nothing has." And it hadn't, not really. He just had another reason to understand why she'd held back earlier when he'd pushed about her family. She must be terrified.

"Be careful, man."

"I plan to. We're only two minutes away. I'll see you in a few." He cut the connection and pulled out the earbud.

He understood her reluctance to tell him now. She was alive only because she'd kept her head low and she didn't want him hurt either. How isolated she must feel not being able to share her life with anyone.

"Julia?"

"Yes?" She paused a moment and turned toward him. She paled and whispered, "No. Tell me you don't work for him. Please god, not you..."

He grabbed her hand. "No. Listen, it's complicated but someone I work with found out who you were. Please don't be afraid. I know and I'll protect you. Don't you see? You don't have to pretend with me, not ever."

She backed against her door, eyes wild. "Oh my god. You're fucking insane, you know that? Do you know what he'd do to you if he found out you helped me? You have to take me back now. I can't see you anymore. I'll have to leave Seattle, change my name again. Oh god." She put her head in her hands and began to cry.

He pulled down the long gravel drive of the lodge, stopping when they reached the house, but waved off Kari and Andreas, who'd rushed out to greet them. Taking off his seatbelt, he moved toward her but she backed up against her door, fear rolling off her in waves.

"Nothing is going to happen to me or to you. I'm not going anywhere and neither are you. Rain, Julia — love, listen to me — I've been waiting my entire life to find you and nothing is going to come between us now. Please trust me and my ability. No one, none of our people, is going to breathe a word about you. Only Phillip and I know, most likely Andreas too, but it doesn't matter. Your father won't find you. Even if he did he can't hurt you. I won't let him."

"Please," she whispered and he reached out to touch her face. "You don't understand. I can't let myself let you in. I made a mistake, I should have said no when you asked me for my number. I always say no."

"I love you. You already have let me in and you know it."

"This is total insanity. How can you love me? You don't even know me. Shit, so now you know my name, big deal. You still don't know me and it's better that you don't. My father and his *associates* are not nice people. I walked away from that world and he'll never let that go. Can you outrun a bullet, Laurent? I was so stupid to think I could have a normal life, a relationship. God, I can't even have my fucking art now. He's stolen that too."

"One, I love you because you're you, period. Two, your name is not you, I know you because you've shown me your true self. Your birth name is immaterial. Three, *my* associates are not nice people when messed with either. Four, I can't outrun a bullet but I can heal extremely quickly and I am extraordinarily fast and agile. Five, normal is in the eye of the beholder. I can't promise normal but, Rain, I am in your life for good. Six and last, no one will take your art from you. If we have to have shows without your being there it'll just add to your mystique. We have lawyers on staff who can advise you on your contracts with Holt as well as how you can go about setting up a blind trust so no one can find out your identity.

"We can do this. Let me help because, Rain, I'm not going anywhere even if you really wanted me to and we both know you don't. Let me in," he whispered and she collapsed into his arms, weeping and hugging him tightly.

They stayed out there for a while, Laurent slowly calming her down until she'd stopped crying. Kari continued to flit around the doorway, clearly seeing that something was wrong and wanting to fix it. Andreas finally came and yanked her back inside and Laurent smiled.

"Shall we go inside, sweetheart?" Laurent handed her a handkerchief.

"I'm sure my face is a total mess. They'll all think I'm a basket case."

He kissed her gently and tipped her chin up. "No, they won't. You look beautiful although your eyes are a bit red. You'll feel better once you wash your face with cool water. They'll love you because I do. It's who they are, Rain. Come on inside, freshen up and let's get a drink to celebrate your show. Don't let your father ruin that." He got out of his door and walked around to hers, helping her down, and Andreas, Kari, Sean, Emma, Jack, Alyssa, Skye, Ryan, Gregory, Phillip and Anna all came out onto the porch smiling welcomingly at them.

Laurent grabbed her duffel. "We'll get your art supplies in a bit, okay?" She nodded and he put his arm around her and they walked toward the house.

Kari came down the steps, stopping to hug Laurent and then Rain. "Hi, I'm Kari Warner-Phinney, it's so nice to meet you. Welcome to Star Lake Lodge." She smiled up at her. "Oh my, sweetie, are you all right? You've been crying." She looked at Laurent, narrowing her eyes. "What have you done to her?"

"It's not him but thanks anyway." Rain said it softly but she wanted to be sure no one thought Laurent had harmed her.

"Someday I'll have to tell you about my first time here at the lodge." And Andreas groaned.

"If you don't mind, can you all let Rain just freshen up a bit before we do the introductions?" Laurent's arm around her was gentle but reassuring.

"Of course, my goodness. Everyone back off!" Anna, taking over, shooed them all away. "Laurent, we've moved you into cabin six. Since Alek is taking over we thought that Skye could use your old room next to Andreas and Kari and that you might like your own place, you know, so you and Rain could have some privacy. We moved your stuff down this morning."

"That was kind of you, Anna." He looked back to the group on the porch and waved a hand at them. "We'll be up in a few minutes."

"Honey, I'm Anna and I've been taking care of this place for a mighty long time. If you need anything just yell, okay?" She hugged Rain tightly and walked back toward the house, telling everyone to stop gawking and get inside.

"Come, the cabins are around here." He took her hand and led her along the path to the cabins. Cabin six was his favorite, it was on the point of the "V" that the cabins all sat along. It was closest to the water and was surrounded by trees. The most secluded cabin, it even had a small flower garden that Jade had put in years ago when she and Tomas lived in this cabin. Andreas' parents now had their own small house near Sean and Emma's.

"It's really beautiful here," Rain said with wonder. "I'm glad I brought my paints."

He smiled at seeing her loosen up a bit. She gasped when he turned down the path toward his new cabin. *Their* new cabin. "This is where you live? My goodness, it's beautiful."

He opened the door, not surprised but still comforted by Anna's thoughtful touches around the cabin. Vases of wildflowers filled the rooms. "I'm just going to put this in the bedroom. Again, no pressure to sleep over." He dropped Rain's duffel in the large master bedroom overlooking the lake. The kitchen was fully stocked.

"Wow, this place is amazing. I'm running out of adjectives here." She walked through the place and went to the sliding glass doors in the master bedroom to step out onto the deck outside. Gregory had put out two Adirondack chairs and a table with an umbrella out there.

"Andreas' family owns the land here, the lake too. Most of his immediate family have houses here. His brother Sean and his wife as well as Kari's brother and his wife and kids too. Even his parents live out here." Laurent pointed out to different places around the shore.

"In the lodge there's Kari and Andreas, their four kids, Skye, Ryan and Phillip. The extended family is gigantic, some days there are over forty people here. Devon, the youngest brother, lives with his wife and son in Portland but they're here all the time. The sisters-in-law are all very close."

He looked to her and saw the confusion on her face and smiled. "I know, it's a lot to take in, but you don't have to know every detail at this very moment. For now, why don't you freshen up? I'm just going out to sit on the porch. Come get me when you're ready."

Overwhelmed by the events of the day and all the information she'd been fed in the last hour, Rain wandered into the bathroom, grimacing into the mirror. Her eyes were puffy and red but at the same time it felt good that he knew the truth. It'd been so hard to live a lie for so long, to not be able to share her life with anyone. Being on guard every moment was exhausting.

She washed her face with cold water and after a few minutes with cool washcloth compresses the swelling and redness went away. She reached into her bag and put on a bit of lip gloss and finger combed her hair. She wanted these people to like her. They all seemed to adore Laurent and she couldn't blame them. He'd been so good to her in such a short time.

The short time thing along with the declaration of his love scared her. She shouldn't feel so much for someone after so short a time. It wasn't normal, was it? Still it felt right. She felt safe with him. She felt a lot of things for him. The chemistry between them was intense. Really intense. When he was near it was all she could do not to touch him or kiss him. She wanted his hands on her every moment. But it was more than lust, he made her warm and fuzzy inside too.

The way he'd told her about Andreas and the gallery, the way he'd assured her the decision to stay or not was up to her—she loved that he thought about that stuff. And she'd pretty much already decided that unless something freaky happened that afternoon she wanted to stay overnight. The whole place was heaven. So beautiful and green. The light was perfect and she couldn't wait to work.

Meanwhile, Laurent sat out on the deck, trying to process his rage. Rain's father had really done a number on her and seeing her in such terror over being found—at the thought of anyone she cared for being hurt—enraged him. Worse, that she imagined having to give up her art, when it was clear how much she loved it—he wanted to wring the man's neck.

On top of that Laurent himself had spooked her. He hadn't meant to move so fast. Telling her he loved her freaked her out, he could tell. Still, another positive thing about converting her was that the change would help make her even safer from her father. The more he was with her the more he wanted to be with her. He'd never thought it was possible to be so totally in love with someone after just two days but the thought that she'd be going back to her life in Seattle while he'd have to be at the lodge made him edgy. He didn't want to be separated from her, not even for a day. He knew he'd have to woo her and all but he wished she was already a werewolf and understood their culture so they could skip the whole dating thing and get straight to the mating bond ritual.

"Hi. It's beautiful out here. I think I'll get a lot of work done in this very spot." Rain came to stand next to his chair. Reaching out, he grabbed her waist, pulling her down into his lap so he could drink her in while he nuzzled his face into her hair.

"Feeling better, sweetheart?" he asked, massaging her shoulders.

"A bit. Oh that feels nice." She snuggled into him.

"Rain, watch it there." Laurent chuckled when she rubbed her ass into his lap as she squirmed, awakening his cock. His anger ebbed, replaced by an onslaught of pure lust.

"Hmmm. Laurent? Is that a pickle in your pocket or are you happy to see me?" She giggled. "Oh I crack myself up."

He groaned. Both at her silly pun and his predicament. He wanted to take her into the bedroom and spend the rest of the day showing her just how happy she did make him. But he knew his Pack. And he knew Andreas was probably holding Kari back bodily to keep her from coming down. They'd been there for half an hour already and by extension Rain was one of Kari's wolves, she'd want to be sure Rain was all right.

"Oh I'll show you just what it is. However if we don't go up to the lodge soon people will start coming down here."

Rain turned around so that she was straddling his lap. "Oh well. I was hoping for some hot, sweaty naked time with you. Like, in how much time will people start coming down?" Her voice was sultry and she stroked the heated softness of her pussy over his cock for emphasis.

He brought his lips to hers and their combined passions united and the flames overcame them. She mewled deep in her throat. The edge of need in the sound drove straight to his groin. Moaning, he pulled her tighter to him, one of his hands moving to cup her breast, the other sliding down to cup the curve of her ass.

Her hands went to his hair and pulled his mouth even closer. His breath became hers. Her head lolled back and he feasted on her neck and bit her pulse, marking her. In response she cried out, jerking back, arching her spine.

Standing, Laurent picked her up and she wrapped her legs around his waist as he carried her into the house, placing her on the counter in the kitchen. Her hands went to the waist of his jeans, yanking at them desperately. "I need you now, Laurent. Please," she panted.

He helped her out of her jeans and panties, spreading her thighs wide, exposing her pussy. He could see how slick and swollen she was and his breath whooshed out of him at the sight. "Shit. Hang on, I need to grab a condom from the other room." He stepped away but she grabbed him, pulling him back to her.

"No. Now. I'm on the Pill. Please, Laurent, I can't wait." She grabbed his cock in her hands and stroked it.

Groaning, he moved back to stand between her thighs, surging into her cunt in one stroke. She gasped, her fingers digging into his biceps, wrapping her legs around his waist. She was safe from STDs as wolves couldn't transmit them, they couldn't crossbreed with humans either so she was safe that way too, not that he could tell her either thing.

Shaking his head to dislodge any thought but of them at that moment, he began to stroke deep into her. Their coupling was hard, fast and wild, born out of fear of separation and acceptance of the intensity of feeling of one for the other. She was tight around him and he knew it wouldn't be long until he came. Her fiery heat surrounding him like a velvet vise drove him to distraction.

Releasing the tight grip on her hip, he moved his hand to her pussy, finding her clit swollen and ready for him. Spreading her honey, he flicked slick fingertips over her clit over and over. Her moans started soft but gained intensity as her hips rolled in unison with the thrust of his own, the heat of her pussy meeting his cock over and over.

The sounds she made, the smell of her hair in his face, the musk of her pussy and the hormonal perfume of their sex pushed at his control. "I'm going to come, come with me, sweetheart," he grunted out and she nodded before her head lolled back.

Her muscles tensed around him as he increased the speed and intensity of his thrusts. His fingers on her clit matched the rhythm of his movement into her pussy.

It hit them both in a screaming, moaning climax that most likely echoed out over the lake. His knees nearly buckled with the overwhelming sensation of her pussy coming around his cock. It seemed like his orgasm would never end. Each time he thought his breath was returning to normal a small aftershock would hit, driving him upward again.

His face buried in her neck, he stayed inside her for long minutes afterward, never going totally soft.

"That was…" Her words were slightly slurred as she panted.

"Yes. Every time with you is exceptional. You're so beautiful and so sexy." He kissed her forehead before pulling out and helping her down.

"I'll just freshen up again and we can go up to the lodge." She grabbed her jeans and underwear and headed back to the bathroom. This time when she looked in the mirror she saw a lush, sexy woman with kiss-swollen lips and passion in her eyes. She cleaned up quickly, getting dressed and redoing her lip gloss and hair.

It was as good as it was going to get. With one last smoothing hand over her hair, she went out front where Laurent waited for her.

"Shall we then, love?" He held out his hand and she took it and they walked back up to the lodge.

"Laurent?"

He turned to her, smiling. "Yes?"

"I'd like to stay here tonight if that's okay with you."

Leaning down, he kissed her quickly but thoroughly. "Okay? I'd be thrilled. Thank you. I'm very much looking forward to waking up with you again."

When they walked in through the side doors of the big house, everyone got up and looked toward them both, smiling.

"Well, you both certainly look better," a tall lanky man with black hair like Laurent's said with a wry grin.

"Rain Foster, this is Skyler Andrews. He fancies himself a comedian. Don't take anything he says seriously."

"Ah, pshaw, Laurent. You can take this to the bank, Rain, you are very welcome here at Star Lake Lodge. We've all been waiting to meet the woman who has so captured Laurent's heart. I can see why he's smitten. Can I just tell you that I've always had a deep appreciation for heart-shaped asses?" He gave her an infectious grin and a wink.

Laurent growled, smacking him playfully. "Hey! Watch yourself."

"Thanks, I think." Rain smiled, unable not to.

"I'm going to introduce everyone. Don't try to remember all the names." Laurent chuckled and Rain felt a bit easier.

"This is Ryan. He and Kari run a computer gaming company out of the lodge."

She smiled at the tall man with caramel-colored hair. Did Laurent know any short, homely men at all?

"Welcome, Rain." Ryan smiled at her warmly and took her hand, kissing it.

"This is Sean, Andreas' younger brother. The lovely woman beside him is his wife Emma. She's a doctor in town."

Emma walked forward and gave her a hug. "I know it's a bit overwhelming but we are all very happy to meet you."

"You have already met Kari and Andreas." Rain looked at the giant man who had the tiny woman folded into his side. They both looked incredibly in love.

"Welcome again. I'm really looking forward to seeing your artwork," Kari said warmly.

"Our house is yours. I mean that truly. Laurent is like a brother to me. This has been his home for over thirty years. By extension you're our family too," Andreas added.

Laurent interrupted quickly. "You met Anna outside. She's sort of the den mother around here. She's an amazing cook. Nothing happens without her." He put his arm around the gray-haired woman who'd been so kind to her outside earlier.

"Are you feeling better, love?" Anna asked her, grabbing her hands. "I've made you a pot of tea, that should help." She smiled and pointed to the older man at her side, "That's Gregory, he's my husband and he does the work to keep this place running."

Gregory tipped an imaginary hat at her, smiling. "Nice to meet you, Rain."

"This is Jack, Kari's brother, and his wife Alyssa. He's a police officer in town. Alyssa does website design out of their home."

They both smiled at her broadly and said their hellos and welcomes.

"Last but not least this is Phillip. He's Kari's bodyguard and has been my right-hand man for the last sixteen years." Laurent indicated a tall broad man with a long strawberry-blond braid.

He walked forward and embraced her and said into her ear, "Both you and your secret are safe with us."

She looked back and up into his face, confused for a moment until it occurred to her he meant the situation with her father. "Thank you."

"Well, that's the basics. These are the people who live here except for the kids, you'll meet them when they get out of school. Jade and Tomas, Sean and Andreas' parents, are away on a road trip right now," Laurent explained.

"I imagine you're hungry. I've prepared some lunch so let's go into the dining room." Anna waved her hands to spur them on and led the way through to a large room dominated by a huge table.

"So Rain just got offered a show in six weeks at The Holt. Diane Holt also offered her another solo show at her gallery in Portland in six months," Laurent announced with a proud smile.

"Really? How wonderful! You know Andreas owns part of The Holt but I imagine that you're like me and glad you got it without influence. You have to watch these guys. They get a bit, shall we say, zealous when it comes to the women they care about. It drives me nuts," Kari said. "It's all with good intentions but still annoying." She winked.

"Yes, I was glad to know I got the show on my own merits. No denying the *who you know* influence in the art world, in fact my friend Shane is the one who told me that The Holt was looking for new artists to begin with. But knowing that I got a show because my art is good, that means a lot. By the way, this is a beautiful place. I think I'll be doing a lot of work here."

"I'll bring your stuff out to the cabin when we're finished with lunch, *mon coeur*."

She smiled at him, he'd called her my heart. "Thank you." The way he looked at her made her feel stifled and free all at the same time. The whole experience was a bit overwhelming, all of these strangers talking to her like she was Laurent's new wife or something when she'd known him all of a few days. It was odd but comforting too. She liked them all very much but she couldn't help but feel slightly wary.

After lunch Kari, Emma and Alyssa took her for a walk around the lake and by the time they came back to the lodge the van with the kids had pulled into the drive.

"Ah, your competition has arrived," Kari said, laughing.

"Helene?"

"Laurent told you about her? She adores him. He's been like another father to her since she was born. I've told her about you and she told me this morning that she was willing to share Laurent with you as long as he always took her to the fair and they still got to have their special days fishing on the lake."

The door to the van slid open and children began running out toward the house. "The tallest boy and little girl in the blue dress are mine. Max and Drea," Alyssa said, waving at them both.

"The tall one with the brown braids is Hellie, looks so much like her uncle Sean. The blond one who looks just like Andreas is Tomas, her twin. The two imps with dirty faces are the youngest twins, Sean and Devon." Kari smiled, watching them tear into the house.

"And the littlest blond boy is Matthew, and the bossy little miss telling him what to do is Jade. Both mine," Emma said.

"Such beautiful kids." Rain smiled, feeling a bit of jealousy that these women seemed so in love and had such beautiful families. While the whole situation and extended family thing at the lodge made her wary, she had to admit she wanted it. Wanted to be a part of something that seemed so idyllic. Could she dare imagine herself here with these women? Laurent at her side, children running around?

By the time they walked back into the lodge Hellie had ensconced herself in Laurent's lap and was busily telling him all about her day. Laurent idly bounced her on his knee, smiling and listening intently.

"If she wasn't so young I think I'd have some major competition," she murmured and Kari laughed.

"Hey, kiddos, this is Rain, Laurent's...friend."

The children waved, holding cookies and milk aloft.

Rain sat down next to Jade and Devon, who proceeded to chat her ear off about the frogs their tadpoles had turned into. She laughed delightedly as the story unfolded with much drama.

"Well hello, Laurent! You're back!" a female voice actually cooed from the doorway.

Rain turned toward it and saw a tall redheaded woman standing there, looking at Laurent like he was a slice of pie. Laurent looked up in surprise.

"Paloma. I didn't know you'd be here."

"Surprised?" She laughed.

Rain's eyebrow rose despite herself. *Who was this?*

Kari sighed and Emma murmured to her, too low for Rain to hear.

Paloma sidled over and insinuated herself next to Laurent. Rain looked to Laurent then, waiting for a response on his part. Something to let the redhead know he was there with Rain.

Kari interrupted quickly, "Paloma, what a nice surprise. Please say hello to Rain. She's Laurent's girlfriend."

At that pronouncement Paloma's pretty face fell into a pout and she turned back to Laurent without even addressing Rain. "Really now? Interesting. Did you tell her about us?"

Laurent sighed deeply. "Paloma, I believe that Rain is waiting for you to say hello."

Rain jerked back at Laurent's silence with regard to what Rain was to him and with whoever the hell this woman was. This was after all the man who told her he loved her and needed her—and yet he failed to make that clear to this chick sticking her boobs out at him.

Kari cleared her throat, raising her eyebrows at Laurent.

The redhead turned and looked Rain over with clear derision. "Hi. I take it you're human?"

Rain laughed but there was an edge to it that every woman in the room recognized. "What else would I be?" *The nerve!* She stood up. "I'm feeling tired, if you'll excuse me," she said and left the room through the sliders on the deck off the dining room and started down the hillside toward the cabin.

"What on earth did you say that for?" Andreas roared.

"Children, why don't you go to the playroom?" Phillip said and Anna came out with a plate of cookies and more milk and led the way through the house to the playroom.

"What?" Paloma said, feigning innocence.

"Of course she's human, you could smell it. You mentioned it just to bait her," Laurent growled out.

"Why is she here anyway? Jesus, Laurent, she's some human mouse. Why her when you can have a wolf?"

"She's my Mate, don't speak of her that way. And I don't want you, I've told you that before," Laurent growled. Paloma put her hand on his arm and stroked it and at that moment Rain came back into the room to retrieve the sketchpad she'd left.

"I think I should be getting back to Seattle," she said to Laurent through clenched teeth.

Laurent stood up. "*Amorueux*, this is not what it seems. Come, little heart, let's talk about it."

Rain snorted and walked out. *As if calling her sweetheart was gonna alleviate the trouble he was in now.* Kari gave an *I told you so* look at Andreas, who'd been squeezing her hand to keep her quiet, but she held her tongue, for which Laurent was eternally grateful.

He shoved a hand through his hair and went after Rain.

When he got back to the cabin she was shoving her stuff back into her duffel bag. Stalking over, he grabbed the bag and put it on the floor. He took her arm. "What are you doing?"

"Leaving. That way you and your redheaded friend can be alone. I'm sure I can catch a bus back to Seattle in town."

"You aren't going anywhere. I don't want to be alone with Paloma, I want to be with you. She's nothing to me, Rain. I was telling her that and she touched me right as you walked into the room. You ran out before I could explain."

"She asked if I was human! She rubbed herself all over you and you didn't do a thing! What kind of man doesn't stand up for a woman he's just told he loves?" She was mad now, which was better than the hurt she'd been feeling. She could deal with anger more easily than heartbreak.

"Rain, I don't know what to do in these situations. I'm not some Don Juan. I've never dated anyone seriously before much less told a woman I loved her, well, other than my mother or Hellie. There is no one else for me, count on it. I *am not* interested in Paloma."

"So tell me what the story is," she said, arms crossed.

"I'll tell you if you tell me about your family."

"You're actually going to try to bargain with me right now? After the way you just acted? You've got to be joking."

79

"Look, it's only fair. I share, you share. Come on, Rain, give a little."

"Fine," she ground out.

"Fine. Paloma is a part of the, um, extended family here. She and I dated a few times but it was *never* serious. The last time I was with her was at least seven months ago. I've told her ever since that I'm not interested."

"The last time you were *with* her? As in, your dick inside of her with her?"

Laurent cringed. "You get vulgar when you're jealous. Remind me to never underestimate you. Yes. She and I had sex."

"A lot or a little?"

"Enough."

"What the hell does that mean? Did you fuck her, like, a hundred times or, like, two times?" *Mousy huh, she'd show him just how opposite a mouse she was.*

"Why is it important?"

"So a hundred times then."

"What? Where do you get that?"

"Your total evasion of the answer." She glared at him.

"Women! We had sex about a dozen times. There, satisfied?"

"Um, no. See, so now I'm expected to hang out with some woman you've had sex with, and she's still obviously in favor of continuing the situation, for the day? Oh no."

"Rain, she is *nothing* to me. It was totally casual and meaningless. You are the opposite of that. Whether she's here or not I am with you. You have to know that. Can't you see how I feel about you?"

"Yes, I saw it when you sat there saying nothing when she was a total bitch to me. Oh and again when I walked out and you stayed to get rubbed on by her. If you *care* for me so much, Laurent, why didn't you defend me? She sat there and insulted me and you said nothing!"

"It's best to ignore her. She likes to push buttons. I'm sorry if I hurt your feelings and made you feel like I didn't want to defend you. I just didn't want to engage with her and make her think anything she said mattered. It doesn't matter. You and I matter, that's it." He reached out to caress her cheek and she didn't pull away. "You drive me crazy, Rain. I want you so much," he said in an anguished whisper and kissed her lips.

She snorted and he started to laugh. "What?" she demanded.

"I used to watch Andreas and Kari and when she'd drive him nuts, just like you're doing to me, I'd think to myself, *I'd never let a woman do that to me*. And yet here I am, right where he was, and I love every frustrating minute of it. Not a single woman on the face of this planet is as beautiful and strong and talented as you are. None can hold a candle to you. I want you and only you. I love you and only you. There are no others for me and there will never be again. Do you understand, Rain?"

"Does she?" Rain challenged back.

He grinned at her. "I stayed back to make that clear. She knows."

She smiled at his declaration and sat down on the couch. He sat next to her and she snuggled into his side. "Now you have a tale of your own to tell?"

She sighed. "So you know that my family is involved in organized crime already. I grew up in a world where women were accessories—daughters, mothers and wives. There are mistresses as well but they have their own world and aren't spoken of. Anyway, from an early age my sister and I were trained to be dutiful daughters. We were sent to college but really only in preparation for marriage. I went to graduate school but only because my mother intervened so hard on my behalf.

81

"My father and his buddies actually arranged mine and my sister's marriages when we were young. My sister married a fifty-five-year-old friend of my dad's, a man who'd saved his life. This man was a widower and has three children, all of whom are older than she is. My sister is twenty-three years old." Rain sighed.

"Anyway. I knew who my husband-to-be was. The son of one of my dad's *associates*. Anthony wasn't a bad guy really, at least he was my age. He's the person who took my virginity at twenty-four, not that the event was very memorable. Anyway, my dad put the pressure on for me to marry Anthony. I resisted. I didn't love him, I wanted to paint. My dad insisted, Anthony insisted, Anthony's father insisted. I agreed but secretly I went to my mother, who agreed to help me run. She started to put aside money for me here and there. My dad knew something was up and started to have me watched very closely. He made me leave my job so I had no money of my own. I agreed to marry Anthony but set the date a year out, saying that we had to plan a bash significant enough for a man of my father's stature. He, being the egomaniacal asshole that he is, agreed and the pressure lightened a bit but I still had no car and no money.

"One day, after a fitting of my dress, Anthony came over and he was high. He had a problem with crystal meth. Anyway, we argued and he beat me up pretty badly. My eye was swollen up and he actually fractured my arm in two places. The worst part is that he did it in a room filled with people and none of them did a thing to help me. My father came in and finally made him stop. He looked at me and shook his head and said, 'Julia, this is what happens when you can't keep your fiancé happy, don't let it happen again' and he turned and walked away, leaving me there. My aunt convinced them to let me go to the hospital and get treated. That's what saved my life. My mom took me and they left us alone. She knew none of them — my father's men — would come to the emergency room for fear of getting arrested. I got treated and my mother and aunt gave me all of their cash, my mom gave me some jewelry, the money she'd saved up, and they dropped me at the bus station with the clothes I had on my back, bruises and all and my arm in a sling.

"I walked in, bought three tickets, one to Salt Lake, one to Florida and one to Boston. I took the bus to Boston and got off halfway there and took the train out here. I never looked back.

"I call my mother once a month at the pay phone near her beauty salon. My dad doesn't know where I am and I don't know how long it will be before he starts to look for me. I think at first he thought that I'd come back when I ran out of money but you know, I'm not afraid to work hard. My first few months here I picked apples in Yakima on weekends for extra money. I got the job at The Black Cat about eight months ago after meeting Harrison and Andrew and moving in there. I have a small amount of cash, enough to split if I need to. I won't go back but I can't involve anyone either. My father won't hesitate to hurt people to get what he wants."

By the time she'd finished Laurent trembled with rage. The thought of anyone putting his hands on Rain, of hitting her so hard her bones fractured—it was enough that he felt his wolf chafing to rise. He had to take a few deep breaths to drive it back down.

"Bet you're sorry you met me now, huh? Listen, just drop me in town and I'll get back to Seattle. Pretend you never met me. I'll be gone in a day. I'll choose another city and another name and be out of your life."

He looked at her then, anger in his eyes, and she flinched. "No, Rain. Never fear me. I would never raise a hand in anger toward you. *Never*. I love you, I want to cherish and protect you. My anger is about your father and this Anthony, it's not toward you. I knew you were strong but, Rain, you're amazing to have done all that on your own. Oh *mon coeur*, my heart, you've been alone for so long, haven't you?"

She choked back a sob. "Yes."

"Not anymore. I'm your family now, Julia."

"I'm not Julia anymore. Julia is dead. I'm Rain."

"Okay, Rain. Why Rain by the way?"

She smiled. "I got off the train at Union Station in downtown Seattle. I'd been on the train and panicked with fear. But despite being downtown, despite how tired I was, the rain hit my face and everything sort of washed away. The rain took the weight from my shoulders." She shrugged. "It just seemed appropriate."

He smiled, leaning in to kiss her temple. "I like that. Now we will all have to put our heads together and find a way out of this. You cannot live in fear any longer." He threaded her fingers with his own.

They were sitting there, watching the light dim and the pinks and purples of the sunset stain the sky when they heard a quiet tap at the door.

Laurent called out for whomever it was to come in and the door opened, Ryan standing in the frame.

"Is everything all right? Phillip and I brought Rain's art supplies down for her. Shall we just leave them here in the living room?" Phillip came into the room holding the bag with her pads and Ryan put the case carrying the paints, brushes, charcoals and pencils down beside it.

"Thank you both, you're very kind," Rain said. "That's an understatement but I mean it genuinely."

"I'm afraid you haven't been shown much hospitality," Ryan apologized.

"Ah, what's one jealous bitch? The rest of you have been lovely," she said, getting up and stretching.

Laurent laughed and Ryan and Phillip joined in. "You'll fit in with the other women here just fine." Phillip came over and hugged her. She realized that they *felt* like family.

"I'm going to go out on the deck to sketch for a while, the light is so pretty right now." She grabbed her watercolor pencils and a sketch pad and headed outside. Settling down into one of the big chairs, she tucked her feet beneath her body and flipped her hair back over her shoulder before getting to work.

"She's gorgeous, Laurent," Phillip said as they watched her sketch, totally lost in her own head.

"Spunky too. I imagine that since you are still able to walk without a limp that you were able to explain the Paloma situation to her satisfaction." Ryan wore a wry grin.

Laurent sighed. "Women! Why on earth she'd be mad when she's my Mate is beyond me!

"Because if some man was rubbing himself on her you'd be freaking out. Admit it, Laurent. You can't expect her to just know anything. And I seem to remember you telling Andreas all of this back when Kari came to us," Phillip said, smiling, remembering back to the first days that Kari had come to the Pack.

"If some man rubbed any body part against her he'd lose it." Laurent growled dangerously and Phillip and Ryan laughed.

"Kari, Emma and Alyssa took Paloma aside earlier. I think she'll be behaving for now at least. While it's more diverting to have a few unmated females with us now, it's also troublesome at times like these. Too many bitches," Ryan said and Laurent and Phillip nodded energetically.

"When do you plan to tell her?" Phillip asked, meaning about being a werewolf.

"In time. She just told me the story of how she ran from her family and that's enough trauma for a bit."

"Bad huh?"

"I can't talk about it right now I'm so angry. It's bad, very bad. We will have to brainstorm to see what we can do to keep her safe later."

"Okay. Don't be late for dinner or you know you'll have half the Pack down here." Ryan and Phillip went back out the front door and Laurent followed them, chatting for a few more minutes while the sun set and Rain finished her sketching.

Rain came back into the cabin and went into the bedroom to change her clothes. She put a bit of goo in her hair to tame the flyaway hairs and keep the curl, dabbed on some lipstick and mascara and changed into a skirt. She opted for a pale blue dress shirt hanging in Laurent's closet though. She put in some hoop earrings and used a tortoiseshell clip to pull some of the hair off her face, fastening it at the nape of her neck. That was about as good as it got—she didn't wear a lot of makeup.

"Hey there," she called out, joining the three of them on the front lawn. She paused a moment as she caught sight of Laurent and his friends. The moment seemed perfect. Tiny white lights lit the trees around the lodge and along the path, the moon was three quarters and hung large and low in the sky, painting the scene with silver and hues of gold. Laurent's hair was loose, how she liked it, shimmering in the light.

Their united masculinity hung in the air. She could almost smell the testosterone between them all. She envied their connection to each other, loved the sense of brotherhood they seemed to have with each other.

The best thing though was the way Laurent's face changed when he caught sight of her. He made her feel like the most beautiful woman alive. How lucky was she? Suddenly everything seemed to be all right. Because of how he looked at her.

Laurent turned and his heart stopped for a moment, looking at her. She was so feminine and soft and yet so strong. He smiled when he saw she wore one of his shirts. He wrapped an arm around her, pulling her into his side.

"You look beautiful. I like this skirt a lot." The skirt sort of wrapped around her, leaving a slit up the side. Nothing daring but very sexy. Her hair hung in curls down her back. He leaned in and breathed in her scent and calm overtook him.

"I like the shirt myself." She gave him a sexy smile, eyes dancing with mischief.

"I like what's under it," he said into her ear and she laughed, a rich throaty sound that sent shivers down his spine.

"That's enough, you two! As if Kari and Andreas weren't bad enough." Phillip chuckled.

"Let's go up to the lodge, dinner will be ready soon. Would you like a drink?" Ryan asked, falling into step next to Rain and Laurent.

"Yeah, a drink would be nice."

"A celebratory drink, in honor of your show," Laurent said and Phillip agreed.

"God, this morning seems so long ago."

"I'm sorry that today has been such a trial. You've dealt with a lot."

She shrugged and he wanted to make everything better for her. He would if it was the last thing he did.

"Rain, wanna play Chutes and Ladders with us?" Hellie asked as they walked into the house. She came to grab Rain's hand, looking up at her expectantly.

"Oh yes. I love Chutes and Ladders! You'll have to take it easy on me though, I'm sure you're all very good at it." She allowed Hellie to lead her into the great room where her brothers were gathered around the board already. She sat on the floor with them, playing for half an hour, laughing and letting them beat her. Laurent sat on the couch, his knees touching her back, and watched, smiling.

"Dinner is ready, come on in here!" Anna called out and Rain helped the kids put away the game. After a tussle and some negotiation, Tomas held her hand as they went into the dining room, little Devon on the other side, both gazing up at her adoringly.

"It appears that you've got some competition, Laurent." Phillip chuckled as he watched Rain interact with the boys so easily.

Laurent laughed and grabbed the boys, one under each arm. "Sorry, boys, Rain is taken. You'll have to find your own female." They giggled at Laurent's gruff growls.

The kids all had their own table next to the main table and Anna laid out a less ornate dinner of chicken fingers and mashed potatoes for them while the adults got chicken divan and rosemary-and-garlic-roasted potatoes and grilled vegetables.

Andreas stood up and looked down the long table, smiling and holding his wineglass aloft. "A toast, to Rain, on her first art show, and to Laurent, for being lucky enough to have been starving and having begged me to pull over at the next place, that place being the restaurant where he met Rain."

"Hear, hear!" Laurent said and they all raised their glasses and toasted. Even Paloma, who still looked disgruntled at Rain and covetous toward Laurent.

After dinner they all sat in the great room and had drinks while talking and laughing. Rain drew funny portraits of the children, to their immense delight. Laurent loved seeing how well Rain fit into their family. He also made sure to sit curled around Rain all night and to avoid looking at Paloma at all.

"Time for bed, kids," Kari called out, the children's moans and protests meeting her pronouncement. Sean and Emma took their two home, saying they'd be back the following day. Alyssa and Jack followed with their two as well, leaving Kari and Andreas' rowdy lot, who begged and pleaded until their mother allowed Rain to read them a story.

Rain went upstairs and after the children had all changed into pajamas and were tucked into their beds she sat in the middle of the room. But instead of reading she made up a complicated and action-packed story about a prince and princess who were really superheroes and traveled the universe saving people.

Andreas stood in the doorway with Laurent. Laurent didn't miss the way both his friends looked at Rain. His woman was something special. He looked at Kari whose eyes twinkled, knowing the way to her heart was through the children. Rain was so naturally loving with them they responded back, sensing what a genuine person she was. Even Hellie who hadn't had to share Laurent since the moment she was born seemed to adore Rain.

Rain leaned over and delivered smooches to each child before leaving the room with a promise to see them all the next day.

"You're a natural with them. They'll be so upset when you go back to Seattle," Kari laughed as they went back downstairs. "You know, you could always move up here, heck, you could even have a cabin of your own for a studio for your art."

Rain laughed and squeezed Kari's hand. "Your children are wonderful but my life is in Seattle. I have a job and a place to live. I'm sure I'll be back again."

Laurent scowled at Andreas over Rain's head. He was annoyed that Kari brought up Rain moving in so fast. He wanted to slowly introduce the idea of her moving to the lodge, not scare her even more. Andreas merely shrugged as if to say, 'hey, you know Kari, I have no say'.

"Come on, Rain, let's go for a walk," Laurent said, flashing an annoyed glance at Kari who raised one shoulder and grinned back at him.

"Sounds lovely." Rain took his hand.

"I think a run sounds even better," Paloma purred, giving Laurent a meaningful look.

"Isn't it sort of dark for a jog?" Rain asked.

Phillip narrowed his eyes at Paloma and Skye grabbed her arm and dragged her out of the room.

"What was that all about?" Rain stopped in her tracks, looking between the people left in the room.

"Nothing," Laurent growled.

Lauren Dane

"She's really going to jog at this time of night in the dark in the woods? And what's with all the growling anyway? You all do it so much."

"With Paloma who knows? She's odd." Laurent avoided the question about the growling.

"You're up to something, Laurent. I can tell when people are hiding something. What is it?" Rain cocked her head and put her hands on her hips.

He gathered a very stiff Rain into his arms and showered kisses all over her face. "So suspicious! What could I possibly be hiding? How about that walk?"

"Yes, a walk sounds wonderful. Andreas and I would love to come as well." Kari cast a glance back to where Skye animatedly explained something to Paloma.

Rain looked at the three of them and back around to where Skye stood with Paloma. Something was up and they were all trying to cover it up. Suspicion sat like lead in her gut. "No, thank you. I'll be going back to the cabin. If anyone here would like to tell me the truth I'll be glad to hear it." She pushed out of Laurent's arms and stalked out.

"What could I possibly be hiding!" Rain mumbled, imitating Laurent. She shouldn't have come up there. She was trapped now and she wanted to get home, away from all of these people. They were all very nice and she felt an unbelievable sense of rightness about being there. But there was something not being said, something major, and she had had enough of being lied to.

Once Rain stalked out Laurent growled dangerously, looking toward Paloma. "What on earth do you think you're doing? You know she doesn't know about us yet. You're deliberately making trouble, Paloma. I should point out to you how stupid that is when as my Mate Rain will outrank you in Pack hierarchy. Then what will you do?"

"If you *love* this human so much why haven't you told her about what we are?" Paloma spat out, saying the word "human" with loathing.

"First of all, Paloma, I was human before I came here too. I have had enough of your anti-human talk. I am your queen, am I not?" Kari asked angrily.

"You're different. This human is not fit to be mate to our Third."

"It is not up to you to decide that!" Andreas roared and assumed his full height and width. The hairs on Laurent's arms rose up at the power spilling out of his Alpha. "If you do anything to upset Rain again I will personally expel you from this Pack, do you understand?"

Paloma fell to the ground and prostrated herself at Andreas' feet in total submissiveness to her Alpha's authority.

"Go to Rain, Laurent. You have to tell her soon."

"I can't tell her tonight, Andreas. She's had enough to deal with for one day."

Andreas looked at Laurent, smiling and shaking his head. "I seem to recall you telling me that things had to be done when Kari was brought over, that it was too late and had to be dealt with."

"Yes but she was already made. Rain hasn't been. The situation is different," Laurent said, his chin out stubbornly.

Kari laughed and kissed Laurent's cheek, rubbing her face along his jawline. "She'll have to be told sometime. The sooner the better. It's easier if you tell her here now than back in Seattle."

Laurent sighed and stalked out of the room, heading back to the cabin. He walked in and discovered that Rain had locked herself in the master bedroom. "Rain? It's Laurent, let me in." He knocked softly on the door.

"I'm trying to sleep. I put your clothes in the spare room. You can take me back to Seattle in the morning."

Laurent frowned and clenched his fists. "Rain, open the door!" he ordered through a clenched jaw.

"Good night, Laurent. That is, unless you plan to explain to me just exactly what is going on here."

"You're being stubborn. I am not hiding anything!"

"You're full of shit, Laurent Cole! Just be sure to wake early, I need to get back to the city first thing."

"You don't have to be back at work until Sunday, I wasn't going to take you back until late tomorrow afternoon."

"Hmm, well I don't remember asking for your permission."

"I will not discuss this with you through a closed door!"

Silence. He pounded on the door. More silence. "Rain, love, let's talk."

"Are you going to tell me the whole truth?"

"I'm not hiding anything." Laurent knew she'd be pissed off when she heard the whole story but he truly didn't think she was ready to know he was a werewolf, not after the whole drama about her father had unfolded earlier that day.

"Good night then."

He banged his forehead against the door several times. This mating business was frustrating. Why couldn't Rain just accept that he knew what was best for her and trust him? He stiffened, he could smell her tears and hear her quiet sobs. "Rain, please, I can hear you crying. Let me in."

"NO! If I let you in we'll end up in bed and I'll hate myself for being so weak. I can't abide this, Laurent. You're lying about something and the rest of your friends are helping you hide it. I don't want to be a part of that. You will leave me alone and take me back to Seattle. In fact, why don't you just take me now?"

He sighed. "I'm going for a walk. Stay inside. We'll talk tomorrow."

"Say hello to that bitch Paloma," she called out, a hitch in her voice.

He wanted to howl in frustration. "I won't be seeing Paloma, Rain. Why don't you come for a walk with me?"

"Why don't you piss off?" she hurled back and he wanted to laugh but wisely stifled it. Despite the situation, he had to admire her balls.

He left the cabin and walked to the edge of the woods. A run would take the edge off his anger and frustration. Shedding his clothes, he dropped to all fours and closed his eyes. His human self sank beneath the waves and his wolf rose and he transformed. The world was black and gray but the scents painted a vivid portrait of the world. Deep, loamy earth, bright, clear skies, the sharp scent of pine, the musk of animals and his Pack—nature called to him and, shaking himself out, he answered, taking off at a run.

* * * * *

A few hours later Rain opened the door and peeked out. She crept through the cabin, quietly peeking into the spare room, snorting with rage when she saw that Laurent was still gone. It had been four hours! It was after one a.m. Where in the hell had he gone? She threw on some jeans and a sweatshirt and slipped on her tennis shoes before heading outside. The night was clear and cool. She walked toward the lodge but the lights were out. Reversing direction, she walked along a path toward the edge of the woods and came to a halt at the manicured edge of the forest. She peered at something moving in the breeze. Upon closer inspection she saw it was clothing. Laurent's clothing. She walked closer and saw more clothes, women's clothing. She gritted her teeth and stood there, waiting.

Laurent walked out of the woods, tall, regal and naked, and met the angry eyes of Rain, who sat next to the tree where his clothes hung. Paloma followed and Rain's eyes widened and then narrowed instantly when she saw that she was naked too. She stood up, eyes flashing dangerously. Pain and fury warred inside her. She'd never trust her judgment again.

Laurent put his hands up. "Rain, what are you doing here? I thought I told you to stay in the cabin."

Rain's eyebrows flew up and she snorted. "Oh, sorry to interrupt your little naked party. I'll be packing. You can take me back when you get finished with whatever it is you're doing." She spun around and ran back toward the cabin.

"Rain, let me explain," he called out when he caught up to her at the cabin.

"Fuck you, Laurent Cole! Oh my god, how could I have been so stupid? I slept with a total stranger and let him bring me hundreds of miles from home." She started shoving clothes back into her bag and Laurent followed her into the bedroom.

"Rain, let me explain." He tried to touch her but she pulled away.

"Don't. Touch. Me," she gritted out and zipped her bag up. Sweeping past him, she grabbed her art supplies. "You will take me back to Seattle now." She walked past him and he grabbed her arm to stop her.

"You aren't going anywhere, Rain. Let me explain what you saw."

"How stupid do you think I am? I may not be sophisticated but I am intelligent. You walked out of the woods *naked* with a woman who was rubbing herself all over you earlier in the day. A woman you admitted to *fucking*. Were you collecting mushrooms for dinner tomorrow? Oh, I know, you were bird watching and it scares the birds if you wear clothes!"

"SIT DOWN!" Laurent thundered and she jumped. "Please." His voice softened.

She sat down and the shame washed through him as he saw and tasted her fear. He sighed. "This is going to sound farcical and ridiculous but here goes. I'm a werewolf. Everyone here is a werewolf. We were running tonight, as

94

wolves. Skye and Philip were running too, they came out of the woods after you ran off. You need to be naked when you change, that's why we were naked. Nudity before and after a change is necessary or you ruin your clothes. It's not a big deal to us."

Rain shook her head, her hands trembled in her lap. "I'm going to just call a cab. That way they can take me to town and I'll get back to Seattle from there. I'm sure Harrison will come and get me. Don't bother to contact me. I won't be taking your calls." She stood up and walked out the door. He grabbed her arm in panic and his wolf fought to surface.

"Rain, I told you the truth. Please, let's talk though this."

She tried to break free of his grip but he held onto her, worried for her safety, not wanting her to run off, horrified that she'd been afraid of him. Wanting to comfort her and make her all right.

"You're hurting me!" she yelled out and Skye came out of the shadows.

"Laurent, let go of her arm, you'll bruise her that way," he said softly, his hands up, trying to be non-threatening. But all Laurent felt was the threat of another wolf moving toward his frightened Mate. Protectiveness roiled up through his system, nearly blinding him.

Laurent growled at him and Rain's eyes grew huge. "Stay out of this, Skye."

"You're a lot bigger than Anthony is. I'm sure you'll break bones instead of just fracturing them. Is that what you want, Laurent? Are you just like him? After all of your sweet talk are you going to bully and hurt me too?" Rain asked, a hitch in her voice. She trembled, her pupils wide with fear.

Laurent wrestled his wolf back and felt as though he'd been slapped. Chastened and horrified he'd scared her, he let her go quickly. "No, no, baby, I'd never hurt you." Emotion choked his voice.

She pulled up the sleeve of her shirt, showed where he'd ripped it at the shoulders. He also saw the pale red mark where his thumb had been. Remorse and horror slid through him and he wanted to throw himself to the ground and howl. If he bruised her he'd die of the shame. "Oh god, I'm sorry. Please believe me, Rain. I didn't mean, god, I'm a werewolf, I'm so much stronger than any human. I shouldn't have grabbed your arm but I did not mean to harm you. You have to know that. Please, come back inside. Let me get Kari, she was human once too, she can talk to you about us."

She made an anguished sound and broke into a run, back toward the gravel drive that led to the road. Phillip caught up to her and stopped her, bringing her into his arms. She started kicking and screaming, pounding at him with her fists. "Let me go! You're all crazy!"

Phillip tightened his hold on her and said into her ear, "Please, sweetheart, calm down. You'll get hurt. I know you're afraid but you can't just run off into the forest. You don't know where you are, you could get lost or something could happen to you."

Laurent and Skye approached and Laurent looked like he wanted to kill Phillip for holding Rain so close and stroking her hair. Kari and Andreas burst out the front door. "What is going on?" Andreas bellowed and Rain's trembling worsened. Laurent moaned in anguish, wanting to comfort her but knowing he'd just make it worse.

"She saw us coming out of the woods, naked. Paloma was running with us. Rain ran off and Laurent told her about us but she's frightened. Laurent grabbed her and he hurt her, her shirt got ripped. Not on purpose," Phillip added quickly. "She apparently got beaten up by her fiancé before and she's just very scared."

"I want to go home! You can't k-keep me here!" Rain sobbed and Phillip held her tightly, nuzzling the top of her head under his chin, trying to calm her down.

Kari approached slowly. "Rain, why don't you come into the lodge with me? All of the guys will go away. We'll have hot chocolate, talk a bit. All right? I've been where you are right now. I *know* how scared you are. But no one here would ever hurt you, I promise."

Phillip let Rain go and she turned, pulling on the sleeve of her shirt, showing where it'd ripped. Her creamy skin bore a fading red mark where he'd held onto her so tightly. Thank goodness it didn't look like it would bruise. "Oh yeah? Just what is your idea of not being hurt?"

Kari looked back at Laurent, who looked so crestfallen she knew he hadn't meant to use so much strength on Rain. Kari reached out gently and took Rain's hand. "Come on, let's go inside. If you want to go back to Seattle we won't stop you but promise to hear me out."

"NO!" Laurent roared and Rain winced and her tears started anew.

"Andreas, deal with your Lieutenant!" Kari hissed. Andreas stalked over and hauled Laurent away, Ryan helping.

"He's gone now, Rain. How about that hot chocolate? Anna makes really good hot chocolate. Phillip is going to come inside with us but he'll leave the room while we talk, okay?" Kari spoke in gentle tones.

Rain looked at Kari and nodded slowly. She didn't resist when Kari took her hand to lead her back up the steps and into the lodge. Phillip threw a worried look over his shoulder before following.

"Just what the hell do you think you were doing, Laurent? How could you hurt her like that?" Andreas barked as they got inside of the cabin.

"I didn't mean to! She was freaked, she was panicked and leaving and I just grabbed her arm to stop her," Laurent said, his face in his hands. "I didn't mean to use that much strength on her. Don't you think I'd take it back if I could? I've never,

ever hurt a woman. I love her. Damn it, my wolf rose, she was so scared and I wanted to protect her. I just reached out quickly. I'm not trying to excuse what I did but I didn't mean to harm her."

"He saw me and it agitated his wolf on top of everything else. He felt threatened by another male who was trying to protect his Mate," Skye said, flopping into a chair.

"You can punish me for it. Before the whole Pack. I'll take it because I deserve it."

There was a collective intake of breath. Public punishment of a Pack member was an old custom rarely enforced. To volunteer to be beaten before the whole Pack was a huge deal.

"No one is going to beat you. You're doing a good enough job yourself, Laurent. Once she talks to Kari, hopefully she'll understand and forgive you. Hell, one of my Pack nearly killed my wife and she forgave me. It wasn't on purpose and you didn't do it in anger. It's a ripped shirt and a red mark that doesn't even look like it'll bruise. The damage is inside. That's slower to heal than a bruise." Andreas scrubbed his hands over his face.

"Kari had no right to promise to let her leave." Laurent's wolf was restless and possessive, trying to fight to the surface to keep Rain any way it had to.

"Kari is your Alpha, Laurent, she has every right. You can't win this fight by forcing Rain to stay here while she's terrified," Andreas said.

"Oh is that so? Hmm, let's see, Andreas, and how did Kari come to be here? Did you let her go when she asked?" Laurent snarled.

"No, it was different, she had been bitten. Plus aren't *you* the one who told me to be honest with her about everything?"

"You wouldn't have let her leave after she transformed even if she wanted to."

Andreas sighed. "You're right. You'd better hope that Kari can talk her into staying, Laurent."

Kari settled Rain on the couch. Anna came out looking worried, bringing a pot of hot chocolate and placing it on the low table before the two women.

"Rain, Laurent loves you. I know you're shocked by what he's told you but can I show you something?" Kari asked softly.

Rain nodded. Kari called out, "Phillip? Can you come in here please? I think that this could all be taken care of with a little demonstration."

Phillip came into the room and smiled softly at Rain. "Rain, I need to take my clothing off, all right?"

"For what? Just what sort of demonstration do you have in mind!" Rain sputtered and moved away from them.

Kari laughed and said softly, "I was this difficult too. Just wait a moment, all right? Plus, well, Phillip is pretty nice to look at when he's naked."

Rain stared at Phillip as he disrobed, arms across her chest. Her heart thudded in her chest and she felt like she'd pass out from the stress of the entire day. Still it was apparent that Laurent wasn't the only above average-sized man staying at Star Lake Lodge.

Phillip got to all fours and stretched, the air around him seemed to ripple and shimmer, Rain blinked in disbelief as a huge reddish-gold coated wolf trotted over to her and pressed his nose into her palm. She ran her hands through the soft fur in amazement.

"Holy shit. I'm going to stroke out now," she whispered. "It's true?"

Kari smiled at her. "No stroking out. Take a deep breath and get yourself together. Yes, we're all werewolves. Laurent was *just* running tonight, Rain. I've known Laurent for four years, he's intensely loyal and honorable. He would not cheat on you, least of all with Paloma. He loves you. Werewolves are far stronger than humans and when Laurent saw you so afraid and panicked his wolf tried to take over to protect you. When he reached out he grabbed your shirt and it ripped. He would not hurt you on purpose. He even managed, at a time of high stress, to rein it in to protect you from any real physical harm."

Rain looked down at the ripped sleeve and saw the red mark he'd left was already nearly gone. While she'd been afraid of all he'd said it was more that she thought he was crazy and a cheater than her being afraid he'd actually hurt her. The realization was a huge relief.

For long quiet moments Rain continued to think, sitting there trying to process it all, absently stroking the fur of the wolf at her side that would have easily stood four feet high. "He's so beautiful," she murmured, nuzzling her face into Phillip's soft fur. He rumbled his approval and licked her face.

"Yes, I've never seen another wolf with a coat like his. They're all this big though, except for me, I'm smaller. Can you understand why Laurent hesitated to tell you? It's not something easy to believe. I know."

"How do you know?"

Kari sighed. "I was walking to my car after leaving a nightclub and I was attacked by what I thought was a dog. It turns out that it was a wolf, a werewolf, and Andreas' cousin Michael. They took me to the hospital and my doctor turned out to be a Pack member, Elaine Kennedy. Anyway, they saw that I was manifesting symptoms of the change and they brought me here. I was *so* not happy. They kept me locked up after I refused to believe any of their werewolf nonsense. Heck, they even told me I was their queen! I escaped my second night and almost got to town when someone stopped to help me, turned out it was Ryan and he brought me back here. I was livid." She laughed at the memory.

"Anyway, Skye changed for me, to prove what they'd been saying was true. A few days later I transformed at the full moon and, true to their word, I am indeed the *reine du loup*, the werewolf queen and the female Alpha to Andreas' male Alpha. I was destined to be with him. When I accepted that I realized that I had loved Andreas from the first moment I saw him. I've never been happier in my life, Rain. This Pack is my family and it will be your family too if you just give us a chance."

"Wait, you *were* human? Being bitten changes humans into werewolves? Were all of your children bit then?"

"Yes, I was human and I was bitten and transformed. Some shifters are born that way. In fact, all male Alphas of Clans are natural wolves. They're the strongest in each Pack. Laurent, Andreas, Skye and Phillip are all natural wolves, as are the children. Tomas, Andreas' father, was the Clan Alpha before Andreas, and his father before that and so on for generations."

"How can I be Laurent's Mate if I'm human?"

"At some point in your family tree, you've got wolves in your family genetic code. It means you are able to change safely. Being bitten is hard on humans, many don't survive. Those who've got wolves in their family are able to survive the change and many are able to bear children. Before you ask, we know this because when you licked the page you wrote your phone number on you left your DNA and we have a pretty sophisticated records system."

"Oh this is fucking freaky. Are you telling me that Laurent plans to turn me into a werewolf? Was he even planning to ask me?"

Phillip put his face on her legs and whined a bit, sensing her distress.

"I'm sure he was going to ask you but yes, being his Mate would mean that he would change you. Hopefully you'd agree to live up here, Laurent is Andreas' Third in command. He's very high up in Pack hierarchy, he needs to be where Andreas is."

Rain stood and turned as Laurent came into the room.

"Baby. I see that Phillip has transformed for you. Do you believe me now when I tell you I wasn't with Paloma?"

She took a step back. "Yes."

"Why do you cringe away from me? I am so terribly sorry that I hurt you. Did it bruise? Oh god, please tell me it didn't."

She pulled her sleeve up and showed him the place on her arm, where the mark was finally gone. "No. The mark is gone."

"Thank god," he sighed in obvious relief. "We have much greater strength than humans do, I got scared that I was going to lose you and I forgot that for a moment. When you transform you'll be as strong as I am."

"When I transform? You know, Laurent, you might try actually *asking* me things. Who do you think you are? You don't have the right to simply make choices for me. I just met you! You push your way into my life, declare that you love me and bring me up here. Surprise, you spring a slutty ex-girlfriend and the fact that you're a werewolf on me. It's a bit much, you know."

"I'm your Mate, I will do what I have to to keep you safe," he growled and Phillip bumped him with his large body.

Kari looked at Laurent. "Laurent, human women are not as malleable as shifter females. You can't just order them around."

Laurent sighed and tried to ignore Andreas' amused glance. "Rain, love, I'm sorry for assuming. I just want you to be safe. I want us to be together. The change will give you more strength, more speed and agility. It'll protect you better against anything that may come up, like your father or his men. And she's not my ex anything, nor did I spring her on you." He shoved a hand through his hair. "We're meant to be together, surely you can't deny that."

"She's totally slutty and I'm not going to discuss her one second further!" Rain's voice rose and Laurent heard the strain there. She was close to losing it again. "I don't know what to think. I am in over my head and I have to have some space to work through it."

"What does that mean?" Laurent asked suspiciously.

"It means I want to go home, back to Seattle. I want you to back off and give me time to work this all through. I need to think."

Kari sighed softly and Andreas grabbed her hand. "Rain, why don't you stay here for a while? I promise that we'll give you space."

"I want to work. I have a life, in case anyone here actually cares about what I want and need. I have a gallery show to prepare for. I have rent to pay, a job."

Phillip had loped over to his clothes and transformed back into human form. "Rain, your father has started to look for you. It's not safe."

She turned to look at Laurent. "He has? Did you know that?"

"Yes. That's why it's imperative that you stay here where I can protect you."

"You knew that and you didn't tell me?"

He sighed and ran his hands through his hair, which was probably standing up by now from the number of times he'd repeated the gesture. "I knew you were upset and that you'd be safe here. I was going to tell you later today, after breakfast."

She shook her head. "You just can't seem to lie to me enough, can you? I begged you to tell me what you were hiding earlier tonight, remember? You said to my face and through the door that you weren't hiding anything. You made me feel like I was going crazy for suspecting you! You knew that I ran from a system that made choices for women without consulting them and you did the exact same thing. I'm going back to Seattle. If one of you won't give me a ride I'll walk."

"I'll take you," Laurent said sadly. He hoped he could change her mind on the long drive back.

"Fine." She turned back to Kari. "Thank you for your kindness."

"Please come back soon. Don't let this one thing make you give up the love of your life." Kari hugged her tightly. "If I had done that I'd be so lonely now. I know it's scary but listen to your heart."

Andreas hugged her next. "Rain, please come back soon. You're welcome here any time. You're one of our family now. Laurent loves you, he's a good man, give him a chance. We all make mistakes."

She turned and walked out of the lodge and got into the truck. Skye brought her stuff from the cabin and loaded it in for her, patting her hand. "Please don't turn your back on him," he murmured and walked back to the porch, touching Laurent's shoulder as he walked past.

* * * * *

The ride back to the city was quiet. Laurent had tried to take her hand but she moved farther away from him. She couldn't believe that he'd lied to her. He was making plans to turn her into a fucking werewolf and had just assumed she'd be all for it. He was a werewolf! Holy cow. And he knew her father was looking for her and didn't tell her. Such total disregard for her feelings on big decisions irked her and pushed all of her buttons.

"Rain, won't you stay at my apartment? You're safer there. You can work there all you like."

"No."

"Baby, won't you forgive me? I did what I did to protect you. Yes, I'm sorry, I realize now that it was wrong and that I should have told you. But I did it because I love you and I didn't want to hurt you." Laurent felt like he had something stuck in his throat. The last time he'd felt this miserable was when his mother had died.

"I need some time to think, Laurent. I need to work through this all, on my own."

"I can help you."

"Laurent! In the past not even week, I met a man and fell in love with him, I found out that he's a *werewolf*, not to mention finding out that such things exist to begin with. I tell the first person in a year the truth about my family, I also find out, via a third party, that my father is looking for me. I find out that you knew these things and didn't tell me, and that you want to turn me into a werewolf and hadn't even consulted me. Give a girl a break." She sighed.

"You love me?" Laurent asked softly.

"Yes. But you know, love isn't always enough, Laurent. I cannot, no, I will not live a life where someone else makes decisions for me."

"Rain, I love you so much. Don't shut me out." His heart was breaking. To have found his Mate after forty-four years and then have her turn away from him was excruciatingly painful. Knowing he was a big part of why was even worse.

Rain turned toward him. "Laurent, I am not shutting you out, even though I'm not sure I shouldn't just run as fast as I can from you and my father and all of this. I'm asking you for some space to think about things."

"You aren't breaking it off with me?"

"No. I just need some time. I'll call you when I'm ready. I just plan to work and build up my body of paintings. I need to work, I need to think. I can't do that with you around. You're so big, you make me want to forget about things and just be naked and let you do whatever you want. It's disconcerting."

Laurent smiled and the squeezing pressure on his heart eased. "Baby, you belong naked with me doing whatever I want to please you. We're meant to be together. You know that." He pulled up in front of her house and turned off the ignition.

"I know a few things, yes. That, strange as it sounds and feels, I love you and that it feels so right to be with you. I also know that you have totally rolled over my life and you seem to do whatever you want without regard to my opinion on the matter. I can't reconcile those things."

Laurent slid across the seat to get closer to her. "I can't say I'll always be the best at seeking your input. I'm sorry, I'm a male werewolf, we're not designed that way. I can promise you that I love and respect you and that I will always try to consult you and listen to you. You are not my pet, you're my Mate, my equal. I just want to protect you."

He kissed her temple and she melted into his embrace. She turned her face to his and his lips crushed hers in a kiss laced with love, fear, desperation, joy and pain. She put her arms around his neck and her hands through his hair. He moaned and pulled her into his body. "Stay with me," he whispered into her mouth.

She pulled back and kissed his forehead. "No. Let me have some time please. I'll call you, I promise."

She opened her door and pulled out her bag. He brought her supplies into the house for her. At the door he faced her, reaching out to touch her lips. "This is the hardest thing I've ever done. Please don't stay out of touch long," he whispered and she nodded.

After he left she crawled into bed and cried herself to sleep.

Chapter Four

ॐ

Rain spent the next two weeks in a haze. She worked double shifts at The Cat and when she wasn't there, she painted. She spoke with The Holts and had read over and signed a contract for her show. Harrison's brother was an attorney in town and had helped her with all of the legalese.

She missed Laurent. Even though he'd only been a part of her life for such a short time he'd become instantly integral to it. She felt his absence acutely. Harrison and Andrew hadn't pushed but watched her anxiously, knowing she was working through something major.

In the meantime, Laurent spent the days watching Rain. He stayed back but there was no way he was going to leave her unprotected now that her father was looking for her. He was happy to see that she paid no attention to the men who flirted with her at work. She looked as tired as he felt. When he needed to be up at the lodge, Drew took over and guarded Rain for him.

* * * * *

Rain sat in the Japanese Gardens at the Arboretum. She often came to write in her journal and sketch but it wasn't working today. The quiet and cool didn't bring her solace and soothing. She'd decided the night before to call Laurent. She missed him and she wanted him back in her life. She'd thought long and hard about his lies and behavior, she couldn't agree with what he did but she could see that he'd done it to protect her. And he'd backed off when she asked and let her work through everything on her own. But she had the feeling he'd set guards on her. It just seemed like his nature to make sure she was protected. With her father out there looking, she had to admit it made her feel safer.

Putting aside the blank page she'd stared at for the last hour, she went to the pay phone and dialed his mobile.

"Laurent," he growled.

"Hi."

"Baby? Are you all right?" His voice went from gruff to gentle.

She sighed. "I will be once I see you again. I miss you, Laurent. I forgive you and I think that if you agree to respect me and include me in our life, we can give this relationship a try."

He laughed, relieved that she'd reached out to him at last. "Where are you? When can I see you? I'm in town." He knew he was lying about tailing her, he was watching her at that moment and he ached to run to her but he couldn't. This one last thing out of the way and he could protect her openly.

"I'm at the Japanese Gardens at the Arboretum."

"Are you hungry? We can go and grab lunch if you like. I can pick you up in the main parking lot, did you drive or ride the bus or your bike?"

"Laurent, come on now. You know exactly where I am, don't you? You've either had me guarded or are doing it yourself, aren't you?"

He sighed and she fought back a smirk.

"How'd you know?"

"Ha! I knew it! I just had the feeling you wouldn't leave me unprotected with my father out there looking for me. For what it's worth, I'm glad you told me the truth. I probably would have been really pissed if you hadn't."

"You're not mad? I didn't interfere with your life. I know you needed time to think. But I couldn't bear the thought of you being unprotected."

"I know. I'm not mad. It made me feel safe. Now come on. I'm here with my bike."

"I'll meet you in about three minutes." Quickly, he moved to his truck and drove over to where she waited. He got out of the cab of the truck and leaned against the hood, greedily watching her as she rode toward him.

"Hi," she said a bit shyly.

"Baby, I've missed you so much," he said as his gaze drank her in. He reached out and touched her cheek.

"I'm all sweaty, I rode several miles to get here. I should shower."

"You're glowing, your sweat smells clean. I want to lick you up," he growled, pulling her into him. "But I can do that in the shower too."

She had to fight to keep her eyes from rolling back into her head at the pleasure of his embrace. "Mmm. You feel so good, I've missed you so much." The sight and feel of him affected her the same way as always. Physical desire snaked through her veins, she wanted him. More than that, she felt possessive of him, she wanted to breathe in his scent, to run her tongue along his skin, to take his essence into her body.

"I'm glad I haven't been the only one dying the last two weeks." He picked her bike up and placed it in the bed of his truck. "Let's get you back home."

She broke away and jumped up into the truck while he went around the cab to his side.

She barely waited for him to throw it into park when they arrived to start dragging him toward the front door. "I need to shower then I'll let you take me to dinner. I'm starving." They went into the house and he watched while she gathered up clothes and a towel.

"Let me help you get the hard-to-reach spots," he said suggestively.

"That's been my assumption all along. I'm sure my back is all sweaty and in need of a scrubbing," she murmured, raising an eyebrow.

Laughing, he shoved her toward the shower, locking the door behind them. He yanked his shirt off but his hands lost momentum at his jeans as he watched her peel off her shirt and bra, letting them fall to the ground. Her nipples tightened at his attention. The beauty of her body hit him like a fist and his grin softened and fell away. She kicked off her shorts and tiny pink panties and he pulled his jeans and boxers off.

"I don't know if the shower is big enough for the three of us," she whispered, looking at his cock greedily.

He laughed suggestively. "Perhaps one of us can fit inside of the other. You know, to make room for the other two."

"You're such a humanitarian." She stepped into the shower and back into the spray, sighing as the warm water washed over her body. He followed her, nuzzling into her neck, worrying over her tendons with his teeth. She moaned as he rubbed against her softly. "I've missed you so much."

"Me too, Rain. I can't believe I'm here with you at last." Reaching around her, he grabbed the sponge and soap, true to his word, scrubbing her all over. Sensuous and lithe, Rain leaned back and shampooed her hair, arching to rinse.

Her breasts, wet and slick, were too much to resist and he leaned down with a growl to take a nipple into his mouth, grazing it with his teeth.

"That's very nice," she said, her voice hitching. "I've missed that."

"Let me show you a few other things you may have forgotten about." Without preamble he picked her up and entered her. Reaching down, he helped her wrap her legs around his waist. "Oh god, you feel so good," he grunted out as he slid into her, the heated walls of her pussy tight around him, welcoming him home.

She sighed at the pleasure of it all. He was back with her, where they were meant to be all along. The time away from him had helped her realize that, freak happening or not, she loved Laurent Cole.

The cool tile against her back served as a sharp contrast to the heat rising from his body. Her palms slid over his pectoral muscles as they flexed and released with each thrust. Those well-muscled arms held her up, supported her weight easily and the flat, hard abdomen bunched and rippled as he moved within her.

His scent rose with the steam, teasing her senses, tantalizing her. Wet strands of his hair clung to her skin, married with her own. "You need to come, Rain. I love the way your pussy feels when you come."

All she could manage was an incoherent moan in the affirmative.

"I'm holding you up, touch yourself," he murmured into her ear.

She froze for a moment, she'd never masturbated in front of anyone before. But this was Laurent, her man, and she needed to come, wanted to so very bad.

His eyes were glued to her hand as it slid down her belly and between slick labia. His breath caught when she began to circle her clit slowly.

"Show me what you like, Rain."

Watching him watch her, she caught her bottom lip between her teeth as the metallic energy of her climax began to build. His cock filled her up over and over as her fingers stroked her clit, harder and harder, faster and faster.

"I," she began but it ended in a soft cry as climax rolled over her, through her, echoed through the walls of her pussy as he continued his hard, digging strokes.

"Shit…that's so good. I love you, Rain," he whispered as his own moment slammed into him, making him see stars.

She stayed wrapped around him until the water turned cold. Laughing, he set her down, gently helping her out of the tub. They dried off quickly amongst stolen kisses and embraces.

"Just to clarify something, we can't get STDs. I couldn't tell you up at the lake, before."

"Oh well, that's nice to know. I felt sort of stupid afterward. One of those heat-of-the-moment decisions. I'll refrain from commenting about that woman."

Laurent cringed. "Rain, she's a Pack member. You will see her around. I'm sorry if that upsets you. I truly am."

"I don't want to talk about her. I'm so hungry all of a sudden and she'll ruin my appetite. Let's get dressed and go to eat. I'd make something here but we're in desperate need of a grocery run and none of us have done it." She laughed as he slung her over his shoulder and carried her back to her room and tossed her onto her bed.

"Well, I think I need more sustenance from you before we go anywhere." He winked at her, moving to settle between her thighs.

"Huh-uh. I'm starving. You got an appetizer in the shower. Come on, a girl has to keep her strength up for a big guy like you." Rolling away from him, she pulled a pair of clean underwear out of a drawer and pulled them on, laughing at his pout.

"Fine, but I'm collecting after we eat."

"Like I'd argue." She picked up a pair of jeans from a pile of clean laundry and got dressed quickly. He smiled when he noted she was wearing the red blouse Drew had sent with him that first day they were together.

"I'll have to tell Drew how beautiful you look in the shirt. Or he can see you in it himself soon, I hope. We should probably talk about what we're going to do, what our next steps are." He moved to her, braiding her wet hair, nibbling on her neck as he did it.

"Okay. Let me get some calories into me, maybe a beer or two, before we start that discussion."

He sighed dramatically and pulled his shirt and jeans back on. She cocked an eyebrow when he left his boxers off. "Easier access for you later. I'm all about your ease, baby."

She burst out laughing and they walked out the door but the phone rang so she turned back, dashing to answer it.

"Hello?"

"Julia? Is that you?"

With a strangled gasp, she dropped the phone. Alarmed, Laurent stalked over, picking the receiver up.

"Hello?" Laurent smoothed a hand up Rain's arm, trying to look into her eyes.

"Who is this?"

"I think I'll be the one asking questions here," Laurent growled. He tipped Rain's chin up and kissed her gently. "Are you all right, baby?" he asked her softly and she shook her head.

"It's him," she whispered. "Anthony."

His vision went red a moment but he found calm in his rage. "You're the fucker who beat my woman?"

"Put my fiancée back on the phone, asshole! You don't know who you're talking to."

"You're talking to her fiancé, you piece of shit. I know exactly who I'm talking to, you puny excuse for a man. If you harass or upset her in any way, I'll make you sorry. What do you want?" he gritted out.

"Julia has been away from home long enough. She's got to come back to her family."

Laurent looked down at Rain. "Do you want to talk to him, baby?"

She nodded and took the phone back. "What do you want, Anthony? I'm not coming back there, not ever. I have a life here now." Her voice trembled slightly and she held onto Laurent like he was her lifeline.

"You don't have any choice. You're promised to me. Now get your ass back here, you fat fucking whore, before I have to come out there and drag you back here."

Laurent stiffened. His hearing was acute but Anthony's screams over the phone were loud enough for normal human hearing to pick up. With a forced calm that belied the killing fury that rode up his spine, he took the phone from Rain gently. "Did you just call my beloved a whore?" he said softly but so dangerously he heard the breath in Rain's throat catch. He stroked fingers up and down her spine to calm her. She wasn't the focus of his anger.

"Your beloved? I own that bitch. She's mine. You don't want to cross me, dude. Julia is spoken for. She needs to get her ass back home and take care of business. If you were smart you'd put her on the next plane to New York and forget you ever met her."

"I will tear your entrails out with my teeth and eat your fucking heart, you piece of woman-beating shit. You had better find another wife, this one is spoken for. If you threaten her or frighten her in any way they won't even find your shadow. Don't mess with me and mine and make no mistake, Julia is mine."

"Who do you think you are?" Anthony screamed out. Laurent could taste his fear through the phone and a slow, predatory smile broke over his face.

"I think I'm the man who just told you to back off and leave Julia alone for good. If she wanted to come back to you she'd have done it. Take my word for it, Anthony, just back off and leave her alone or I'll make you sorry."

"Do you know who I am? Do you know who her father is?"

"Question is, Anthony, do you know who I am?"

"You've been warned, asshole!" Anthony shrieked and hung up.

Laurent slammed the phone down. "The guy shrieks like a pussy." He shook his head. "Honey, they know where you are, at least your number. We have to get your stuff and leave. You can't be here. It's not safe anymore."

"Laurent, what about Harrison and Andrew? I am so stupid. I've put them in danger." She held back tears as she tried to think up a plan.

"Baby, let's think about this. You can't run forever, you need to be free of them. But for right now, since we don't know what they're planning, we need to clear out of here and do some thinking. Figure out our next steps. Do you know where they are? Harrison and Andrew?"

"Um, Harrison is probably out somewhere. Andrew's in rehearsal."

"Can you get in contact with them now? Tell them to lay low for a few days? Even to have this number disconnected?"

"How could I have done this to them?" A fine tremor took over her muscles then.

Laurent grabbed her arms and forced her to look him in the eye. "This is not your fault. You've been living here a year. God knows how he found you but it's done. You have to get hold of yourself. Can you get hold of Harrison?"

"Let me try." Rain picked up the phone and called Harrison's mobile.

Thank goodness he answered. "Hello?"

"Harrison, it's Rain. Can you meet me at the Teapot Dome in half an hour?"

"Is everything all right, babe?"

"No. And don't go home just yet. Come straight to the Dome, all right?"

"All right. Thirty minutes. Are you safe?"

"Laurent is with me. Yes."

"Good. Take care, all right?" he added before he hung up.

"Now, baby, try Andrew."

She nodded and dialed but got his voicemail. "Andrew, when you get this message don't go home, call Harrison ASAP," she said and hung up.

"Let's get you packed." Laurent guided her into her room. "I'll get your art into the truck. I promise to be careful with it. We can store it at Drew's. He's a member of my Pack, a Cherchez wolf. He can be trusted."

"Okay," she said in a small voice but he watched, relieved, as she gathered herself together and began to throw her things into suitcases and boxes.

Laurent put the earpiece to his cell phone in and called Drew while he moved Rain's art.

"Drew?"

"Ever since I was born. What's up, bro?"

"Rain's in trouble. They've found her. Can we store her paintings at your place?"

"Of course. Shall I meet you and pick them up? Janine is here, she can help if she's needed."

"No, keep her out of it. Do you know the Teapot Dome?"

"On Queen Anne?"

"Yeah."

"I do."

"We'll be there in half an hour. Can you meet me?"

"I'll be there."

"Thanks, brother."

"Any time," Drew assured him and hung up.

Rain busily took loads of her belongings out to his truck, packing them behind the seat and in the bed. She saw him and shrugged. "That's it really. I didn't have a whole lot, in case I did have to run again someday. My passport and a bit of money are in a safe deposit box near the bus station."

He pulled her to him and kissed the top of her head. "You're so smart. Help me with the rest of your canvases."

She followed him back into the house and brought out the last four paintings and they left to go and meet Harrison, who was already waiting inside the tea house.

"Let me tell him," she murmured to Laurent as they went in and sat with Harrison.

"Okay, sweet thing, what is it?" Harrison asked as he hugged her.

"Harrison, I don't even know where to start. I'm so sorry but I'm not who you think I am."

"I know, Julia."

"What! You knew?"

"Yeah, I knew from day one. I did an exposé on organized crime a few years ago. You're the daughter of a very connected man. Of course I saw your picture. I have a photographic memory, I remembered you. I figured you were running for a reason so I never pressed."

"I'm so embarrassed. My ex-fiancé, the man who beat me up, he's found me, or at least my number. I've moved all of my stuff out of the house and I've left you cash to cover my rent for the next two months in an envelope under your mattress but I'm afraid for you. I'm so sorry to have brought this into your life." She wrung her hands.

Harrison smiled and took her hands, kissing each one. "You are a goddess, Rain. You've been so much fun to live with. But I can play the game. If they come to look for you I'll tell them I don't know where you've gone. I'll add that you've skipped your lease and left me some money but no forwarding."

"Harrison, I'm so sorry. I've put you in danger. These men aren't likely to just let it go."

"I'm convincing. Plus, hell, you did skip your lease and I won't know where you've gone since you'd never be silly enough to tell me. Although I'm not taking two months' rent

117

so forget about it. I'll put it aside for you. I'll talk to Andrew and fill him in. Go, Rain, be safe. Don't look back."

"I can't bear to think of you being unsafe because of me. I should have just lived alone. And I'm not taking that money back."

As they stood, Harrison gathered her into a hug and said softly into her ear, "You've helped me heal, babe. You've made me feel again after feeling empty for so long. Go, love, be happy. And yes you are." He kissed her forehead and looked at Laurent, who nodded his thanks.

Drew came then and took Rain's paintings. Janine had come, of course, nothing could stop her from getting the chance to help and to meet Laurent's Mate whom she'd heard so much about.

Harrison left quietly. "If you need me, call me at my mailbox at the *Times*, all right?"

"Okay. Thanks, Harrison."

She watched him stride off and get into his car and drive away.

"I'm going to put a guard on them. Don't worry, Rain. I promise we'll do all we can to keep them safe," Laurent said quietly in her ear and she leaned back into him a moment.

A tall, lithe blonde smiled at Rain, holding out her hand. "Rain? I'm Janine. I'm Drew's wife. Why don't you let me help you get back into the truck? You and Laurent need to go. I'll see you again in a few days when Drew and I come back up to the lodge. It was very nice to meet you and I promise to keep your paintings safe." She smiled and patted Rain's hand as she led her outside to Laurent's truck.

"I don't know what to say. Thank you seems inadequate."

"We're family, that's what family does. Thank you is just fine." Janine smiled and handed her off to Laurent.

"Come on, baby, let's get going." Laurent helped her get into the cab, closing the door after her.

Feeling somewhat numb, Rain waved at Drew and Janine as Laurent pulled out and headed for the freeway.

She leaned back into the seat and sighed.

"We'll stop and get something to eat in an hour or so, all right?"

"Okay," she said softly.

"Why don't you nap? I'll wake you later." He brushed a wayward strand of hair out of her eyes and tucked it behind her ear.

She nodded and curled up into the seat, closing her eyes and drifting into sleep quickly.

He concentrated on driving and making sure they weren't followed. It looked clear and he hoped it stayed that way.

* * * * *

Two hours later he pulled into a diner on Highway 2 and gently shook her awake. "I hate to wake you but you should eat. We won't be back at the lodge for another hour and a half."

She stretched and looked up at him, totally trusting. "Okay. I could eat."

They ate a quick meal and got back on the road. He called the lodge and spoke with Skye, filling him in on the situation.

"Maybe I should just go. I don't want to bring danger back to the lodge."

"Rain, several things. First of all I love you, deeply, passionately, intensely. I will protect you to my dying breath. I'd never leave you unprotected. Second of all you are part of the Cherchez Clan, we protect our own. Third of all Kari would never forgive me if I let you run off. Lastly, I want to have sex with you nonstop for at least the next week and I couldn't do that if you left. So get any plans of running off out of your head. We'll find a way to deal with your father, just give us time to find some weak spots to exploit."

She laughed and he rejoiced in that small amount of levity. He hated that these men terrorized his woman, his Mate. Anthony Vargas and Pietro Margoles would pay for that.

When they pulled onto the long gravel path to the lodge, Rain had just gotten off the phone with The Cat and had quit. Luckily they had enough staff to cover and understood her family emergency. Her boss had even offered to let her take leave so that she could come back but she'd said that she wanted to devote her time to painting full-time when she got finished with her family crisis.

Laurent hadn't wanted to tell her that he had plenty of money and that she could indeed devote her time to painting full-time but he would later when she was feeling better. Not only did he receive a generous salary for being Pack Lieutenant that he'd invested wisely, he'd inherited a large sum of money when his mother died and again when his father passed two years before. Laurent Cole was a very rich man, not filthy stinking rich like Andreas but very, very comfortable.

When Laurent's truck had come to a full stop in front of the lodge, the wolves of Cherchez Clan had filed out, moving to help unload all of Rain's belongings and move them into their cabin. The art supplies were taken to cabin fourteen, next door, which Kari had ordered turned into a studio for Rain's use.

"I'm so glad you're back here. I understand that before that awful phone call you and Laurent patched things up. I'm so happy for you both." Kari hugged her tightly.

"Thank you. Thank you so much for the beautiful studio and for being so welcoming. I don't know how I can begin to repay your kindness."

"Oh Rain, you don't know how happy it makes us all to see Laurent this way. He loves you. That in and of itself is worth everything. He's saved my and Andreas' lives more than once. He's loyal and kind and he's been so good to this Pack and to my family. You make him happy."

Rain smiled at the small woman. Hellie, Tom, Devon and Sean came scrambling out of the lodge and tumbled into Rain's open arms. "You're back!" they squealed.

"I am. I told you I would be. Sorry I cut out on you without saying goodbye the last time. How about a game of Chutes and Ladders later? I haven't played in so long."

"Oh yeah!" Hellie squealed and played with Rain's hair while chattering on and on about the new puppies that their dog had just delivered.

"We'll be up to the lodge in a few minutes. Let Rain get settled in a bit, all right?" Laurent said as he gently ushered everyone out of their cabin. He closed the door, leaned against it and looked at Rain, smiling. "I think the kids love you more than me," he said wryly.

"I doubt that. Those kids happen to think you're the coolest guy ever to walk the earth." Rain laughed.

He came to her, sitting on the couch, bringing her with. He pulled her hair loose of the braid, the scent of her shampoo filling his senses. "Rain, have you given any thought to coming over? To me making you into a werewolf? I don't want to push you but I really think it will make you safer plus, well, it will seal our bond, marry us. I'd like that very much."

"You want to marry me?"

"Hell yes. Since the moment I saw you in The Cat." He smiled into her hair, inhaling deeply. "I won't lie. It'll hurt. You'll be out of commission for about two days, maybe three. Emma is a doctor, as is Sean. They'll keep you here at the lodge, here in our cabin even, if all goes well. Then you'll garner more and more ability until the full moon and your first transformation. After that you'll be able to change at will. The full moon is in six days. I'd like to do it as soon as possible."

"You don't need to marry me to get me into bed." she said, teasing. Hearing him say he wanted to be married to her made her thrill to the tips of her toes.

He laughed. "I know. As much as I like fucking you, I want it all. I want you to be my wife. We'll do a human ceremony as well, any kind you like. Perhaps we can do a quick justice of the peace ceremony first. I'd like your family to know we're married according to human law, to add a layer of protection for you."

During their time apart she'd given a lot of thought to changing. She'd decided that she was willing to do anything she had to to be with Laurent. Being stronger and having more safety against the threat of her father and his people was appealing too. She turned to him and kissed the dimple on his chin. "Yes."

He looked down at her. "Truly?"

"Yes. Let's do it."

"Okay. We can do it tomorrow. I want you to rest for tonight. In fact we know the local justice of the peace in Star Lake. We'll call him and get married in a human ceremony tomorrow first thing, then we'll come back and I'll start the change."

"It'll hurt, huh?" That part sucked.

"Yes. I'm sorry to say it will. I have to bite you in wolf form. The bite has to be deep enough to cause a certain level of trauma and reaction in your body. Kari and Andreas will be there with you in human form, to hold your hand and soothe you. I wish we could have you knocked out when we do it but the adrenaline is a big factor in the change for some reason."

She trembled a bit. "Okay. I trust you, Laurent, with my life."

He kissed her deeply then, his soft lips covering hers like they were made just for kissing her. He pulled her onto his lap, angling himself to grind his cock into her pussy. Moaning, she stretched at the pleasure of it.

Taking advantage of her stretch, he slid a hand up and under the hem of her shirt, questing up to cup a heavy, braless breast. "Mmmm." She arched into his hand and bright threads of pleasure shot through her when he pinched a nipple between thumb and forefinger.

Her hands went to the waistband of his jeans and moisture pooled at the sound of his zipper descending. She felt like Pavlov's dog and she stifled a giggle at the pun. Instead she tucked her hand into the open gap of his jeans, grabbing his cock, squeezing lightly.

"Rain." Laurent gasped and arched into her hand.

"Laurent! Darling boy!" A woman's voice broke the moment as it drifted in through the door.

Laurent groaned and let his head fall back against the back of the couch. "Jade." He still had a hand up her shirt. Annoyed, Rain slapped it away, leaving him to zip his own fly, not wanting to cause physical damage.

"You must be Rain! I am so happy to meet you." Rain turned, struggling to get off Laurent's lap, but he held her there fast with an iron grip. Rain saw the tall blonde woman who looked to be about fifty and smiled.

"Yes, I'm Rain."

"Jade Phinney, this is Rain Foster. Rain, this is Jade, Andreas' mother and, up until this moment, a woman I thought of as mine too. She has a history of just barging in on people without knocking." He said the last bit rather pointedly and Rain slapped him on the arm for being so rude.

Still struggling to get free of his grip, Rain pinched his side until he let her go with a yelp. Quickly standing before he could recover, Jade immediately enveloped her in a hug.

"I'm so happy you're here! Welcome to the Cherchez Pack. My goodness, you two will make gorgeous babies!" Jade said, clapping her hands together in delight, sending an armful of bracelets clanging against each other. "I've been blessed to have raised Laurent since he was eleven. I've known him since he was born. I've never seen him look so dreamy. You're good for him. His mother would have liked you. She looked a bit like you, only her eyes were blue instead of brown and her hair was short and curly."

Rain smiled and nodded her head, not able to get a word in edgewise. Laurent cleared his throat. "Well, Jade, does she pass inspection?"

"Oh my yes! Gorgeous and talented. I saw some of her artwork earlier. My grandchildren adore her and she's tamed you. Looks like I have another fabulous daughter-in-law." She looked back to Rain. "Please, think of me as your mother-in-law, we most certainly view Laurent as our son. I'll let you two get back to having sex. We're waiting up at the lodge for drinks, dinner in two hours. Come when you are ready." She giggled. "No pun intended." She smiled and left with a flourish of bracelets.

"Wow."

"She's something else. The women in this Pack are all pretty unique, headstrong. A lot of humans who came over. Perri, Kari and Emma, all three wives to the Alpha family males, were humans. Human women are different, more, um, feisty. Although a bigger pain in the behind at times. You should have seen Kari when she first came here." He laughed at the memory. "Then again, Andreas swore to me that I'd get my own back when I laughed at him then and he was right." He scowled playfully. "Now where were we?"

Rain stood up and went toward the door. "I can't now! Sheesh, it's like they're all waiting up there with a scorecard or something."

"Well, one thing you should know is that werewolves are very casual about sex and nudity. Especially around the time of a Gathering. That's when the Clan comes together, we do it at least once a quarter. Anyway, you'll see naked and very scantily clad people lounging around. As I said you need to be naked when you transform. Plus, well, sexual mores are more relaxed. Some mated couples will share at Gatherings. And in the interest of full disclosure, many Pack members seek comfort through sex, in human form and wolf form."

"Um, okay. I suppose the comfort part makes sense. I imagine werewolves share some characteristics with wolves, right? So pack animals would naturally seek comfort from each other. But back to the whole sharing thing. What do you mean, share?"

"Um, yes, as in have sex with other members of the Pack. Both unmated males and females and members of mated couples."

She narrowed her eyes and crossed her arms across her chest, bringing those beautiful breasts even higher. He groaned at the sight. "You mean that skanky redhead is going to think she can just sample you any old time she likes?"

He shook his head vehemently. "No, no, no! Not all couples do it. I must make it clear I have no intention of sharing, especially at a Gathering. Andreas and Kari don't, although I do know they've been with Phillip a few times. I can't say what the extent of the experience was. Others do from time to time. If we ever decided to do that it would be something I'd want to discuss in detail."

"Well, I'm glad you feel kind enough to inform me that you don't plan to pass me around like a party favor." She smirked and he cringed. Human women were a trial.

"You are the main course, Rain, and only for me. As I am only for you."

"So wait." He winced. He knew what was coming but he knew he had to tell her up-front after seeing the disaster after Andreas didn't tell Kari and she found out by accident and it almost broke up their marriage. "Obviously it was more than just red. *The skank.* Who else have you slept with in the Pack, Clan, family, whatever?"

"Not all of the females of course, but several of them. Mainly in wolf form but some in human form. I've dated some of the unmated females and I've been with, in a limited sense, Ryan and Phillip."

She cocked an eyebrow. "So I'm expected to hang out with your prior sex partners? Oh and after that, I want to hear *all* about Ryan and Phillip."

He relaxed at the last statement and the glitter of desire in her eyes. "Yes. As I said, we have a relaxed view of such things. As my Mate you outrank all but Kari and Emma. You have *nothing* to worry about, I have no desire for any other female, not since the first time I saw you."

She snorted, he recognized that snort from Kari and fought not to roll his eyes.

"Tell me who, now. I don't want to be sitting next to some woman who you've had sex with and not know it."

He sighed. "Well, you know about Paloma. There's Meg, she's also an unmated female in the Pack. Ellen, who is mated to James, and Luna, who is mated to Shane. She used to get around a bit but is now quite monogamous." He left out Perri, whom he had slept with before she Mated with Devon and joined the Clan. He wanted Rain to like the females in the inner circle and he had a feeling that it would be hard for her if she knew about Perri.

"And all of these women are here now?"

"No, Paloma is." He avoided her eyes, knowing what her face looked like at the mention of Paloma. "The others will come at your first transformation. Andreas will call a Gathering and the entire Clan will come to welcome you to our ranks and to seal the Mating ceremony."

"Mating ceremony?"

"Yes. Well. You and I will run, transform into our wolf forms. We run for several miles to a lake. I'll mount you and the Pack will witness and seal it. You will be mine and I will be yours."

"Mount? As in sex? In front of people?"

"In front of the Pack. Your wolf will not have a problem, trust me. It's natural, Rain."

"And will you be mounting anyone else or anyone else be mounting me?"

"If anyone else tries to mount you my wolf would kill them." He actually had the gall to harrumph at her and she stifled a laugh. "And I have no interest in mounting another. It's all you, Rain." He kissed her lips softly.

"Cripes. This is all a bit much. The mob looking for me. Crazy ex-fiancé, new fiancé who's a werewolf. All in a day's work. All in a day's work."

He snorted. "I know, baby. But after the initial stuff it calms down a lot. And I'll deal with the mob and ex part. Now since you've burned up all of our sex time with chatter," he winked at her teasingly, "let's go to the lodge. Perri and Devon are here and I know Perri is dying to meet you. Perri, Kari, Emma and Alyssa are pretty tight. I imagine that they're all too anxious to bring you into their evil quartet."

She sighed. "Lead on."

He threaded his fingers through hers and they walked up to the lodge together. When they walked in Hellie attached herself to Rain's side, sitting in her lap when she settled in next to Laurent on a couch in the main room.

A tiny flame-haired woman who looked like a fairy approached, grabbing her into a hug, squeezing Hellie too. "Hi! I'm Perri, Devon's wife. You must be Rain. I've been dying to meet you." She tried to sit next to Rain but Hellie and Laurent weren't budging. "Fine! Hellie, won't you share with Auntie Perri?"

Hellie snuggled tighter into Rain's side, burying her face into her long hair, and Laurent chuckled. "As you can see, Perri, she's won over the most important woman in the Clan."

Skye came over and sat at Rain's feet, leaning back against her legs. "Hey there. I'm glad you're back." He stroked along her leg and she raised an eyebrow but Laurent seemed calm enough.

"Oh and I forgot to tell you, in case you hadn't noticed, werewolves are a touchy-feely lot. Some touching is offensive, you'll know it when you see it. The way Skye is stroking your leg now, Hellie burying her face in your hair, nuzzling and cuddling, that's all normal comfort behavior. As the Mate of the Third, most in the Pack are subordinate to you, which involves another level of touching. Many will seek reassuring touching from you," Laurent said and closed his eyes, enjoying the way she stroked a hand languidly through his hair.

"What if I don't want some woman rubbing herself all over you?" she asked, eyebrow arching.

Skye burst out laughing and Perri patted her knee. "Paloma."

"Yeah. I don't want her rubbing or stroking on you, Laurent. It isn't comfort she's seeking."

"That, my love, is an example of the difference between appropriate touching and offensive touching. Touching of a sexual nature with another's Mate without permission is offensive, you'd be entirely within your rights to knock the shit out of any female who touched me in a sexual manner," Laurent said, eyes still closed. "But Kari touches me all of the time, as do Emma and Perri. Emma and Kari are higher in rank than you and I. You take on my rank when we mate. That's another thing you'll learn. Werewolves are a very rule-bound, hierarchical culture. We sit at the dining table according to rank, we eat according to rank. Our relations with each other are bound by rank."

She sighed. "And I thought organized crime families were complicated."

Laurent and Skye laughed and Kari came over, plucked Hellie up and sat in her spot. "Hey, Momma, I was sitting there."

Kari kissed Hellie's head. "And now I am. You can't share?"

"No!"

Rain patted her lap and Hellie scrambled onto it and snuggled into her, bringing Rain's hair around her shoulder and wrapping it around a small fist, smiling.

"You and Laurent will spoil her!" Kari laughed and Ryan joined them.

"Laurent was giving me werewolf etiquette 101. You're all so complicated," Rain moaned.

"You don't know the half of it. I've been Alpha for over four years now and I still don't know it all. If you need help or have a question, just ask. Any of us will be happy to help."

"I'm going to bite Rain tomorrow. After we go to Judge Fortensky's chambers and get married," Laurent said, eyes still closed, his full weight against her, totally relaxed.

"Really! Well, uh, thanks for just sort of slipping it into the conversation like you'd relate a new pair of shoes. Jeez, Laurent. We'd like to plan something, a party. At least let Andreas and I be witnesses. We'll have a reception and any kind of ceremony you want after your first transformation." Kari looked at Rain, smiling. "Drew is a genius by the way. He designed my wedding dress and my maternity clothes too. I'm so happy you're here! We can get into so much trouble together!"

Perri laughed, nodding enthusiastically. "Every two months we all make a weekend in Portland."

"Sounds fun!" It had been years since Rain had real girlfriends.

"And every six months we go up to Vancouver to see Ellen. The shopping up there is fabulous," Kari said.

Rain stiffened. "Oh."

Laurent opened one eye and met Ryan and Skye's. He nodded.

129

Kari patted Rain's hand. "Laurent told you then? It was a shock I'm sure. It was for me too. But know that Ellen is a wonderful woman who loves her husband James deeply. They go about their mating differently than Andreas and I do but she wouldn't ever attempt any untoward behavior with Laurent. She's not the type. Laurent has made it absolutely clear that he's in love with you and has no intention of sharing, even though some males who shall remain nameless did ask him right off."

Laurent glared at Ryan and Skye. Skye winked at Rain and she blushed, flicking his ear.

"That's how you have to handle Skye, Rain. He's a total flirt. But he's generally harmless – to those he loves anyway."

Anna came in to announce that dinner was ready and they all stood up to go into the dining room. Andreas and Kari went first, followed by Sean and Emma, Laurent and Rain, Devon and Perri and so on. Rain was beginning to get the idea about the whole hierarchy thing. As bodyguards, Phillip sat next to Kari and Alek sat next to Andreas. Rain couldn't help but feel a bit smug at how far down the table Paloma sat. It was also a relief that Laurent never even glanced her way but doted on Rain's every movement and word. The kids all sat at their own table to the right of Andreas and within reach of both him and Kari.

After the meal people got up and milled around, chatting and visiting with each other. A tall gray-haired man who had to be related to Andreas pulled Devon out of his chair to sit between Rain and Perri, putting his arms around the backs of their chairs.

"Welcome, my lovely new daughter-in-law-to-be." He kissed her right on the lips, the sly fox! She quirked a smile at him and laughed.

"You must be Tomas."

"Yes, I see my reputation precedes me." He laughed and gave Perri a smooch too. "I'm old, Rain, but never too old to appreciate a beautiful female. Lucky for me each of my sons has married an absolutely stunning woman and you all seem to fit a different part of the feminine spectrum. Every one of you a man's dream." He winked.

"Watch it there," Laurent growled and they all laughed.

"Are you telling me you never noticed how sexy Rain's lips were?"

"I noticed. When she gets up, check out her ass, it's perfectly heart-shaped," Skye added helpfully.

Laurent threw a roll at him. "No one needs to check out Rain's bottom, thank you very much."

"I've noticed both the lips and may I also say that your body is so lovely and lush, all curvy and sexy?" Ryan added with a wink.

Andreas laughed so hard his eyes watered and Kari smacked his arm. "What are you laughing about? You don't think it's funny when they do it to me."

"Exactly! Yes, I told Laurent that he'd get his comeuppance when he met his Mate and brought her here. He thought it was funny to join in the fun when they pulled this sort of thing with you and I had to grit my teeth. Well suck it up, brother of mine, the piper's come to call." He started laughing again and Laurent growled, making an anatomically impossible suggestion.

Kari leaned across the table. "Don't worry, Rain. They don't mean anything by it, they do it all the time. They can't help but act like twelve-year-olds." She rolled her eyes and Emma and Perri nodded sagely.

"Well, it's not like it's a horrible fate to have the stud patrol here compliment you on your appearance." Rain laughed and shrugged. Laurent hauled her into his lap.

"Stud patrol?"

"They are all quite stunning, aren't they?" Perri asked as the four of them looked around the room at the men sitting there.

The women burst out laughing and Laurent picked Rain up, sweeping her out of the room. "See you all tomorrow morning," he said as they left.

"Wait! Uncle Laurent, Rain is going to tell us a story," little Devon cried out and Rain had to stifle a laugh at Laurent's anguished groan. He set her down with a dramatic sigh.

"Okay, you can borrow her for a while. I need to talk to Phillip anyway." He kissed all of the kids and then laid a long, lingering kiss on Rain's lips. "Very sexy indeed," he murmured into her ear.

As Kari and Rain were herding the kids upstairs, Paloma called out, "Don't worry, I'll keep him entertained for you."

Rain looked back at the woman and narrowed her eyes. "Try it and you'll discover the true meaning of pain."

Paloma sat there with her mouth open and Rain turned back to Kari, who gave her a thumbs-up. "That's how you have to handle it. It's a reality with all the unmated females here," Kari murmured as they got the kids settled.

Rain sat in Hellie's bed with the kids all snuggled around her and gave chapter two of the superhero story she'd told the last time she visited.

Afterward she met Kari, who sat at a table in the hallway playing cards with Phillip.

"I can't tell you how wonderful your children are."

"Oh please! It's you. Honestly, they've never taken to anyone else this quickly. Even Tommie adores you and he's such a daddy's boy. By the way," Kari said, turning to the man who had joined them when Andreas came up the stairs, "have you met Alek? He's Andreas' personal bodyguard."

"It's nice to meet you. I hear you've taken Laurent's old spot, he speaks very highly of you."

"Coming from Laurent that's high praise. It's very nice to meet you, by the way, welcome to the family." He rubbed his face along the line of her cheek and she stiffened at first and then went with it. She'd have to get used to it sometime.

"Have you seen Laurent?" she asked Phillip.

"Last I saw he was in the study with Ryan and Skye, brainstorming about what to do with your father and that bastard Anthony. I heard what he did to you and what he said to you today. I'm surprised that Laurent hasn't flown back there and torn him apart with his bare hands."

Rain smiled. "Well, let's hope he doesn't do anything so stupid. Anthony isn't worth murder one." Saying her good nights, she wandered down the stairs and into the study where Laurent, Skye and Ryan sat, drinking scotch and talking about her situation.

Laurent looked up, smiling when he saw her, and warmth spread through her veins at his attention. "Hi there, handsome." She sat next to him and took a sip of his scotch before tucking close into his side. Skye snuggled into her other side and Ryan pulled her feet into his lap. "It's like a werewolf sandwich," she said and Skye laughed.

"Hmpf." Laurent raised his eyebrows at Skye and Ryan but they both ignored him. "Punks. Rain, we're going to wait until after the conversion and you're officially brought into the Pack with the Mating ceremony before confronting your father directly."

Rain's eyes widened. "Are you sure that's a good idea? Can't we just ignore him?"

"Baby, it has to be done. I won't have you living in fear for the rest of your life. I'm going to make contact with the Eastern Seaboard Clans and get them onboard. Your father has to know that you're married to me now, that you don't want any contact with him or Anthony and that should any harm come to you or anyone close to you damaging information will be sent to the police and the newspapers. We do need to gather that information, I'm assuming you have some?"

133

"More than I want but yes. Why involve the other Packs on the East Coast though? I hate making anyone else a part of this."

"Insurance. I want them to be watched, even just casually. Any word about you or harm to you and yours will be reported to me immediately and dealt with. Werewolves have been around a lot longer than organized crime. If Anthony wants to play rough I *will* make good on my threat to him today without remorse. You need to understand, Rain, I'll do anything to keep you safe. Killing a waste of skin like Anthony Vargas wouldn't cause me even one moment's grief."

"Okay. I can't say that it doesn't scare me to have you talk like them but I'm happy to say you're on my side."

"I don't hurt innocents, Rain. That's the difference between me and your father and Anthony. But I can rip out a throat in ten seconds and I will, without hesitation, to protect you or anyone else I care about."

"Uh, okay," she murmured and put her face into his neck and breathed him in. She felt better as the warmth of his body rolled over her. "Mmmm." Suddenly things tightened low in her gut and a warm wave of desire oozed through her.

"Rain, watch what you're doing, love," Laurent growled softly. Instead Rain moaned and snuggled into his side more firmly. The heat of his skin called to her. Unable to resist, she slid her hands up under the hem of his shirt, stroking over his bare skin.

Something about the man just drove her to distraction. She never felt like a sexy siren in her entire life and now he had her feeling him up in public. A laugh bubbled up at the thought of ripping off his clothes and ravaging him right there and then. But the laugh was low and velvet, startling her.

"What have you done to that sweet shy girl you brought here a few weeks ago?" Ryan asked with an eyebrow raised.

"I don't know what he does to me. I can't keep my hands off him," she answered as she nibbled on his earlobe and he growled and electricity arced down her spine and landed in her pussy as honey gathered.

Laurent's nostrils flared. "We need to take this home. I need you." He got up, picking her up, and she wrapped her legs around his waist.

"Okay. Whatever. Wherever." She rolled her hips, grinding herself over his cock, and he drew in his breath.

"Damn," Ryan said and got up and had to adjust himself. "I need to look at some human women. First Kari, then Emma and now Rain. I'm missing something for sure."

"'Bye," Laurent called out, striding from the room, Ryan and Skye laughing in their wake.

* * * * *

Laurent kicked the door of the cabin open and slammed it shut behind him. His eyes glowed with heat as he deposited Rain onto the bed. She watched, speechless, as he ripped his shirt off and stripped his jeans from his body.

He growled low and carnal as his eyes greedily took in Rain's movements as she rose to her knees. Slowly she pulled her shirt off, exposing her breasts. Her hands went to her jeans but he shook his head.

He stalked to the bed and pushed her onto her back. Grabbing an ankle, he pulled her to the edge of the mattress and made quick work of her jeans and panties. Eyes on her pussy, he dropped to his knees and kissed a hot, wet trail up the inside of her thigh until he reached just where she wanted him most.

"Sweet, sweet, Rain, I love you so much," he murmured and kissed her passionately. Kissed her pussy like a lover — licking, laving, sucking across fevered, swollen flesh.

Rain's breath left her body in a gusty sigh as she reached down to thread his hair through her fingers.

His fingers joined in the erotic assault on her pussy, one hand tickling the star of her ass while the other slowly slid two fingers into her, hooking until he stroked over her sweet spot.

No one had ever made her feel so good, feel so much at once. It was more than the combination of his mouth and hands, it was *him*. It was the two of them together that made it so hot between them, she was sure of it. Even the stroke of his hair over her belly and thighs turned her on.

Liquid pleasure stole over her, built and built until she nearly overflowed and still he continued. Continued as she softly cried out his name, rocking her pussy against his mouth because she could do nothing else.

"Mmm, now then." Grinning, he stood up and pushed her back a bit on the bed, still between her thighs. While her cunt still fluttered and her skin was still flushed with pleasure, he guided the head of his cock to her gate and plunged deep into her.

Rain cried out again, wrapping her legs around his waist, and he felt the flutter of an echoing orgasm round his cock. Laurent just about lost his mind as Rain's velvet heat surrounded him over and over.

He loved how responsive she was to his touch. Looking down at her, he smiled at the shine of her lips as she licked them. Her eyes, half lidded with desire, were passion-glazed. Her hands had been stroking over his back until he increased his speed and the strength of his thrusts, and then her nails dug into the muscle of his thighs. The edge of pain added spice to the encounter.

His hair, loose, swept over her bare skin. Over the curves of her delicious breasts and across her nipples. The juxtaposition of the dark hair over the creamy skin of her breast and the coral pink of nipple and areola was disarming and unbelievably erotic.

"Laurent! Oh!" she gasped as he changed his angle and stroked across a different path of nerve endings. She fluttered around him and he fought for control, a fight he was quickly losing. "Yes. Oh god yes," she moaned as yet another climax hit her. The power of her inner muscles fluttering and pulsing around him was too much and it pulled him in with her and he came with a hoarse whisper of her name.

Pulse after pulse he released his pleasure, his love, his joy into her and she received him. He felt as if he'd come home. She was his safe harbor. He fell to his side and moved her with him, staying buried within her, not wanting to leave the tight heat of her flesh.

She let out a long breath. "I love you, Laurent."

"I love you too."

"So you never did tell me about you and Phillip and Ryan. Are you bi?"

He shrugged. "How much detail do you want?"

She laughed. "Are you kidding me? Give it to me, all of it."

He kissed the top of her head. "It was just a few times over the years. I don't know if I'm bi or not. I certainly enjoyed myself so if that makes me bi I guess I am. I'm not much hung up on definitions. Anyway, like I said, sometimes sexual touching is a comfort. Werewolves are very sexual creatures. There are times when we're up here for weeks at a time and don't leave the area. If I'm horny and Phillip is horny too there's no reason not to work that out."

"Holy shit. Can I watch?" She sat up. He started to laugh but found the idea was one that titillated him.

"I hadn't planned to be with anyone else but you. But should I ever feel the need for another cock in the equation I'll be sure to have you there. Would you like that?"

"To see you with another man who looks as good as Phillip or Ryan?"

"To *be* with another man who looks as good as Phillip or Ryan."

"Oh." She pursed her lips. "I don't know. You're saying you'd be okay if I fucked another man?"

He sat up with her. "Fucked? Probably not. Although I don't want to fuck another man or woman either. Mess around? Naked, sweaty, hands and mouths? Yeah, I'd be okay as long as I was there and as long as the other wolf was subordinate."

One of her eyebrows rose and he scented the ripening of her body as desire rose again. Grinning, he took her to the mattress with his body. "Ahh, you would like that then? To have me fucking you with another male in the bed with us? His cock in your hand or maybe your mouth? His mouth on your pussy when my cock was in your mouth? Hmm?"

"Oh," she said, rather breathlessly. "I, well, my!"

"One day at a time. For now I plan to be all you need. But in the future, if the opportunity comes up, we can talk about it again. Now then, your pussy is wet and ready and as a coincidence, I'm hard again."

He took her again, hard and fast, and after they'd both come she fell asleep within moments, her body tucked against his, a smile on her lips.

Chapter Five

✿

"She answered but some dude got on the phone and threatened me," Anthony Vargas said into the phone to Pietro Margoles.

"Where is she?" Margoles roared.

"The phone number my source got me is in Seattle."

"Why aren't you there then? Anthony, why haven't you gone to get my daughter and bring her back here so she can marry you?"

"She said she didn't want to come home, that she didn't want to marry me. The dude said she was his fiancée," Anthony whined.

"I don't give a rat's ass what she wants! She's been told what to do and she needs to do it. No wonder you couldn't hold her here, Vargas! You don't let a woman tell you what to do. The woman does what you say. Now get your ass out to Seattle and bring her back. And Vargas, keep your hands away from her face. I understand you need to instill a bit of discipline in her but no more broken bones or I'll break a few of yours. As for this man who claims to be engaged to her, do with him what you will but make it clean."

"Fine, I'll go out there." He huffed and slammed the phone down.

* * * * *

"Wake up, baby, we have a wedding to go to," Laurent said, kissing Rain's pert nose.

She pulled him down to her lips and he gave her a proper good morning kiss that left her breathless. "Now a girl could get used to those kinds of good mornings," she said, sitting up.

"Damn, who is that?" he muttered when he heard a knock on the door. "Get up, baby, and grab a shower. We should grab breakfast and then head to the courthouse. We're on his calendar in a little over an hour. Then we'll come back and start the transformation," he said, leaving the room.

"Like shopping for a new sweater. Hey, let's just bite you and change you into a werewolf this afternoon. Jeez," she muttered and loped into the bathroom. Turning the water on and getting it extra hot, she stood there for a few minutes to wake up. Her muscles were sore in all the right ways. That made her smile.

Afterward she wandered back into the bedroom to find clothes to wear but instead found Drew and Skye standing near the bed, talking to Laurent.

She raised an eyebrow as they all stared at her naked body. "Hello, doesn't anyone say, 'put some clothes on before you come out of the bathroom, Rain'?"

Laurent growled and pushed both men out of the room. "Stop staring! That's my Mate."

"I thought you said nudity was natural." Rain followed him out, amused by his agitation. After the whole thing with Paloma, a little turn of the tables was in order.

"Well it is. On a run. You look, well, damned sexy with that just-out-of-the-shower flush of your skin. Get that dress on! Drew brought it for you today," he growled and pushed her back into the bedroom, shutting the door behind her.

She could hear Skye laughing as she opened the protective bag around the dress hanging in the bedroom. She stilled, touched that anyone would think something so beautiful should belong to her. Carefully she pulled it out and ran a reverent hand over the material.

She stepped into it, pulling the snug bodice up and buttoning it. The blood red material set off the honeyed tone of her skin and complemented her hair. The neck scooped just enough to accent her breasts but not embarrass. The skirt, in contrast to the bodice, flowed and moved around her legs fluidly as she walked. Twisting this way and that, she took herself in through the mirror. She looked beautiful and sexy and feminine. She felt like a woman should feel on her wedding day, like a princess.

She pulled her hair up in a series of twists at the back of her head, fastening it with pretty pins. Sexy red shoes and a bit of clear gloss on her lips completed the outfit. She wished she had her jewelry from home but she had better — her freedom and a man like Laurent to love her forever.

She walked out into the living room and all three men turned to stare at her openmouthed.

Laurent came to her and got on one knee. "Rain," he shook his head, searching for words, "you look amazing. I didn't do this very officially when we arranged it all so let me do it right." He pulled a black velvet jeweler's box from his pocket and cracked it open, revealing an oval diamond solitaire and a band set with baguettes of alternating diamonds and rubies. "Rain, will you marry me?"

Tears sprang to her eyes as she knelt to face him. "Yes. I don't have a ring for you, but will you marry me?"

He smiled and put the solitaire on her finger and put the band back in his pocket. "Always and forever. I don't need a ring, I have your heart." He stood and pulled her up. "Let's go and grab some breakfast. And remember, we'll do this in style after the dust has settled."

She nodded and smiled, following him out and up to the lodge where Anna had prepared a huge breakfast.

"We're all coming to the ceremony. I can't believe you haven't given us any time to plan a big party but we'll make do today and have a big bash in a few weeks." Anna waved them to the table and Laurent smiled as he made Rain a plate.

"That dress is gorgeous! You look like Snow White, only a sexy version," Ryan said as he came into the dining room, and Skye and Drew nodded in agreement. Phillip kissed her cheek and went to sit down with his coffee. A very vivid picture of a lot of naked male flesh, loose hair in many shades and lots of moaning hit her and she had to close her eyes a second until it passed.

"I just want to thank you for being so kind to me," Rain said, looking at them all, each face open and warm. "I haven't ever had a family where I've felt free to be who I was and, well, you all feel so right to me. So thanks," she finished, blushing.

"No, it's we who should thank you. Now that I have Kari I know how truly empty my heart was before she came to me. You've filled Laurent's life with so much joy. Thank you, Rain." Andreas smiled at her, winking.

"Is that a ring I see?" Kari gasped and jumped up, Emma, Alyssa and Perri joining her. Rain nodded and held out her hand.

"Laurent gave it to me this morning. Isn't it beautiful?"

"Gorgeous!" Emma said and the other three agreed. Laurent was secretly proud that Rain was so excited about the ring but tried to look irritated by all of the girlish squealing. He failed miserably when a huge grin broke over his face.

"You are in so deep, Laurent," Sean said mildly as he watched Emma hungrily.

"You should know." Laurent snorted.

"Hell yeah. I like being in deep. A woman like Emma keeps me on my toes and I can keep her on her back," he added sotto voice but Emma heard him and raised an eyebrow his way and they all laughed.

"You two are next." Laurent lifted his chin, indicating Skye and Ryan.

Laurent stood after they ate, pulling Rain up beside him. "Well, off we go. Anyone who cares to come along will probably fit in chambers. Close your eyes," he said to Rain, who did. She smelled the heady scent of roses before she felt the bouquet in her hands. "Open."

She looked down at the most beautiful bouquet of red and silver roses she'd ever seen, tied with a red bow the same color as her dress. "Laurent, they're gorgeous!" She buried her nose in the flowers and breathed them in.

"I know today's just a quick deal and that we'll do a bigger ceremony later but I wanted you to have some of the bits and pieces that women seem to like," he said, slightly embarrassed.

"Thank you." Rain touched his cheek.

Laurent led Rain out of the lodge and to his truck, helping her inside, and they took off toward town.

The judge was easily eighty years old but a randy old flirt who winked lasciviously at every female in the room, including the bride. They had to use Rain's real name to be sure the ceremony was totally legal and Andreas had already contacted his attorney to start the name changing procedure, to change from Julia to Rain. The ceremony was over in just ten minutes. When they walked out into the early autumn sunlight, now married, Rain had never in her life been so happy.

Chapter Six

৯০

Back at the lodge Skye and Andreas argued with Laurent that one of them should bite Rain because Laurent loved her and it would be far too difficult for him to hurt her. Laurent felt that it was his responsibility because she was changing for him.

Kari and Rain watched the whole thing unfold until Rain stood up, put her fingers in her mouth and whistled shrilly. "ENOUGH! Oh my god. Listen, people, let's get on with this already. I'm nervous enough knowing that I'll be attacked by a wolf so severely that I'll be out of it for at least a day or two." She crossed her arms over her chest. "Laurent, love, Andreas and Skye are right. When they bit Emma it was Phillip who did it. Can you really hurt me that severely? Can you really shove your face into my skin and tear at my flesh?"

Laurent went pale. He couldn't but it seemed such an intimate thing he wasn't sure he wanted to allow anyone else to do it either.

"Laurent, you're our brother. Let one of us do it and take on this burden for you. That way you can be with her the whole time she recovers. You'll feel guilty enough, I know I did and I couldn't even be there to hold Kari's hand."

Laurent exhaled. "All right. I'll hold her while you do it. Andreas, let it be you. You're the strongest and largest of us, you can do it quicker and cleaner." Laurent looked at Rain, who had changed into sweats and a button-down shirt for the bite. "Is that all right with you, baby?"

Rain snorted and kissed Laurent tenderly. "Honey, I trust you and you trust Andreas. It'll be fine. Let's just do it already because I'm losing my nerve here."

144

Andreas moved to one side and removed his clothing. Rain looked at Kari and winked and waggled an eyebrow. Andreas was built like a giant Greek god. Kari laughed and held one of Rain's hands. "You're a glass half full girl, I see."

Rain shrugged. "Hey, take your pleasures where you can."

Emma walked forward with a smile. "Lie down here, Rain. It'll hurt. I'm sorry about that. There'll be a lot of blood as well. Rest assured though, I'm here and Sean and Elaine are here too—three doctors, and two of us have been through the change and survived. Scream if you have to, okay? Let's get your shirt off, it'll just get ruined anyway. Strip down to your panties too."

Quickly, Rain removed her clothes down to her panties and lay on the low table covered in warm linens Emma had indicated.

"I'm going to restrain your arms, Rain. We don't want you attacking Andreas or hurting yourself more than necessary."

Laurent wiped a tear. Seeing her so pale and frightened ate away at him. He hated that she had to do this. It was the only way she could live as his Mate and the best way to keep her safe from her father. Sean approached him and Ryan and Phillip did as well.

"Laurent, we're going to hold you. Fight your wolf, do not change. If we feel you start to change we'll have to remove you from the room. Just remember that Rain will survive and four days from now, under the silver of the moon, she will be bonded to you and you to her."

Laurent leaned forward and kissed Rain's lips. "I love you, baby. I'll be here for you. You'll wake up soon."

Rain fought back a sob as she began to tremble. Andreas had changed and padded over to the side of the table she lay on. He licked her hand and whined and she looked at him, eyes wide. "My god, you are so beautiful," she whispered and suddenly he snarled. Sharp white teeth shone for a moment as time stretched. Those teeth met the soft flesh of her belly, tearing it open. The pain was unbearable, she screamed and tried to get free, struggling against the restraints that held her arms as the others held her legs. She screamed for Laurent to help her, begging. The searing pain faded, numbing as her consciousness began to feather and float away.

Laurent struggled to free himself from the hold Sean, Phillip, Ryan and Skye had on him. He screamed and growled, trying to get to her, trying to help her.

"Hold on, Laurent!" Sean yelled into his face. "You have to control yourself. She's going to be all right. If you interfere now you'll hurt her."

"She's unconscious," Emma said over the din.

Laurent slumped down the wall, tears streaming down his face, sobs wracking his body. His Mate lay on the table, pale and bleeding profusely. The scent of her fear, acrid and bitter, clung to the air. Andreas had changed back and Kari helped him clean up quickly before he went to Laurent, putting an arm around his shoulders.

"Why aren't you helping her?" Laurent demanded as Emma and Elaine watched Rain bleed out.

"We will. You know this has to happen. Her body has to suffer the trauma for the virus to work. I will not let Rain die, you know that, Laurent." Emma kept her eyes on Rain but reached out to touch Laurent, squeezing his hand briefly.

Standing there as the minutes passed and the trauma took over Rain's system nearly killed Laurent. The room spun as he swayed on unsure legs, watching her approach death. Closer and closer.

The heart monitor was out of control and then suddenly it slowed down to next to nothing. He would be haunted by her screams to help her until his last breath.

"Now!" Emma said and they began to move. Elaine gave Rain a shot of something and Emma cleaned her up. Before stitching her up Emma checked her internal organs. "You perforated her bowel, Andreas. Ripped through one of her kidneys and her spleen. Everything is healing now," she said, looking up with a relieved smile. "Laurent, it's looking very good."

Laurent slumped but Andreas and Sean held him up. Both men knew the terror Laurent was facing. He leaned forward and kissed Rain's brow. "I love you, baby. You're going to be all right. I'm here. I won't leave your side."

Phillip brought Laurent a chair and helped him into it. They attached an IV for fluids to Rain's hand and put a gown on her before moving her to a bed. "She's doing well, Laurent. Her vital signs are improving and steady. I'll be back in a few minutes to check on her again. Just yell if you need me before that." Emma kissed Laurent's temple and brushed the hair from Rain's shoulder.

Over the next hours, Laurent didn't leave her side any longer than a few minutes here and there to go to the bathroom.

Anna brought him meals and sat with the two of them for a while here and there. She knit as the day deepened into evening. "You know, Laurent, you were always such a serious boy. You've grown into a serious man, a protector who's always put others' lives before his own. I've always been very proud of you, thought of you as one of my own. But this sweet girl, she's brought a light to your eyes. There's a playfulness to you I've not seen since your mother was alive. It's a joy to see it. She's something special, your Rain. She's going to be fine you know. The two of you will have a long and happy life and bring this Pack more children."

"I was just thinking that too, Anna." Kari came in with Andreas and handed Laurent a mug of tea. "Drink that, sweetie. Do you want to take a break? Stretch your legs? I promise I'll stay right here."

Laurent smiled at them, at his Pack, his family. "I'm fine. And Anna, I've always considered myself one of your own too but thank you for saying all of that."

* * * * *

Over the next two days Laurent read to Rain. He told her stories about his life growing up. He promised to take her to the Paris cemetery where his mother was interred and his father—who never remarried or fell in love again—now lay next to her. He told her that he couldn't wait for her to have his children. He talked about traveling and about how much he loved her.

All the while she got stronger and he felt the return of her spirit more each passing hour. Her color improved and she even squeezed his hand a few times. His woman would be waking up any moment and the rest of their lives stretched out before him.

Rain finally opened her eyes on the third day, early in the morning. She watched the light coming through the window, dust motes floating on the air. Slowly she turned her head, Laurent's scent drawing her attention.

He lay there sleeping, head on her bed, nestled against her side. His hair was an ebony spill over his face and shoulders. Most of his body rested in a chair next to the bed. Reaching out, she gently pushed the hair out of his face and his eyes fluttered open.

"Rain? Baby?" He sat up, blinking and finally looking into her eyes. She smiled weakly and nodded.

"Who else would I be?" she croaked.

"How do you feel?" He kissed her fingers, joy radiating from him.

"Like I got attacked by a werewolf. Oh and I need to take a shower and brush my teeth," she said, her voice coming back.

"Hang on, baby." Laurent got up, walked to the door, opened it and bellowed out, "SHE'S AWAKE!" He walked back over to her and kissed her forehead.

Rain chuckled. "I'm sure you didn't need to wake up the entire house."

Emma came into the room and smiled. "Of course he did. I'm happy to see you awake at last, Rain. You look good. Laurent, move for a second so I can check her out." Emma pulled the sheets back and opened the gown Rain wore. "As you can see your wound is totally gone. Not even a scar from the stitches." She took Rain's pulse. "Good. Nice and strong."

Kari and Andreas came into the room, as did Sean and Phillip. "Is she okay?"

"Yes, she's doing excellent. That extra day she was out made a huge difference. She has no scarring at all, the site of the bite is totally healed," Emma said, tucking the sheet around Rain as she stood.

"I need a shower," Rain said with a wince.

"Oh man! Do I remember that," Emma groaned. "You'll be shaky for the next day or so. I'm going to have Anna make you some broth and tea. You'll feel completely better by this evening. You can eat regularly tomorrow and tomorrow night you'll transform and you'll feel better than you have in your entire life. As for now, don't overdo it, as in Laurent, you can't have sex. Save it for the bonding tomorrow."

Laurent raised an eyebrow at the sex comment. He may be a werewolf but he wasn't an animal. He knew Rain needed TLC. But the truth was, three days without Rain and he wanted her desperately. "I'll take care of her. Can she shower?"

"Yes, someone will need to be nearby to help just in case."

"Don't do it, Laurent. I helped Kari after she came home from the poisoning and she ravished me right there in the stall." Andreas chuckled.

Kari started laughing while she blushed.

"I don't care who does it. I feel grungy and sticky," Rain said, sitting up as Emma removed her IV.

"I'll do it," Skye said sighing dramatically. "It's a chore but someone has to help Rain stand naked, wet and slippery in the shower." He winked at her.

Laurent growled at him and he only laughed harder. "I'll do it. I can control myself, for heaven's sake. No one is going to be handling Rain in the shower. You have no idea how sexy she looks all wet and covered in soap bubbles," he said, eyes glazing over at the memory.

Rain rolled her eyes and snorted. "Whatever! Whoever it is, help me into the bathroom and then leave for a few moments while I do my business. Then you may come back in and stand guard outside the stall. Laurent, if it is you, you can scrub my back and help with my hair," she said softly, cocking her head. Lauren went to her, bumping Skye out of the way and letting her take his arm.

Once she'd gone to the bathroom, he made her sit while he heated the water and laid out towels and a fresh change of clothes for her. Stripping down, he moved to help her out of her gown and panties and into the shower stall.

The shower was harder than he'd thought it would be. Hell, *he* was harder than he'd thought he would be. His relief at her recovery made him desperate to be inside her. He wanted to be close to her like that, to have their special bond reaffirmed. She was alive and unharmed and she'd survived the ordeal. On top of that she was wet, nubile and the sexiest thing he'd ever seen.

Gritting his teeth, he stepped out and grabbed a towel to help her dry off. He bent to dry her legs and his cheek brushed her nipple. The scent of her body, the feel of that taut peak against his skin, made him groan in frustration.

"Laurent," she gasped.

"No, baby! You heard Emma. We can't. Tomorrow though, all bets are off." He helped her pull on a robe and picked her up. "I'm going to carry you back to the cabin. I'm sure Anna has been down there already."

And she had of course. Steaming mugs of tea and broth waited on a tray and Anna had set up a little nest for Rain in their bed. Laurent smiled at her thoughtfulness.

"Are you mad at me?" Laurent whispered as Rain slowly sipped her broth.

"For not making love to me against doctor's orders? No, silly, why would you think that?" She laughed.

Laurent shook his head. "No, about the bite. You screamed at me to help you but I didn't." He hung his head.

She moved the tray aside and turned to him, taking his face in her hands and tilting it to see his eyes. "No. I was out of my head with the pain. It was horrible. I was terrified. The logical part of me knew that it had to be done and I'd be okay. It's just that my terror took over. I'm sorry I made you feel bad," she whispered and pulled him to her.

"Don't apologize. My god, you let yourself get torn open by a wolf for me. You trusted me. What a beautiful gift. Rain!" he exclaimed as she wormed her hand into the waistband of his pants and grabbed his cock.

"I'll be on top. We can be gentle," she said and he shuddered with repressed desire.

He moved her hand reluctantly. "No. We can wait."

She rubbed herself over him like a cat, a cat in heat. Her robe was open, he felt her nipples through the material of his t-shirt. "I don't want to wait. I want you, Laurent," she purred and he grabbed her and set her away from him and he re-closed the front of her robe.

"Eat and stop tempting me!" he said gruffly. "Siren." He growled and she winked at him. She loved his growls.

"Fine. Reject me then." She sighed dramatically and he snorted but put the mug of broth back in her hand.

"Eat. Drama queen."

"I should call Harrison to check up on things. It's been several days," she said as she finished and he took the tray into the kitchen.

"That's a good idea. Call him at the paper though. Don't risk calling him at home or on his mobile."

"Yeah. Bring me my wallet please, his card is in there."

Laurent dug through her purse and found her wallet, bringing it to her. She rifled through the business cards and pulled one out and dialed the number and his extension.

"Harrison Watts."

"Harrison! How are you? Is everything all right?"

"Rain! My god, are you all right?"

"Yes. Laurent and I got married. I'm great."

"Well, congratulations to you both. But, Rain, a man was here. I think it was your ex. He came to the house three days ago. I told them that I came home from work and you'd skipped but had left me cash to cover rent. I told him your name was Rain Foster and that I had no idea who Julia Margoles was. He seemed to be satisfied with that and told me to call him if you came back around. I told him you'd been seeing some guy who lived in Portland. He had a gun, Rain. I could see it through his jacket. He had two guys with him, big, blond, not too bright. Anyway, he called me yesterday and asked if I'd heard from you. Don't call the house."

"Jesus. I'm sorry. Be safe, all right? Tell him everything if you have to, don't risk your life for me," she said and Laurent took the phone.

"Harrison, it's Laurent. Listen, I'm going to be contacting her father to work something out. Rain's right, don't get yourself hurt to protect her, that's what I'm here for and she can't hide forever. You still have my mobile number, right?"

"Yeah, I memorized it and threw away the paper a long time ago. But I'd never betray Rain to those bastards. Laurent, I lost someone very dear to me and I'd never take the chance of losing Rain. You can trust me. If anything else happens and you don't call I'll contact you."

"Okay. Thanks a lot, Harrison."

"No problem and remember how lucky you are to have a woman like Rain. Do something to deserve her every day," Harrison said softly before he hung up.

Laurent hung the phone back in the cradle and looked to Rain. "Now rest. You're transforming tomorrow night. I'll give you a bit of history and culture 101 when you wake up," he said, tucking the blankets around her and fluffing her pillows. He kissed her forehead and by the time he got to the door she'd fallen asleep.

Phillip, Andreas, Skye and Ryan waited for Laurent out on the porch when he came out of the bedroom. He noted the tray holding breakfast and a carafe of Anna's coffee and hightailed it to join them.

After he'd poured himself a cup he grabbed some bacon and toast and sat back, relating the details of Harrison's call. Andreas told them he'd compiled all of Rain's information and had sent it to several different people across the country and even to their Father Clan back in France. Rain had given them Pietro's personal business line number and Laurent would call him first thing the morning after Rain's transformation. They wanted her to officially take her place in the Pack and have their protection before they moved.

After they'd spent a few hours brainstorming and planning, business gave way to gossip and trash talking.

"She did well. I'm happy to see she came out of the recovery from the bite so strong," Andreas rumbled. "She's an excellent mate for you, Laurent."

"Better than I deserve. I hope that I can make her half as happy as she makes me."

Skye smiled. "Dumbass, she adores you. Don't know why, I'm ten times more handsome but for some reason you push her buttons. I thought she'd just jump your bones the other night in the office."

Laurent smiled slowly at the memory of his sweet Rain being so bold. "Yeah."

"Get that sly smile off your face!" Phillip smacked his arm. "Care to enlighten me?"

"And me too," Andreas agreed, eager to hear that story.

"The other night in the study Rain came in and was sitting in between Laurent and me, her feet up on Ryan's lap, and she started moaning and nuzzling into Laurent's neck. Next thing her hands were up under his shirt and she was sucking on his earlobe and rubbing herself all over him."

"In front of you guys?" Phillip asked.

"Yeah, that sweet heart-shaped ass was actually rubbing into my thigh. If she'd been anyone other than Laurent's mate he would have had to share her. All of those sexual pheromones she was emitting were pretty hardcore."

"What happened?"

"Laurent growled and picked her up and carried her out of the room, her legs wrapped around his waist."

"Sorry I missed that. Who'd have thought? Our sweet shy Rain." Phillip grinned.

"Oh she was hot," Ryan murmured and they all sat silent for a moment thinking about her.

"Enough! I know you're all imagining my Mate. Knock it off! She's been living in a very repressed place for a long time. She's freeing her sexuality for the first time and there's a very sensual woman under the surface. I also think there's a nuclear combustion of chemicals between us. The sex is, well, mind-blowing. Suddenly I understand why Kari and Andreas are always so damned loud."

Andreas laughed. "It's all Kari, she's just loud in bed, what can I say? And suck it up, Laurent. I've had to live with you perverts fantasizing about my Mate for years now. It's your turn."

"Well, it's a fortunate thing she's Mated to a wolf so strong. Anyone lower than Fifth or Sixth would have a sore trial trying to hold on to a female like Rain," Skye said and they all nodded in agreement.

"What are you all up to?" Rain said, still sleep soft, standing in the doorway. "You look like trouble." She arched an eyebrow and they all laughed.

"Come on out here, baby. The fresh air will do you good. You have socks on, right?"

She laughed as she came out onto the porch. "Yes, I have socks on. You know my feet get cold."

Laurent pulled her down into his lap and into the shelter of his body. "Let me keep you warm then. You look better, did you have a good nap?"

She wriggled to get closer to him and he gritted his teeth as her lush ass rubbed against his cock through his jeans. "I'm fine. I'm hungry though and not for broth either. I can't remember the last time I felt like I could scarf up an entire cow." She laughed and kissed the inside of Laurent's elbow and Laurent saw Skye send an arched brow to Andreas as if to say, "See what I mean?"

"Rain, you need to stop that," Laurent growled into her ear and she laughed a husky taunting laugh that teased over his skin and straight to his already throbbing cock. "You're playing with fire."

"So burn me, Laurent," she said into the skin of his neck. "Why is it that I just want to eat you up? I want to bite right here," she said and bit down over his pulse, his tendon between her teeth, and he groaned. "And I have the strangest urge to drag my tongue up your neck and taste you. Like this." She drew the flat of her tongue from his shoulder to his ear. Gooseflesh broke out in the wake of her warm, soft lick.

"God. Rain, honey... Ohhh, that feels so good," he murmured as she licked over his ear, dipping the tip of her tongue inside briefly.

Moments later he opened his eyes to see the others staring at them, openmouthed. "Rain, I think it's the reaction of our two pheromone compounds. It's combustible, it's why Mates are for life. Sweetheart, we have an audience."

She undulated into him, the heat of her pussy branding him even through her pajama bottoms and his jeans. He only barely bit back a growl.

"I know, I can't help it. They need to go and you and I need to go inside," she said, swaying from side to side, brushing her nipples over his chest.

Andreas burst out laughing and it shook her out of her stupor. She sighed. "Okay okay, I'll stop. But I can't sit on your lap and not do anything to you so I should go up to the lodge and hang out or I'll molest you," she said as she bit his bottom lip.

"You shouldn't let us stop you. If you need to ride Laurent like a pony we won't get in the way." Skye winked and Laurent tossed his mug at his head.

Laughing agreeably, Rain stood. "Maybe later, when I know you better." She turned to Laurent. "I'm going to change and head up to the lodge. I'm feeling better, not that anyone will let me do anything once I get up there."

Which was why he agreed to let her go up to the lodge. Anna and Kari would make sure she put her feet up and rest.

They all remained speechless as she went inside and came back a few minutes later, dropping a long kiss on Laurent's lips before swaying up to the lodge.

"Good lord!" Ryan gasped out. "I think I may have come in my pants like a fifteen-year-old boy."

Laurent waggled his brows, grinning. "My Mate is so hot. Oh yeah. And from what I've observed between Kari and Andreas it doesn't seem to wear off."

"No, thank goodness, it's like being in heat every day. My desire for Kari hasn't waned one bit over the years. Man though, Laurent, Rain does have a mighty fine ass," he murmured as they all looked up the hill to watch her climb the stairs and go in to the lodge through the French doors.

They all laughed and continued to talk for a while before following in Rain's wake back to the lodge for dinner. Emma even let Rain eat mashed potatoes and chicken, much to her delight.

"So what about the sex?" Rain whispered to Emma when the women had moved into the great room after dinner.

Emma laughed. "Oh I see, it's hit you hard hasn't it?"

"What?"

"I don't know that it has an official name. In my case it's Sean Lust. I've been with him for nearly four years and I still can't get enough of him. Just smelling his skin drives me nuts. Kari and Andreas have it too. Perri and Devon have it. Good lord, they'll get down just about anywhere anytime. They were nonexclusive at gatherings for a long time though. I think it's just a part of the fit between two Mates. That combination of DNA and pheromones, it's just a sex brew."

"It won't lessen with time? I mean, I wasn't an overly sexual person before I met Laurent and now I crawl all over him at the oddest times. He's like a drug." She looked in Laurent's direction and he sent her a heated glance over the rim of his glass.

Emma laughed. "Well, it hasn't lessened between Jade and Tomas and they've been together for fifty years." She shrugged. "I'm not complaining, it's like the first three months of a relationship and it never lessens. Knowing I'll have a sizzling hot sex life at eighty makes me a happy girl."

Kari came over and sat down. "All of this whispering must be about sex."

Emma and Rain burst out laughing and the men turned to eye them suspiciously.

"What are they up to?" Andreas rumbled to Laurent who raised an eyebrow and shrugged.

Sean laughed. "My money says sex." He sent a lascivious grin and wink at Emma and she blushed, bending her head to talk with Kari and Rain again. "Yeah."

"Jeez, as if having the four of them wasn't bad enough. Rain evens things up more," Jack said, coming to sit with them as Alyssa and Perri went to the circle of whispering women.

Devon agreed as he sat down with a sigh, watching Perri.

"We're all in big trouble," Andreas chuckled, watching the group of beautiful women bent in laughing conversation.

"They're getting nervous over there," Kari said, laughing. Rain stole a glance back at Laurent, who looked so darkly handsome and masculine that her insides melted.

"Good. I walked into a conversation they were all having earlier about my ass and about how hot our sex life was. Laurent, Andreas, Ryan, Phillip and Skye were all out there chatting away. Oh and I hear you're loud in bed." She tipped her chin toward Kari, who burst out laughing. As a group they all turned slowly and looked back at the men as they continued to laugh.

"Now I'm seriously worried about what they're up to," Devon said. "I've been Mated the longest among us and I tell you, they get into a lot of trouble when they get together."

"Human women. Couldn't be nice wolf females, raised to understand things. Nooo, had to be human women, raised to be independent," Andreas groused.

Laurent threw back his head and laughed. "And I wouldn't have it any other way."

"Hey, my woman is natural wolf. She's just as big a pain in the ass as my sister is," Jack said.

Fire and Rain

"No one is as big a pain in the ass as Kari," Phillip said and they all laughed.

"So you're talking about the lust?" Perri asked the other women.

"Yes, is that what you call it?" Emma asked.

"Yeah, we call it wolf lust," Alyssa said.

"I just was saying how it totally shocks me. I'd never felt like this about sex or a man before. Just smelling the skin at the hollow of his throat makes me crazy," Rain said.

The other women moaned. "Yeah, it seems that certain spots on the body are stronger conductors of the pheromones than others. The neck, the shoulders. For us I think it's the neck and the curve of the breasts, the back of the knees," Emma said.

"Oh and the skin on the inside of Laurent's elbow." Rain shivered.

"How could I have forgotten!"

"So? Can I or not?" Rain asked.

Emma laughed. "Yeah, I did on my first night after I woke up."

"Oh thank god!"

"At least he's not Alpha. Andreas and I couldn't have sex the night before I transformed because his boys were sacred and he had to save them for some sort of fertility thing. Of course he did go down on me so one of us got off. Oh and wait until you get pregnant, it's even worse!"

"Oh yeah," the other women agreed loudly.

"Poor Andreas, toward the end he and I were having sex like four times a day and he was getting me off in other ways at least four other times and I still couldn't get enough. He was actually complaining that he had carpal tunnel." Kari laughed and they all looked at him over their shoulders.

"What in god's name are they discussing?" Andreas growled.

"When I was pregnant with Drea I would just show up at Sean's office and make him have sex with me in between his appointments. I'd wake up an hour before he left for work to fit in at least one round of fucking and a blowjob."

"You guys are scaring me," Rain said, laughing. "But now that I have the go-ahead I'm going to grab my husband and make a run for it. All of this talk has only made things worse." She stood up and they all hugged her. "See you tomorrow morning."

Rain turned and looked at Laurent, her pupils dilating, lips parting. She sent him a wave of sensual awareness and he looked as though he'd been physically hit. He stood up and without even saying goodbye grabbed Rain and stalked out the doors.

"Wow," Skye whispered in awe.

"If you will excuse me, I believe that my wife and I have a prior engagement," Sean smiled at Emma and they both got up and met at the door where he pulled her to him and brought his lips down to hers in a passionate kiss.

"Yeah, what Sean said." Devon stood up, Perri was already running for the door.

Kari and Andreas stared at each other for a few moments and she smiled softly. He walked over to her, swept her into his arms and started up the staircase toward the master suite.

"That leaves us, babe," Alyssa said to Jack who smiled and started to walk to her, that is until Max came in and said he needed help with his homework. Stifling a groan, he put his arm around his adopted son and assured him he would be happy to help with his homework. They all walked out of the dining room as a family, leaving Ryan, Phillip and Skye sitting alone at the table.

"Dibs on Paloma," Phillip said quickly and got up in search of the only unmated female at the lodge.

"Damn," Ryan and Skye both said and grinned at each other. "Well, the Gathering has been called, Meg and Lissa will be coming out tomorrow. We'll have to grab them early, Alex has a thing for Meg."

"In the meantime shall we go and grab a beer in town? Human women are still fine specimens."

"Yeah, first round is on you," Skye called out as they left the lodge.

Chapter Seven

ॐ

"Dare I ask what you females were discussing?" Laurent said as he walked back to the cabin with Rain.

"Lust. Sex. Desire. Fucking. Blowjobs." Rain laughed. "It started when I asked if we could have sex and it turned into a whole discussion about it. Apparently the overwhelming lust I feel for you is something common between Mates."

"You feel overwhelming lust for me?" Laurent growled as he followed her into the bedroom and caught the shirt she tossed off.

"Laurent, before our first date — when, if you remember, I had sex with pretty much a total stranger — I hadn't had sex in nearly a year and I wasn't really that bothered by it. It wasn't that I didn't like sex, I certainly liked coming. Still do." She winked. "But no one really made me crave it before. Suddenly you come into my life. Laurent, you make me wet when I just inhale your skin. I crawl all over you and lick you in front of people I barely know. Yes, I feel overwhelming lust for you."

He followed her down to the mattress, tossing off his clothes to the pile where hers were. "Good, I wouldn't want to be alone. I can't stop thinking about you." He nuzzled his face in the valley between her breasts. "So?"

"Hmmm?" Rain asked, distracted by the hard-bodied man lying across her naked body.

"Can we have sex tonight?"

"Oh yes," she said and in less than a minute Laurent had entered her and began to fuck her slowly and thoroughly. "Oh! I like a man with follow-through." He chuckled and leaned down to capture a nipple in his mouth.

"You taste so good, like berries and cream." He laved her with the flat of his tongue.

"Berries and cream? Really? Must be my new soap."

"Your taste is fresh, sweet. Reminds me of summer mornings."

"Oh that's very good. With lines like that your bed must have not been empty much." She grinned.

Suddenly he withdrew and she whimpered in alarm at his absence.

"Hey!" she cried. "You have work to do. Where do you think you're going?"

"I don't want to lie across your stomach, you had a serious wound there. Plus I want to try another position. Turn over."

She blushed, rolling onto her belly. "I've never done it this way before."

"Have I told you how much it turns me on that I get to be the one who shows you new things?" He stroked questing hands all over her body and she arched into his touch. "Ass up, head down," he said and a thrill rode her system. The position felt very submissive.

His hands took her hips and helped her into position. "Good god, you have such a luscious ass." The wiry hairs on his thighs prickled the backs of her legs as he moved just behind her on his knees. Her hands fisted and released the sheets with anticipation.

The blunt, fat head of his cock nudged against her gate and slipped inexorably back into her cunt. A long, low groan escaped from her as he hilted completely and pulled back out, nearly all the way.

"Oh that's the ticket."

She heard the strain in his voice. The power of knowing she tested his control roared through her.

"I must agree with that assessment," she gasped out.

163

"It lets me look at that gorgeous ass. God, I just want to bite it." She jumped when he slapped one cheek with the flat of his hand. "Sweet." His fingertips danced down her spine, over the crease of her ass and tickled the star hidden there. She froze at first but gasped as the warmth of the touch radiated to her pussy.

He chuckled. "So much to you, Rain. So many things to try, to touch and taste." The touch faded as he traced down her thigh and moved to hold her hip. "I love your pussy, all cocoa pink. In this position it's bare, open and accessible to me in any way I want or need it." His other hand moved to her clit, bringing fingertips to stroke over it for a few moments before tracing up her belly to pinch a nipple as her breasts swayed with each thrust he made into her.

"And here is another part of you I love to touch. This way I can just reach up while I'm fucking you and play with your nipples. Make you squirm in that sexy way you do every time I touch them." Rain shivered at his words followed up by action.

"Deeper," she gasped.

"I don't think I can get any deeper, Rain." The fingers on the hand at her hip dug into her muscles as the strength of his thrusts increased.

"No, I mean, you get so much deeper this way." She moaned as he rolled a nipple between thumb and forefinger.

"Oh yeah," he agreed, sliding a hand down her stomach, stopping at her clit, which he mashed with an experienced thumb. "So wet and slippery, your clit. Like a hard little button." He chuckled as she writhed back against him. "One I like to push over and over."

"Ohmigod," she murmured as orgasm swallowed her up, blinded her to anything but his cock deep inside her and the hands on her body. The way the man could make her come always surprised her. He knew his way around a woman's pink parts, that was for sure.

"God that feels good," he whispered as he pressed into her one last, hard, deep time and came.

Long moments later he brought them both to the mattress, not withdrawing from her but moving to the side so his weight wasn't on her. She lay on her side in the curve of his body, his cock still embedded within her, and it seemed like no moment had ever been more wonderful.

"I love you, Laurent. By the way, do you ever get soft? Is that a werewolf thing?"

He chuckled, clearly startled by her questions. "The way you change subjects. I can't say I've ever met anyone else like you. To answer your questions—I can't say, baby. It's not something that's come up. Did Anthony get soft? Did he bring you pleasure at all?"

She laughed. "Yes he got soft and no he brought me no pleasure. He was an in the dark, only as naked as an unzipped fly, shove it in without regard to me being ready kind of guy. Thrust four times, come and get soft and zip up and be done. I told you that you were the first person to give me an orgasm, well, other than myself."

"Another reason to dislike him then. Watching you come is the most beautiful thing I've ever seen." He nuzzled into her neck and breathed in deep. "Tomorrow night at nine, baby, you'll transform and our wolves will mate for life. I can't wait."

"Does it hurt?"

"Transformation or mating?"

"Transformation."

"Well I was born a wolf so I can't say from experience. It's very natural for us and totally painless. But Archer, one of the Pack members who was transformed some years ago, says the first time is painful, like bad growing pains. The long bones are especially hard hit by the shock of the transition. What happens when we change is as much metaphysical as it is physical and biological. It's hard to put into words but it's like

165

you slip your consciousness as a human off and slide into your wolf. Archer says after the first time it's not nearly that bad."

"Okay." She chewed on her lip thoughtfully. "Can we talk to each other? While we're wolves?"

"Well, not in words but the Pack is connected in a very real way. We can send bursts of feeling and images. There's a lot of bumping and nipping. I'll guide you by moving you with my head. There's also howling and barking, growling and whining."

"Growling like in anger? Or that sexy way you growl at me?"

He laughed. "Mainly in anger or agitation. I save the sexy growl just for you." He sighed. "Sometimes fights break out. Almost always within a Pack fighting is over position or a female. There are times females fight each other. Like when an unmated female presents herself to a Mated male. Blooding is usually what it takes to make the other wolf back down. Sometimes it has to go further and you have to incapacitate and, very rarely, kill."

"What! Are you telling me that I might have to kill someone?" She scooted away and he slipped out of her. Sitting up, she clutched the sheet to her body.

"Not *someone*. Your wolf might have to kill another wolf to save your life or mine or someone else you care about. If a wolf doesn't back off after blooding and keeps coming after you it's kill or be killed. If you don't fight to protect yourself you'll die and where would I be then? Chances are I'd die too because after the bonding ceremony we'll be very connected to each other."

"Remind me to get back to the connection thing later. Laurent, I don't know how to fight! I know you probably think I do because of how I grew up, but we were sheltered from the violence of my father's world."

"I think no such thing. It works this way—Mates are generally the same level of strength as the other. So for instance even though Kari is a tiny thing in comparison to the rest of the Pack she's got strength, agility and speed comparable to Andreas'. No one messes with her. Mostly because she's an Alpha but also because she had to kill another female on her transformation night. That female was five inches taller and outweighed her by at least forty pounds and yet Kari snapped her neck like a twig. You'll have my strength, speed and agility. I'm Third. That means I rank higher than everyone in the Pack but Sean and his mate Emma, and Andreas and Kari. You'll be Third as well. No one other than Kari or Emma could stand a chance against you. Your wolf will know what to do."

"You said something about presenting? What's that?"

"Ah well." He shifted his eyes and she narrowed hers in response. "It's when a female offers her rear flanks to a male, tail up and exposing her sex. Presenting herself for mounting."

She sighed and rolled her eyes. "Okaaay. So is there anything else I need to know?"

"Don't pay any attention to any other males who attempt to approach you sexually. You're within your rights to snarl and smack the hell out of any male who tries to mount you or even who attempts to sniff you too long. Of course you won't have to because I will if anyone even tries." He sniffed indignantly.

"This all sounds so surreal. I can't believe I'm a freaking werewolf. Now tell me what you mean by the comment that after the bonding we'll be so connected."

"It's hard to put into words really but I'll do my best. Right now you and I are married according to human law. As werewolves we're together because we're a mated pair. The attraction between us is chemical as well as biological. We have a strong attraction. Right?"

She nodded and gestured to the rumpled bed. "Duh."

"Okay. So we could go on and have a lifelong relationship. Have kids. Be together until we die, blah, blah,

blah. But as a part of the transformation ceremony you'll be bound to me as well as the Pack. It's sort of like a magical spell that marries our souls as well as complementing the marriage we've made in our hearts. We'll feel each other's emotions more easily. The connection between us will be very strong and lifelong. My father never remarried or sought another after my mother died. He never wanted to. She was it for him. He never rejoined a Pack either. His heart died when she did."

Rain took his hand. "I'm sorry. I love you, I do. And I simply can't imagine losing you. But I'd live for our children. I want you to know that."

He got to his knees and looked deep into her eyes. "You don't know what that means to me. I loved growing up here and I love the Phinneys. But..."

"But it feels like your father died when your mother did. You feel like he didn't think you were worth fighting for."

He sighed and his mouth twisted in a ghost of a smile. "You know me." He brought her hand to his chest, over his heart. "No one has ever known me like you do. It means...it's everything."

She kissed him slowly, pouring all her emotion into it. Wanting him to know what she felt. "I love you, Laurent. I'm honored to know you, to love and be loved by you."

"You're too good to be true, Rain Cole."

She winked. "Keep that in mind. So can I turn any time then? Not just the full moon?"

"Of course. The full moon is the trigger for the first time you change. But your transformation will enable to you to change at any time you wish after that."

"Will the children be there?"

"No. Children aren't able to change until puberty. They'll all be at Sean and Emma's tomorrow night. The lodge will be, erm, *quite lively* tomorrow. Definitely not a thing for children to see.

"Although they do grow up around a lot of nudity and casual attitudes about sex and sexuality, they aren't around on Gathering evenings. Until they turn twenty-one, they have no official ranking in the Pack. They have the years from first transformation until twenty-one to finish school and find a place in the Clan. Sometimes they have the ranking level of their parents, sometimes not. Generally the higher the rank of the parents, the higher the natural ability and resultant rank of the children. Tomas, Devon and Sean, Andreas' sons, will definitely be Alpha level in ability. I don't know how it'll all shake out with three of them. One will most likely show more strength like Andreas did."

"What about Hellie? She's so smart."

"Females hold no rank outside the rank of their mates."

Her dark eyebrows shot up as her body stiffened in outrage. "No way! You're telling me women can't be Alphas unless they're Mated to one?"

"Yes."

"How completely absurd! That…that's totally sexist. And stupid. In all of the generations of werewolf culture a woman has never stood up and called bullshit on that?" She was indignant and god help him it turned him on.

"Well interestingly enough there's a move right now to bring about greater rights for female werewolves and to create better relations between the shifter races."

"Shifter races?"

"Yes, there're more than just wolves. There are werebears. Big cats, weretigers, panthers and jaguars. At least one Clan in Canada and one just east of us have unmated female Seconds. Things change I suppose, over time."

She stood up and began to pace, speaking with her hands. Her movements had become more graceful and fluid since she'd been bitten but he knew that he'd be committing a fatal error to stare at the beguiling way her breasts swayed. So he tried to sneak-ogle her.

She rounded on him, eyes flashing. "Laurent Cole, if you think our daughter is going to always be held down, tied to what some man does or is, you are out of your mind! Don't some wolves just opt out of the Clans? Go it on their own like your father did?"

He scowled and crossed his arms across his chest but admittedly the way her eyes moved down to take in his muscles pleased him and took the edge off his anger.

"My father was in a Pack, he just chose not to live with them. He affiliated his child with a Pack as was his responsibility, even if he should have done more. Those wolves who belong to no Pack at all are feral and if they encroach on the territory of an established Pack without permission they are executed. We've existed as long as we have because we keep our numbers low. We have a system of sophisticated laws, Rain.

"We don't attack humans unless we're changing them and the change is limited by our laws to those Mates of natural wolves. Those wolves who violate that must be eradicated.

"I'm the Pack Lieutenant. I'm the chief lawkeeper. It's my job to enforce discipline should anyone step out of line. If a feral comes into our territory it's my job to hunt and dispose of him if necessary."

He stood and pulled her back into bed with him. "Get back to bed, woman. I miss you."

"I'm hungry. All of this thinking is so hard!" she teased, acting dumb.

"I'll make some popcorn. And, baby? If we have a daughter she'll be raised to be the best she can be. Maybe she'll be the first unmated female Lieutenant. But female children are very rare. In fact, Cherchez is very unique to have two sets of twins and four female children. Before Helene and Tomas there hadn't been a set of twins born in any Pack for over a hundred years." He kissed her lips quickly before jumping up to get popcorn started.

"I still think it's ridiculous that females get such a bad deal. I think I should sit on the gender equality committee." She followed him out into the kitchen.

"You think it's a bad deal to be my Mate?"

She snorted. "Don't you change the subject, Laurent Cole! If I was a wolf and hadn't found my Mate I'd have no status at all, is that correct?"

"Well, unmated females have a special status, because they're unmated and a part of a Pack. Unmated females are actually a hot commodity and Packs offer them incentives to get them to join."

"Oh goodie. So they're like air-conditioning or a sunroof. But could they decide to challenge and move up?"

"No. And you're making it sound worse than it is."

"No I'm not and you know it. The system is utterly dumb. No wonder Paloma is such a bitch. I'd be a bitch too in her place."

"It's the way things are."

"Oh the dreaded way-things-are line." She waved her hands around animatedly. "The way things are holds no water with me, buster. Slavery was the way things were for thousands of years across many cultures. We know it's wrong now, don't we?"

He sighed, defeated. "Yes we do, Rain. You should be more active in shifter politics if you so desire. You won't have to work anymore. That is, you have time to devote to painting now instead of having to work a day job just to afford to paint," he said, making the save at the last minute.

"What? Oh I hadn't thought of that. Painting full time? What a luxury. Really? You wouldn't mind?"

"Rain Cole, I love you. More than that, I'm a rich man. Making you a rich woman. And yeah, partly due to community property and all but I'm sure you'd do the same for me in your place. Plus when you become a star and you get rich with your painting you can be my sugar momma." He pulled her to his body and wrapped his arms around her waist. "You're incredibly talented and have two shows—just two of many in your future—to get ready for. I'm happy that I can do this, that we can do this. I admit that I love the idea of you working here at home or at least at the lodge."

She smiled at him and kissed his shoulder. The scent of his body rolled over her and she shuddered as a soft moan broke from her lips. "Thank you. Oh!" she said brightly, hearing the bell of the microwave. "Popcorn is ready."

He chuckled and padded over to get it. "Go on, get back in bed. I'll be there in a sec." Moments later he brought a bowl of popcorn and two large glasses of ice water.

"Membership has its privileges," she said, finding her place against him as they ate the popcorn and watched a movie.

Chapter Eight

ଚ

Anthony Vargas was an irritated man. An angry man. Julia had quit her job without any notice and no one knew where she'd gone. Fucking flake.

She'd arranged with her boss to give her last paycheck to Harrison Watts to cover any outstanding bills. The other roommate was a gay guy who appeared to be totally clueless. Anthony hated gays, thought they should be rounded up and sent out of the country. He shuddered.

No one had seen her with any men and Harrison said she had dated a man only once or twice that he knew of, the guy from Portland. Anthony had combed Portland from one end to the other and hadn't heard a damned thing about Julia, or Rain, whatever the hell the bitch was going by these days. He'd had to hire some outside people to check things out.

Mile after mile of tree-lined roads lulled Anthony. His only thoughts were vengeance and getting back what was rightfully his. The ringing cell phone startled him out of his reverie.

"Yeah?"

"Got a lead, boss. Seems that she was an artist or painter or whatever. She's got an upcoming show at a gallery in Pioneer Square. A place called The Holt Gallery. Do you want me to dig around there?"

"No, I'll do it. Good job, Pete." He hit the *off* button, wearing a cruel smile. Oh he'd find that bitch and after he beat her within an inch of her life he'd drag her ass back home and marry her. His place in the organization would be cemented and he'd remind her what the penalty for disobedience was every chance he got.

* * * * *

Rain appreciated Laurent's wake-up calls. She smiled to herself, wearing an ear-to-ear grin as she sat drinking her coffee. Even better, Laurent's long fingers stroked the back of her neck idly. Hellie was currently ensconced on Laurent's lap and Tomas and Devon were sharing Rain, a kiddo on each thigh. Sean sat with his namesake across the table as his own children scarfed up breakfast with their mother.

"Hi, you must be Rain!" A woman threw her arms around Rain, nearly knocking her out of her chair. "I'm Ellen! Kari has told me so much about you. Welcome to Cherchez Pack."

Oh. Her. "Hi, Ellen. Nice to meet you." It wouldn't do to take an instant dislike to the woman, who seemed pretty nice. Two adorable children ran into the room, the little girl, who looked to be about eight, jumped into Perri's lap and the boy, who looked to be about four, headed out to the lawn with the other children who'd finished eating and scampered out to play.

"This is James. Don't mind the black eye, he got it at practice this morning. It'll be gone in a few hours."

"Practice?"

Laurent leaned over toward her. "James plays hockey for the Canuks."

"Cool! I love hockey. Although I have to admit I'm a Maple Leafs fan," Rain teased.

"Well we'll have to fix that! You know anyone who can get you perfect seats at a Maple Leafs game? 'Cause you know someone who'll get you great seats every time you come to town to see a Canucks games," James countered.

"That's very generous, James." Laurent put his arm around the back of Rain's seat and she realized he was jealous. This from the man who'd fucked the woman currently all gorgeous standing in front of Rain! After that, Laurent was jealous of the dude with the black eye? Men.

Ellen got to her knees and rubbed her face along Rain's knees, followed by James.

Laurent explained when he saw Rain's confused look. "You're higher in rank, a part of the Inner Circle of the Pack. James and Ellen are showing their respect by greeting you this way."

"Oh. Thank you." She reached out and touched both of their heads and caressed their jawlines as she'd seen Kari do.

They both smiled at her and got up to grab food. Jade and Tomas came into the room and a river of children followed Tomas who grabbed a plate of toast and bacon and scurried back out, children in his wake.

A tall, regal-looking man with hair of burnished gold came into the room. "You must be Rain. My brother has told me so much about you. Although he couldn't have begun to describe your beauty accurately." He dropped to his knees and rubbed her knees with his face and kissed her hands.

Laurent growled and the man laughed. Laurent pulled her tighter against him. "This is Alex, he's Alek's brother. He's a general pain in the ass and for a long time I wouldn't have trusted him as far as I could throw him but as it happens he's a pretty decent guy. Although one who needs to move his face out of my wife's groin or risk permanent disfigurement." Laurent underlined that by leaning over Rain's shoulder and smacking the top of Alex's, both of them laughing. What was funny about smacking the crap out of someone Rain didn't know but they both seemed to think it was hilarious so she just rolled her eyes at Kari, who snorted.

She caught sight of Drew and Janine and they both hugged her and then showed their submission to her, which freaked her out, but she got that it was a culture she had to learn a lot more about.

A buxom blonde and a café-au-lait-skinned woman with long braids came in next. "I'm Lissa. Pleased to meet you, Rain. I've seen your art by the way and I think it's amazing."

"You have? Thank you. Where did you see it?"

"I'm an intern at The Holt, I saw it there. In fact, I brought you some samples of the mailer they want to send out for your show. Diane wants you to pick one and get it back to her. She doesn't know you're here, she just knows that Andreas knows you," Lissa quickly added when she saw the panicked look on Rain's face.

"Whew! Thanks, Lissa."

She met the rest of the Pack, so many wolves she lost track of names and faces. "Wow, full house," Rain said, taking in the crowd.

"Another reason to be glad we live away from the lodge. It gets so chaotic in here during a Gathering," Laurent said quietly, pulling her close. His breath on her neck sent shivers through her. He noticed his effect on her and chuckled, biting her ear lightly.

"I'm going to get you back for this later you know," she said to him in an undertone.

"I'm counting on it." He picked her up and placed her in his lap. "In less than ten hours you'll transform, Rain. Are you excited?"

"Excited and scared both. Curious too." She wriggled into his lap, stroking across his cock with her ass. She threw him a look over her shoulder and he grinned back at her.

"I can't wait to run with you. I'd hate living in the city. Here we can walk fifty yards away from the house, change and run through miles and miles of safe wilderness. I thought I'd go insane in Tokyo last year. There aren't words to describe what it feels like to run through the wild, wind in your fur, the loam of the forest floor under your paws. It's wonderful to do it with friends but to experience it with you? I can barely stand the wait."

She turned to face him, straddling his lap. "I can't wait to share it with you." She leaned in and nibbled on his neck and he growled with disappointment when she stood up. "I'd love to keep grinding on you like a dollar dancer but we can't do anything now, the children are all around."

He nodded with disappointment but brightened a moment later. "You're right, baby. Perhaps we can meet back at our cabin in say," he looked at his watch, "fifteen minutes?" He looked at her but before she could answer Phillip came over and whispered in Andreas' ear and Andreas got up and left the room. Laurent got up to follow. "I'll be back." He kissed the top of her head and Kari came over and sat next to her.

"Yeah, that happens. Just when you think you're going to get lucky they go off and do some soooper sekrit guy stuff in the office." Kari snorted. "Listen, I want to warn you that Paloma might try to present to Laurent tonight at the Gathering. Some coupling between non-mated wolves will happen, it always does. Not that you need to worry about it from Laurent. He's in big love with you. Still, you need to guard your territory, and by that I mean Laurent. If any female gets near him tonight kick her ass. If you make the first lessons harsh enough you won't have to make them as often later."

"You sound like you speak from experience."

"I do. I had to kill a female the night of my transformation. I blooded her and she wouldn't back off. She pretended to give up and attacked me from behind. Andreas is Alpha, he's a target for females all the time. It gets old but I guard my fenceposts, you know? Unless you don't mind sharing it's part of the gig. The higher ranked and more powerful the wolf, the more attractive he'll be to others. But he's your Mate and that's obvious from a hundred miles away. He loves you."

"The Mate thing is so cool. Laurent was telling me about the bond ritual thing last night and it's beautiful. I love being a part of something so special. It makes me feel wonderful."

"I think so too."

"What isn't wonderful is how shafted females get in werewolf culture. I mean, has anyone stopped to think that if unmated females weren't in such a catch-22 with respect to lack of position that they wouldn't cause such upheaval in the Pack? And yeah, so generally men are stronger than women but does that mean that it always has to be a male in charge, especially in the Inner Circle? Look at Hellie, she's brilliant! How can she automatically be left without position until she finds a mate? Why not Hellie as Second or Alpha?"

"You're preaching to the choir, sister. This is a major issue now. In fact, there's a Supreme Council of Wolves here in North America and this is something being debated right now. You know, I'm a delegate—well, in Andreas' name of course—but I'll be traveling to St. Louis next month to go to a meeting there, you should come as well. Get involved."

"Really? I'd love to go and be involved. I'll be having my show at the end of the month but after that I'm free for a bit while I build up stock for the next one."

Laurent walked back into the room and leaned to speak in her ear. "Rain, can you join us in the study for a bit?" She took the hand he offered and followed him into the office with Kari right behind her.

"What? What's going on?"

"Anthony Vargas came to The Holt today asking about you. He now knows that Andreas knows you. This isn't a registered address but we'll need to be on the lookout for trouble. Andreas is going to call him back tomorrow afternoon after I speak with your father. I don't want to worry you but I didn't want to hide anything from you either."

Rain shivered. Damn that bastard Anthony! "Okay. We'll deal with it as it comes. I won't let either of them ruin my life."

"You're my wife. No one is going to harm you." Laurent growled and put his arm around her waist.

"They'll all protect you with their lives," Kari said, stroking a reassuring hand over Rain's hair. "Plus you'll see tonight just how kick-ass strong you are as a wolf. You can take care of your own bad self too."

"But of course she should leave it to her husband, *the professional and highly skilled bodyguard,* to do the work," Andreas said, looking at Kari.

"Yeah yeah. That goes without saying. But you know, a girl has to be prepared to protect herself at all times because things can and do happen," Kari said and Rain nodded in agreement.

"I feel good this morning, breasty man-poachers and slimy ex-boyfriends notwithstanding. I'm going down to the studio to work for a while."

Laurent got up. "I'm coming too. I love to watch you work. I promise to behave myself."

"Don't make promises you can't keep, Laurent." Rain laughed and they both walked out, hand in hand.

* * * * *

Laurent worked on his laptop and read the paper while Rain painted. The atmosphere was perfect for her. The light was incredible and Kari had really worked to make the cabin into a very comfortable studio. It touched Rain that the Pack had gone so far out of its way to make her feel at home, to accommodate her and ease her way. It felt good to belong to something.

The growling of her stomach alerted her to a need for a break several hours later. She cleaned her hands and put her paints away. When she came into the studio from the deck she saw Laurent had fallen asleep on the couch. Kneeling next to him, she kissed his temple but he didn't wake. The late afternoon was cool so she walked over to their cabin to grab something to cover him up with. But as she was leaving the front porch on her way back he ran toward her, panic on his face.

"Rain! Where were you?" He grabbed her into an embrace.

"I just came over to get this afghan. You were sleeping and I didn't want to disturb you. Hey, what's wrong?" He hugged her so tight she could barely breathe.

"I woke and you were gone. I thought... I just wanted to be sure you were all right. With Anthony sniffing around I don't want you wandering around alone, especially not until you've transformed." He kissed her face, the top of her head, each eyelid, and the sweetness of his worry ignited the lust that lay coiled inside of each of them.

Somewhat urgently, Laurent reached down and pulled Rain's shirt off, tossing it to the earth behind him.

"Inside," she gasped out.

"Give me a second to undo my pants." He groaned, working at his zipper.

Rain laughed. "Well that inside too, but we need to go inside, we're on the porch."

Laurent looked up and focused, noting where they were. Grabbing her hand, he yanked her inside and they made it as far as the couch.

An hour later they made their way back up to the lodge to grab something to eat. "Lunch has come and gone but Anna always leaves sandwiches in the refrigerator for stragglers. Sit down and I'll get us some and bring them out." She enjoyed the view as he went through the doors to the kitchen.

"Looks as good going as he does coming," Emma said with a sigh and sat down next to Rain.

"Yeah. Honestly, I never in my life imagined that a man who looked like him would even give me a second look. Now I'm married to him. Life is good." She laughed.

"I know, this place is like hot guy central. Even better, they're all so attentive and sweet. Heck, I was this bookish doctor, very shy and restrained, and I had the major hots for this psychiatrist who came to the hospital twice a week. He and I had coffee a few times, I had major fantasies about him. When I was alone, in the dark, in my apartment. Late at night with my battery-operated boyfriend. But suddenly, out of the blue, he asked me out. I was shocked.

"Sean is so sensual but he's playful too. I felt this intense connection to him right off. The first time he made love to me it was like these invisible tendrils grew out of him and embedded themselves inside my body, my mind, my soul. All of a sudden he's inviting me out all of the time. Things got very serious really quickly even though I'd known him professionally for a few years.

"And then one morning he tells me he's a werewolf! I'm thinking he's taking the pain meds or something and needs detox but he changed. Right in my bedroom at ten in the morning on a Wednesday. I don't know, I should have been scared but I wasn't. He told me that he and I were Mates and that he wanted to marry me and to bring me over and have me join his family. Again, I should have freaked but I didn't. I just wanted to do it to be with him.

"Of course when I found out that they'd all slept with many of the other women in the Clan, especially knowing that he'd slept with Perri, it did a number on me. It's hard when you're close with people and you know your man had this connection before you even came along. But he and I worked it out and Perri is such a great friend now. Well, obviously you and Laurent have worked it out because I see you and Perri get along well too. You don't have to worry about me, Sean would kill me before he'd share. Even if Laurent is delicious." She laughed.

Rain felt like cold water had been thrown over her head. "Are you telling me Laurent slept with Perri?"

Laurent chose that moment to walk back into the dining room with the food he'd gone off to get.

"Oh god, I thought you knew. I mean, you knew about Ellen. I'm sorry," Emma said, upset. "Honestly, it didn't mean anything. Perri came into the Pack after she'd been with Devon for a while. She, well she's just different about sex and sexuality. As far as I know she hasn't coupled with anyone other than Devon in several years." Emma's voice trailed off as she saw Laurent standing there. "God, I'm sorry," she said and got up and left the room.

Rain turned and looked at Laurent and her eyes narrowed. "Is there any particular reason why I had to find that out that way?" she hissed, feeling sick to her stomach.

"Baby, I just wanted you to see Perri for the person she is and not feel weird about things. She's part of the Inner Circle and you'll be with her so often, I just wanted you to be comfortable."

Her fingers dug into the arms of the chair she sat in as she pushed to standing. "What is it with you! Lying is not going to make me more *comfortable*. Jeez, Laurent, listen, it's not like I think you were a virgin before I came along. I understand that you slept with other women before I came into your life. Fine. You tell me you've had sex with women in the Clan, okay, less fine but I can get past that. I'm confident that you love me, I'm confident in our commitment. What bothers me is your need to lie to me for things you see as my own good. I have a father, Laurent, one who does that. And I believe I've made quite clear my feelings on that subject. I'm capable of thinking and feeling and working through stuff. I hate that you patronize me and treat me like I'm fourteen years old."

Laurent sighed, putting the tray with the food down. He went to Rain and knelt before her, placing his forehead to her feet. "I was wrong. Please forgive me."

Standing there, looking at this fierce giant of a man who'd knelt in utter submission to her to apologize—this in a house full of wolves he outranked—Rain felt so much love. Relieved and smiling, she ran her hands through his hair and knelt to face him. She bent and brought him upright to look into her eyes. "I forgive you, Laurent. I even understand why you do such things. I just don't want you to do them anymore, all right? Please let's be partners. I love you so much that it freaks me out sometimes."

He smiled and pulled her tightly against him. "I don't deserve you. I promise, equals, although I can't stop wanting to protect you."

"You are so dumb! Of course you deserve me, we're made for each other," she said against his lips as he kissed her.

"Okay kids, break it up!" Phillip said, laughing as he entered the room.

"Are we okay?" Laurent asked her quietly.

"Yeah but, Laurent, don't lie to me again. Do you understand? This is a major hot button issue with me and you know why," Rain said seriously.

"I promise, baby." Laurent stood and helped Rain up. "The sun is going down, dinner will be in two hours. The ceremony will begin at seven. Are you ready?"

"Ready to turn into a wolf and have sex with you in front of forty people? Cake." She snorted.

"Welcome to my world, baby," Laurent said, grinning.

"Rain! Will you walk with us over to Aunt Emma and Uncle Sean's house? We're gonna have a slumber party while you're having your transformation. Mom says that we can't be there but I think it would be so cool to see you change for the first time and also to see you bond with Uncle Laurent. Can I call you Aunt Rain? Will you walk with us?" Hellie bounded into the room, clambering into Rain's arms as she babbled nonstop.

"Whoa there, remember to breathe!" Rain said, laughing, accepting all the hugs and kisses. "Yes I'll walk you over. In fact Laurent will come too. Yes, you can call me Aunt Rain. No you can't come to my transformation but someday you'll have one of your own, when you mature. Lastly, a slumber party sounds so cool! I bet Anna has made you guys all sorts of cool things to eat." She put Hellie back on the ground and held her hand.

"Anna is the best! She makes my favorite oatmeal raisin cookies even though no one else likes them but me. Isn't that nice of her?"

"It is nice of her but you know what? Anna loves doing things for you because she loves *you*."

"I love her too. She's like another grandma. I love you too, Rain. I'm so glad that you love Laurent and you've joined our family."

Rain smiled and looked at Laurent, who watched Hellie with an amused grin. "I'm glad I love Laurent too, honey, and I love you as well. Now let's get to walking. Where are your brothers?"

"Oh those dumbheads are outside already. Devon is muddy not even half an hour after Mom gave him a bath. Boys get so dirty," she said airily, with her nose wrinkled.

Laurent laughed. "Let's go, Hellie bear." He grabbed one hand and Hellie's sleeping bag and backpack and Rain kept the other. When they got to the lawn the boys ran and mobbed them all. Kari and Phillip joined the mile and a half walk to Sean and Emma's place.

Their house was a giant A-frame. The entire front of the house, the side facing the lake, was windows and decks wrapped around the entirety of the house. Children played in the huge, fenced-in play area, set back from the water.

"It's beautiful. Totally an expression of Emma and Sean," Rain said with awe and Kari nodded.

"Isn't it though? I love it here. Emma has done an amazing job at decorating."

When they entered the house through the giant hand-carved front doors, Rain could see what Kari meant. The house definitely had a Northwest style. Beautiful, deep earthy colors, hardwoods and beautiful floor rugs abounded and yet the house was totally touchable too.

Anna came out of the kitchen smiling and holding out a plate of marshmallow crispy squares. Within moments the plate was stripped clean and the kids who walked over with them had scampered outside, happily munching.

"As always, Anna, thanks for agreeing to watch this brood. I just don't know what we'd all do without you." Kari kissed Anna's cheek, following up with a stroke over her jawline.

Anna smiled, watching the kids through the window. "It's my pleasure, Kari, you know that. I'll be sorry to miss your transformation, Rain. But after the rush has died down we'll go on a run together." Anna hugged her tightly.

"Thanks, I'd like that."

"We should get back. Janine is going to handle dinner with Jade. I want to check in," Kari said, accepting a kiss and a cheek rub from Anna.

"I made all the food earlier today. It just needs to be served. No big deal."

"Anna, you're too kind. Thank you so much!" Rain said.

"This is a big day for all of us. No thanks are necessary. Welcome to the family."

Laurent guided her to the door. "I've got something planned for you back at home. Just a little pre-dinner ritual," he whispered into her ear and she laughed softly.

"We just had sex a few hours ago."

He chuckled. "*That's* not the ritual, although it'll be part of what I plan to do to you. It's always part of what I plan to do to you."

Hand in hand they walked slowly, taking in the late afternoon as they headed back.

Back at the cabin Laurent told her to wait in the living room and brought her a glass of wine. Minutes later he came in, his hair down, naked and graceful as he moved toward her.

Her heart skipped a beat for a moment in reaction to his fierce beauty.

"Come, *mon amour*." He held his hand out and she went to him.

The heat of his body enveloped her like a cloak as she followed him into the bathroom. Lit candles lent a golden glow to the room as steam rose from the water in the tub. The scent of almond oil and lavender wafted through the room.

"Wow. This is beautiful."

"You're beautiful. This is just a spot of pampering to prepare you for your big night."

With gentle hands he undressed her slowly, sensuously. He laid kisses on each new bit of skin exposed as he went. He unbound her hair and stepped into the bathtub, bringing her in to sit between his thighs.

She leaned back against him while he brushed her hair in long, languorous strokes, all the while whispering endearments and encouragements in French and English. He softly ran a washcloth over her skin and her eyes dropped closed. Warm relaxation stole over her under his ministrations and she loved that he had that affect on her.

"Mmmm. I wish this moment could last forever," she murmured as he kissed her temple.

"This is a wonderful moment, yes. But Rain, our lives will be filled with many many more such moments. So let's get out and we'll make some new memories now." He helped her out and they dried off and headed into the bedroom.

"You're good with that stuff, Laurent. You say the most wonderful things."

"I have something for you. Hang on." He turned and pulled something from a drawer and handed it to her.

She opened her eyes and looked down at a snow white silk robe that bore an ebony trim. It bore only three buttons, one in the center, at the level of her pussy, one above it an inch and one below it. It was flowing and absolutely the most sexy thing she'd ever seen in her life. The buttons were silver discs with wolves carved into them.

"The trim is wolf fur that Drew braided and embroidered. It's not from a dead wolf, it's not a pelt. It's mine. He's been working on it since the first time you came up here. The buttons aren't silver, the mythology is true and we've got a severe silver allergy. They're pewter and platinum."

"I'm...it's so beautiful." She drew fingertips over the trim, over the softness of the edging.

"Let me help you get it on."

The smooth silk caressed her skin as he slid it on. She turned to look into a mirror and her breath caught in her throat. She looked like another person. Her skin, normally olive-toned, had taken on a nearly golden quality. Her hair hung past her ass, thick and flowing over her shoulders, in contrast to the luminous white of the robe. The black trim sat against the silk of her bare skin and the curves of her breasts. Her eyes had taken on a sort of inner light, the gold ring around the pupil more pronounced.

"What is happening to me?" she whispered.

"It's the transformation. You were already beautiful, Rain. The bite simply makes you *more* of what you were. The skin takes on a luminous quality, the hair gets thicker and softer, your eyes, well I can see a shadow of your wolf. It incites my wolf to see her. My god, that robe makes me want to slide inside you right here and now," he growled.

Shivers ran down Rain's spine. "Do we have time? Because I'm all about you fucking me right now too."

He laughed and the sound stroked over her skin like a caress. "No. We don't. I wish like hell we did but everyone is expecting us. There'll be time soon enough though. I promise."

She pouted a bit but smiled when she caught sight of the robe in the mirror, smoothing a hand over the material. "It's incredible. This robe is so beautiful. Thank you, Laurent. Your fur against my skin is, well, amazing. Is this what I'm wearing to dinner?"

"Yes. The transformation ceremony will begin in ten minutes. Dinner first. Then to the clearing for the actual ceremony and binding, then a run."

"I think I need some underwear and well," she looked down, surprised by her ample cleavage on display as well as her bellybutton, "jeez, you can see to my lower stomach!"

Grinning, he brought out a pair of black silk panties, dangling from a finger. "Here, I bought these for you."

She slid them on and he smiled approvingly and she settled the robe back into place. In the other hand he held a pair of soft satin ballet slippers. "I wanted these black leather spike heels to go with it but it's harder to walk. I bought the heels anyway. They're in the closet for later. For now though, these should fit." He quirked up a corner of his mouth.

He stood back and looked at her, his eyes glittering as he took in the entire package. "You look so damned sexy I think my cock may explode." Wincing, she took his arm and they headed out the door.

They slowly walked up to the lodge. Rain's skin was itchy. "Laurent, I feel odd. My skin feels, I don't know, weird."

"It's nearing time for your change, Rain. Your wolf is rising. The moon calls her."

When they walked in a hush fell over the group. Laurent led her into the dining room and they all filed in to sit in their respective places.

Andreas stood and raised his glass. "To Rain, welcome sister, welcome mate, welcome wolf."

"Hear, hear!" they all responded and drank.

Alek leaned in and whispered, "That is the sexiest transformation robe I've ever seen."

"Thanks." She blushed.

"Laurent, you chose well. That robe is marvelous but the two of you side by side, with your hair down... Man, your children are going to be incredibly beautiful," Devon said and Perri nodded. Perri smiled softly and hesitantly. Emma must have told her about that afternoon.

Rain leaned past Devon and said, "It's okay." Relief rushed over Perri's face and a genuine smile replaced the hesitant one she'd worn moments before.

"That's a nice view," Skye said, raising an eyebrow, and Rain saw that the front of her robe gaped open.

Laurent growled. "Watch it, Skye. Your time will come and I personally can't wait. It seems that our Mates are the female equivalents of the pains in the butt that the males are." He glanced at Andreas who tried to look scandalized but failed. "Your mate will be a doozy, Skye."

"Amen!" Sean laughed.

They ate and drank champagne and finally the time to go into the clearing approached. Andreas stood with Kari and walked out, followed by Sean and Emma, and Laurent led Rain, holding her hand tightly. They walked out into the night, which should have felt cold but Rain was surprised to feel that it didn't at all.

Once in the clearing Laurent took off his clothes and hung them up before turning to help Rain out of her robe and panties, placing them beside his own. He kissed her lips softly and led her into the large circle of bodies the Clan had made. Rain was surprised but she didn't feel awkward about her own nakedness or anyone else's, it just seemed normal.

Laurent stood back and addressed her. "*J'honore mon compagnon.*" I honor my Mate. She looked at him and repeated the words back and he smiled and knelt at her side.

Andreas came forward and spoke. "*Nois faisons bon accueil au loup. Nous celebrons le lien. Nous honorons notre soeur.*" We welcome the wolf, we celebrate the bond, we honor our sister.

Laurent looked into her eyes. "Let it come, Rain. Come and kneel and let the wolf come."

She trembled and got on her hands and knees and closed her eyes. There was a burst of pain as her bones reknit into something else, as her *being* reknit into something else. She felt her humanity slip, it sank like a stone and her wolf rose and burst through her skin. When she opened her eyes the world was black and gray. She shook herself out and got used to her new form. She was a wolf. Blinking in shock, she turned her head and saw a giant wolf next to her. He nuzzled her head and nipped at her flank. *Laurent.* She felt joy and a burst of an image. *Run.* And she did.

She tore out of the clearing hot on Laurent's tail. She got bumped on her side and looked, she was sure the black wolf with the flash of white was Skye. Another smaller wolf jumped across her path, Kari. She felt strong, exhilarated, full of life and joy. She ran and ran and Laurent's giant form ran next to her, sheltering her in the shadow of his body.

The world felt alive to her in a way it never had before. She could smell *everything*. She heard birds and mice, small creatures rustling in the leaves. Finally, a long time later, they stopped at the shore of a small spring-fed lake. She drank from its waters and felt refueled.

Suddenly she felt Laurent at her side and he moved her with gentle bumps of his head. The burst of lust she received from him nearly knocked her over. His for her. Of the way his wolf felt about hers, how the flecks of white on her front paws drove him crazy, made him desire her above all others. She knew the soft, silky feel of her fur against his muzzle made him tremble to be inside of her. How she knew this she didn't know. She just did. It was a little like being in his head.

But suddenly her wolf was solidly in charge. Her human self was far, far under the waves and the predator, the wild animal in her, saw Laurent as the master of his surroundings he was. He was a strong protector and an able provider, the offspring he would give her would be healthy and robust. She desired that and presented to him. He howled and the fur on her back stood on end. He mounted her, his large body against her back, and he thrust inside of her, his sharp teeth biting her neck and holding her still.

Her cells sang out. He was joy, he gave her everything and she sent that back to him. He growled softly as he completed, licking her face as he got off. She got to her belly and crawled that way to his feet. He nudged her, pushing her up to her feet, licking her muzzle before moving her into his side. Where she belonged.

The Pack howled as one and the frenzy of celebration and sex hung in the air like a palpable thing. All around them, wolves rolled, play fighting and mounting each other. She sat back, leaning against Laurent's chest, his body curved around hers protectively, and watched it all.

She noticed that a female had come near and presented in their direction. Paloma. Laurent licked her ear and yawned as if he were bored by the mere sight of the other female.

The hackles on Rain's body rose as she growled low in throat. She laced the sound with menace and violence and she felt Laurent's body harden in response. Paloma yipped as if to call attention to herself and Rain sprang forward, snarling and biting, ripping into the flesh of one of Paloma's rear legs. Paloma yelped and ran off, head and tail lowered in submission and defeat.

Rain turned and padded back to Laurent who mounted her again, fast and furious, driven over the edge by her display of dominance. Afterward he nudged her back toward the path that led to the lodge and they ran back to the clearing.

She should have been shocked at herself. She wasn't a violent person but she had to admit she took pride in how she handled Paloma.

They got back to the clearing where their clothes hung and Laurent changed back. He knelt next to her, pressing his face into her fur, stroking her and speaking softly. Her human wanted him, wanted his touch, and her wolf let go and fell away as her human self rose and surfaced. As she opened her eyes her world was in color again and Laurent stood there holding her robe for her to step into.

"Welcome, Mate," he said into her hair.

She turned and kissed him softly. "Welcome, Mate. Now let's go back to our cabin for a while, I'd like you inside of me and I don't think I can wait any longer."

"You don't have to," he said and picked her up and slid inside of her. Her legs wrapped around him and she moaned and arched her back. He moved swiftly but only made it to the lodge. He propped her against the wall at the far side of the house. "I can't wait any longer. I've got to have you." He groaned and began to thrust in and out of her.

Her breath caught in her throat as her hands sought the softness of his hair. "Then don't. Oh Laurent, you make me feel complete, whole, totally safe and loved." She sighed his name again and held on as he fucked into her body single-mindedly.

"Rain, I love you," he whispered as his release approached. Touched beyond reason by her profession of love and safety, he wanted to crawl into her and never leave. Seeing her as a wolf had only heightened his need for her. The magic of the binding, of the transformation, clung to them both, he could taste it at the back of his throat. Her essence rolled through him so that he was drunk with her and what she was to him.

He reached down and found her clit, slick and swollen for his touch, and flicked it with his thumb. And just that quick, her climax began and he leaned in to grab a nipple between his teeth, swiping his tongue over it as his teeth held it, pushing her all the way just as her climax, grasping and pulsing around him, pulled him down with her.

"What you do to me." He kissed her, hard, as he helped her stand and they walked back to their cabin.

Champagne in an ice bucket was at their bedside, together with a set of glasses. "A toast to you, *mon coeur*." He poured them both a glass and sipped.

"Mmm. This is so good," she said, drinking the sweet bubbly. Laurent lay down beside her, head on her chest.

"So what did you think of your first night as a werewolf?"

"Laurent, tonight was incredible. Being a wolf is like nothing I could have even imagined."

"Rain, I used to think Kari was the most beautiful wolf I'd ever seen but you... Tonight, when you blooded Paloma and she ran I...I don't have words to explain how much strength, violence and sex are so primal and fortifying to our wolves. The white spots on your front paws, the way you run, your eyes, your fur, my god, I am such a lucky man, a lucky wolf."

She smiled at him, reaching out to grab her rings and slide them back on. She'd taken them off earlier so she wouldn't lose them during the run. "I was so alone before I met you. Half a person. Afraid to love anything but my art. You changed that. I feel like a whole person, complete. I love you so much," she said and proceeded to show him, twice.

Chapter Nine

Laurent sat up slowly, trying to get his breath back. "We should get up to the lodge. If we don't everyone else will start coming down here." He stood and handed her a pair of red silk panties. "I bought these too." He raised his eyebrows at her.

"Really? Laurent Cole, I get the feeling that you bought quite a bit of sexy underwear for me to wear."

"Oh I did. I can't wait to see you in each and every thing I bought. In fact, there's a red silk camisole that goes with the panties."

"Oh really? Get it and I'll wear it under the robe. At least my breasts won't hang out."

"The looks you get make me want you in a potato sack up at the lodge," he laughed. Which was only partially true, the other half of him loved how beautiful she was and people's reactions to it. It was a primal thing, a sort of showing off. In truth it turned him on that the other males wanted her.

She walked back and he instantly hardened at the sight. The red silk against the black fur and the white of the robe was stunning, the contrast of textures and colors, skin, hair, silk and fur—she was stunning.

And he wasn't the only one who thought so. When they came back into the lodge most of the Clan had come back and the house overflowed with people. Weaving through the crowd, Laurent led Rain to a couch and sat her down before going to grab some food and drinks for them.

Skye came to sit on one side of her and Ryan on the other. Skye sighed. "Snow White, you look fine tonight. Damn that Laurent for having all the luck." He grinned.

"Are you always so full of shit?" she teased.

"What? I tell it like it is. You're a very welcome addition to this Clan. It's not just that you are *fine*, it's that you're just nice to have around."

"Thank you. It's strange, I feel totally comfortable, like I was meant to be here all along. Everyone is so nice to me. Well, almost everyone," she added with a snort.

"Good job with Paloma. She's off licking her wounds. She won't try anything after tonight's display," Ryan said softly and gave her an appraising look that made her all tingly. All the sexual attention from the males was a heady thing.

Alex came to the couch and sat behind her. Laurent stalked over, putting a plate of food and two beers down before shooing Skye and taking his seat.

He pulled Rain to his body possessively and her sexy growl shot straight to his cock. "What are you mutts doing?" he asked the males gathered around his woman like bees to honey.

Rain laughed and Ryan's eyes deepened in color. "Man, I need to get a Mate."

"She won't be as sexy as my Rain but I hope you find her too, Ryan."

Alex laughed then and threaded Rain's hair through his fingers. "Laurent, you're not planning on sharing the wealth?"

"She is beautiful, isn't she? Sexy and stunning. It's up to Rain if I ever share her. I admit the thought of watching her being pleasured is one that appeals to me. In the meantime it's lucky I don't have any brothers and that everyone above me doesn't share."

"Technically I'm your brother," Devon said from his perch on the arm of Perri's chair across the room.

Laurent laughed and kissed the nape of Rain's neck, their shared desire sparked and spilled out like a warm tide. Skye's nostrils flared.

195

Rain was stunned, caught in what Laurent had just said. They'd teased and used the idea of her being with another man on some sexual level as titillation but Laurent sounded serious. She didn't know what'd happened to her over the last weeks of her life but damn the idea titillated her, made her pussy ache as her clit throbbed in time with her nipples.

His lips on her neck only heightened her need as her head fell back against Alex's thigh where he sat behind her on the couch back. Her hand snaked up Laurent's neck and into his hair, holding him there.

"You two need to quit that," Alex said, sounding annoyed and amused all at once.

"It's unusual, the level of sexual combustion these two put out. When I was younger I remember the Pack had a couple that was like this. It's all about those chemicals and how they bounce off each other," Andreas said as he and Kari sat on the couch across from them. "Frankly I like it. It's nice to see you two so obviously in love." He kissed Kari's hand and she rubbed her face along his jaw.

"Hell, even you and Kari don't spill out this much and you're all over each other all the time," Phillip said and Andreas laughed.

"Kari and I do appreciate someone else coming and removing the focus from our sex life," he said, raising his cigar in a toast to them.

Laurent stroked long fingers along the line of Rain's throat and her collarbone. Just touching her like that calmed him at the same time as it made him ache with wanting her. It seemed right to touch her flesh with his own. "She's so beautiful I can't stop." He wanted to kneel right there and widen her thighs and lick her pussy until she came. Wanted every male in that room to see a glimpse of the beauty he sipped every day.

"Yes, the red of the silk she's wearing under the robe is quite striking," Phillip said.

"I liked it without anything underneath," Ryan commented.

"Yes, her skin is like cream," Skye agreed.

Rain sighed and ran her fingers up and down his muscular thigh. "Hello? I'm sitting right here. No need to talk about me like I am just a piece of furniture."

"Baby, a beautiful woman, never furniture," Laurent said and kissed her and she snorted.

Kari laughed. "Don't take it personally, they all do it. It's part of their dominance display thing. The sexier the mate, the more beautiful, the stronger the male is perceived to be."

"Oh goodie! So I'm like a beaded handbag," she said and Kari and Perri burst out laughing.

"Something like that. Let's go grab a drink and leave these boys to their bragging," Kari said, getting up, and Rain had to step over bodies to get out of the room.

"They're like a werewolf frat sometimes," Emma said dryly as they all walked into the study and sat in the chairs and on the couches. Many of the mated females filed into the room as well.

"Where are Lissa, Meg and Paloma?" Rain asked Kari.

"Meg is with Alek, Lissa is with Carey and Paloma left early. She owes you an apology. If she hasn't delivered one in a week you have every right to demand punishment. Although of course Laurent is Lieutenant and god only knows, perhaps she'd like being punished by Laurent."

"You kicked the crap out of that bitch," Emma said and Rain smiled, her eyebrows raised. Up until that point she hadn't heard Emma say anything mean about anyone.

"She's presented herself to Devon several times."

"Jack too!"

"Yeah, Shane as well. I suppose though, given my past behavior, it's my karmic payback," Luna said with a wry smile.

"Luna, you were a total bitch but look, once you found Shane you turned into a new person. You just needed to find your true Mate," Perri said. "But let's get to the good stuff shall we?" She leaned toward Rain. "So what was all that about wanting to see you pleasured by another wolf?"

Rain blushed and Kari laughed. "Rain, if it makes you feel any better Andreas and I have had Phillip in our bed a few times. He's never fucked me, Andreas is very set on that point. But it's very nice when it happens. If I weren't a wolf I don't know if I'd be all right with it. But it's hot. And it's," Kari shrugged, "I don't know how to explain it. It feels comfortable as well as sexy. Not that I would be down with Andreas being with another female but the sharing thing as far as I've seen with the guys in this Inner Circle has only been with other males."

"Like a bit of bragging. Only way more fun for the female," Emma said. "What?" she asked when everyone looked at her, surprised. "Yes. Sean and I had an, um, interlude with Alex last year after a run. It was hot. But ever since it's been totally normal with Alex too. I worried at first, wondering if things would change, but they didn't."

"I can't believe you never told me!" Kari said.

"You never told me about Phillip," Emma retorted with a laugh.

"Well, everyone knows about me and Devon. We haven't in a long time and he's been with other women too. I've never felt threatened or unsure from it, thank goodness."

"Who would you choose?" Alyssa asked. "And before you all get nosy, yes. With Alex. He gets around." She winked at Emma. "But he's got some skills, I'll give him that."

Everyone laughed and Rain, despite her embarrassment, joined them. "I don't know. I mean, Laurent takes up my every waking prurient thought. They're all sexy and handsome." She shrugged. "Right now it's all just talk."

"So when are you going to start trying to have kids with Laurent?" Emma asked and Rain was grateful for the change of subject.

"Oh I don't know. I'm on the Pill right now, which is a good thing since we've been rutting like monkeys and haven't used condoms since the first time we were together."

"Rain, have you had unprotected sex since your transformation?" Emma asked.

"Well duh! Like dozens of times over the last two days. Has it not been the chief topic of discussion that Laurent and I can't keep our hands off each other?" She laughed.

"Oh Rain. Well, here's the thing, regular birth control doesn't work on us. We've developed birth control that suppresses ovulation but regular human birth control pills are like sugar pills to us."

"NO! You're kidding? Are you telling me I could be pregnant now?"

"Yeah." Emma leaned in and smelled Rain. "You don't smell fertile but you may have been yesterday. You'll know in a few days."

"Days?"

"Oh let me do this one!" Kari said, laughing. "See, werewolf pregnancies progress at an accelerated rate. You'll begin to feel the nausea at about two days after conception. We are only pregnant for four months."

"Oh my god. I can't believe Laurent didn't say anything," Rain groaned.

"He probably doesn't know. I mean you were busy and we've all felt the chemical overload with our mates," Emma said. She reached behind the couch and pulled out a medical bag. "Well, we can solve the question of pregnancy right now. I have test strips in my bag. Do you want to know?"

"Yeah." She sighed and, laughing, Emma stuck Rain's thumb and pressed it to the test strip.

It turned blue and Emma looked at her. "So what are you hoping?"

"I don't know. I mean, I guess I'm hoping it's positive. The idea of bearing Laurent's children is really appealing. It's faster than I'd planned on but still something I want to do with him."

"Well that's good because, Rain, you're pregnant," Emma said and Rain squealed with delight, joined by all the women in the room.

"I thought werewolves had a hard time getting knocked up?"

"This particular Clan is really fertile in this generation. It happens every hundred years or so if the numbers get low. Clans that don't have population explosions at least once a century die out," Kari explained. "And the pregnancies have been from new blood into the Pack as well. Which is also, I suppose, part of nature's plan when certain wolves can crossbreed with humans who come over."

Rain nodded, taking it all in, and suddenly looked panicked. "Oh my god, I'll be having babies, right? Not puppies?"

Kari burst out laughing.

"I think all human women who've been bitten ask that," Emma said, chuckling. "Yes, you'll have babies. They'll be children until puberty, when they achieve their first change."

"I need to tell Laurent," Rain said, standing and going to the door.

Kari jumped up, hugging her tightly, and all the other women did the same thing. "New life for the Cherchez Clan. It's so wonderful! Laurent will be so pleased."

"I hope so," Rain murmured as she walked into the great room where Laurent still lounged on the couch talking with Andreas and the others.

She went to him and touched his arm. His handsome face lit up with a smile when he turned to her. "Yes, baby? Is everything all right?"

"I need to talk to you for a moment. Privately," she added.

He stood up and walked to her, putting his arm around her shoulder. "Of course, let's go on the deck." He kissed her neck and they walked out and down to the far end of the deck away from the doors. "Tell me," he said without preamble.

"I'm pregnant," she blurted out. He looked at her, openmouthed. "I'm sorry. I didn't know that the Pill doesn't work on werewolf females and you know, we've been hitting the sheets pretty frequently in the last two days and well, Emma just gave me a test and did you know that werewolf pregnancies mmfph…"

Laurent had covered her lips with his own as he hugged her fiercely. He kissed her silly and pulled back to look down into her face. "Baby, you're having our child. Why on earth are you sorry? You're happy, right? You said you wanted to have children."

"No, I do! I am happy, it's just a surprise and I didn't know if you wanted to do it so fast."

He picked her up and kissed her again. "Rain, my word, I'm over the moon. You know, I've wanted children of my own since Helene and Tomas were born and I saw how wonderful parenting was. I hope it's a little girl who looks just like you." He didn't put her down, instead he trotted back into the house, still holding her.

"Laurent, put me down," she said.

"No, you need to rest," he whispered.

"I'm pregnant, not disabled. Now put me down. I'm guessing by the look on your face that you want to tell everyone? Well actually, a lot of the females know as they were in the room when Emma did the test. I wanted you to know first but well, I had no idea that this was even an opmmtopf!" Laurent put two fingers over her lips and he put her down and looked over at everyone.

"Rain is pregnant!" he bellowed and all of the males jumped up, cheering and clapping Laurent on the back before kissing Rain's cheek.

"You'll need to deal with her father now for sure," Andreas said quietly to Laurent.

"Yes. I'll call him in the morning. Right now I need to get Rain home to rest. Andreas, I'm going to be a father," he said, watching Rain with Skye, who teased her, judging by the smile she wore.

"Come on, baby, let's get you back home to bed."

She raised an eyebrow and smiled, calling back across the room to him, "Okay, but you do know that's how I got this way to begin with."

He groaned. "No, not that. Sleep." He doubted he could resist her though.

Andreas chuckled. "Oh Laurent, you have no idea. You do remember what Kari, Emma and Alyssa were like when they were pregnant, don't you? Come by tomorrow morning, I want to talk about some business issues with you."

"Of course. I'll see you in the morning," Laurent said but his attention was already focused on Rain, who was tossing heated looks his way. The energy between them arced around the room like electricity.

Laurent walked across the room to Rain. She was it. There was nothing else, no one else in the room for either one of them at that moment. He reached her and his lips came down on hers in a heated crush. She made a sound deep in her throat and it drove him crazy. Rolling his hips, grinding his cock against her body, he whispered her name against her lips.

"Get out of here!" Ryan said, tossing a pillow at them. Blindly, lips still on hers, he picked her up and moved toward the opened French doors and out of the lodge.

* * * * *

Laurent laid Rain down on the bed and she undid the buttons of her robe and parted it, showing him the blood red camisole and panties that he'd bought for her.

"Yeah," he whispered as she got to her knees, helping him off with his clothes. "That's what I'm talking about. So fucking beautiful. Sexy. I love you so much," he said, lips against the flesh of her neck.

"On your back," she ordered and he complied, his hair fanning out on the pillows and over his shoulders and arms as he looked up at her.

"I'm all yours, Rain." His mouth quirked up in one corner.

"I know. Lucky, lucky me." She started at the hollow of his neck, swirling her tongue, tasting the salt of his skin there. Her hair trailed down his skin as she kissed lower and lower, loving the way his muscles quivered as she touched him.

Slowly she took him into her mouth. Her movements were tentative at first. She was still learning his body so she listened to the sounds he made, taking cues from the way he responded to the things she did. When his hands tightened in her hair, when he couldn't help but thrust up into her mouth, when his body seized and he moaned. With each new success she grew more confident. More than anything she loved sucking his cock because it brought him so much pleasure and that made her feel like a goddess. She loved making him feel good.

"Rain, that feels so good," he hissed as she pressed the tip of her tongue into the dip just below the crown. She knew he was close, his muscles were taut and his cock got harder and harder as she moved on him. Taking a deep breath, she took him as far as she could into her mouth and dragged her nails lightly over his balls and he gasped and began to come, his fingers gripping her shoulders tight.

She continued to kiss and lick him for long moments afterward. He picked her up carefully, rolling her to her back, looming above her. He looked into her face, locking gazes with her. She loved him fiercely, this larger-than-life man who showed her nothing but gentleness and care.

"All I could think of at the lodge was kneeling between your thighs and licking your pussy until you screamed." He caressed her skin, ran the palms of his hands over her ribs and across her nipples. "All those males would be watching, cocks hard as they listened to your soft sounds of entreaty. The scent of your pussy rising, the sound of my mouth on you echoing over their harsh breath."

He'd rendered her speechless at the thought. Exhibitionism had never been a particular fantasy but perhaps she'd never had the right man for it.

He kept his eyes on hers as he latched onto a nipple, teeth grazing it. Warm ripples of pleasure broke over her, spreading outward from his mouth. A gasp came from her when he moved on but she moaned soon after as he left hot, openmouthed kisses down her belly before pulling her knees up to open her to him. He settled between her thighs.

The tip of his tongue traced over inner and outer labia, over and over, just barely flicking over her clit as he reached it. "I love your pussy, Rain. So sweet and soft. So hot and wet. I could eat you for days."

A sound came from her but she wasn't sure what she said or where it came from. A sort of low moan of need. Not a whimper, not a whine, but laced with desire and begging.

"What was that, baby?" he teased her, the tip of his tongue moving just above her clit. A whisper of a touch.

"Are you teasing me?" she burst out.

He chuckled and the vibrations jangled her nerves, making her body jerk. "I'm not teasing. I mean to follow up on what I'm doing. But I think you need to tell me what you want."

"I want you to make me come!"

"How?"

"I want you to lick me, suck on my clit, nibble and fuck me with your fingers," she said, breathless.

"Fuck. That was so hot."

Before she could say anything else he obeyed her, stretching her with first one finger and then two, fucking slowly, making sure to hook his fingers to stroke over her sweet spot.

Needing to come desperately, she combed her fingers through his hair, holding him to her pussy.

And then he sucked her clit between his teeth, flicking it relentlessly with the tip of his tongue, and her back bowed off the mattress as her thighs clamped over his ears. Orgasm, sharp, white and intense, sliced through her and his name left her lips in a hoarse cry.

He gentled her for long minutes afterward with small kisses and caresses, finally moving up to kiss her.

The last thing she remembered before falling asleep was the soft play of his fingers up and down her spine and the gentle, reassuring beat of his heart against her ear as her head lay on his chest.

* * * * *

Rain woke to the smell of freshly squeezed orange juice and the mouthwatering aroma of bacon cooking. Her stomach growled loudly and she slipped out of bed and went to the kitchen where Laurent was busily making breakfast.

"Morning."

He came to her and hugged her to him, kissing the top of her head. "You're going to have to put a robe on, I'll never finish breakfast if you don't."

"Why are you cooking?" she asked, grabbing one of his shirts and coming back out. "Without a doubt Anna has got

Lauren Dane

nine thousand eggs and a three pigs' worth of bacon up at the lodge."

"I like having time that's just you and me. I like taking care of you." He glanced back and did a double take, his eyes darkening at the sight of her in one of his shirts. She winked at him and he laughed, turning back to the stove to turn the bacon.

"Shall I make toast?" she asked, rooting through the pantry, delighted when she found a loaf of fresh bread.

"You should rest, Rain. Let me do it."

"Don't be silly. I'm not digging a trench, I'm putting slices of bread in a toaster." She snorted and did it and turned back to the pantry where she saw some homemade preserves. "Anna thinks of everything. Hmm, let's see, strawberry or marionberry?"

"Marionberry. You haven't lived until you've tasted Anna's marionberry preserves."

"Sounds yummy." She put the preserves at the table and poured a big glass of orange juice for each of them. She put the buttered toast on the table at the same time Laurent came to join her with a platter of eggs and bacon.

"Hey!" she exclaimed as he laid six slices of bacon and at least three eggs on her plate.

"You need to eat more. We'll talk to Emma about your prenatal care. It's so much better now that we have a doctor here in town. Before we had to go to Seattle or Elaine had to come up here."

She surprised herself by scarfing up the entire plateful of food and another two glasses of juice. "Wow. So am I going to gain like three pounds in about five minutes now or what?"

"Your metabolism has changed. You need to eat at least another fifteen hundred calories a day as a werewolf and now that you're pregnant it's even higher. Another thing to ask Emma. Kari, that tiny thing, ate like a pig when she was pregnant and she barely gained anything at all until the end

206

anyway. And nursing, if I remember correctly, she had to keep her calorie intake high too."

"Score," Rain said, smiling.

"I need to call your father this morning. Why don't you let me help you shower and dress and we'll go and do it from the lodge."

Rain stood, unbuttoning the shirt and letting it fall as she left the room. At the door she looked back over her shoulder to catch Laurent grinning and heading toward her at top speed.

With his *help* it was another forty-five minutes until they were both dressed and ready to go up to the lodge.

She followed him in and Anna stopped her in the kitchen. "You go on, I'll be in shortly," Rain said to Laurent who nodded before strolling into the study, shutting the door behind him.

Andreas was already at work, on the phone with his broker and working on a spreadsheet at the same time. He nodded at Laurent who went to his own terminal and logged on. He'd been away from work for three weeks, taking off the time that Rain wasn't speaking to him to guard her. He had a lot of work to catch up on.

Andreas hung up and turned to Laurent, tossing an envelope his way. "Here, a bonus for being my right-hand man for sixteen years."

Laurent opened the envelope. It was a deed to fifty acres of the Star Lake property, five acres right on the lake. "Andreas, you're giving me your land?"

"No, I'm sharing my land with you. Hell, I own seven hundred and fifty acres, I only gave you fifty. You're my brother, you've saved my life and my family's lives multiple times. You're going to have a baby in four months, bringing more life to my Pack. You can't live in that cabin forever, it's too small. Build Rain a house. Let her nest and build a nursery for your child. The acreage is on the other side of Sean so the lakefront part is already cleared and ready for building."

Laurent got up and went to Andreas, hugging him. "Thank you, Andreas. It means so much to me. I don't have any biological family of my own anymore but I've always had you and your parents to help me through."

"Correction, you will in four months. You and Rain have started your own family but you'll always be my brother, Laurent."

Rain knocked on the door and opened it at Andreas' bid to enter. "Am I interrupting anything?"

"No, sweetheart. Andreas has just given us fifty acres of land. I am going to have a house built for you and the baby."

Rain looked at Laurent, surprised and happy. Then she walked to Andreas. "Oh thank you, Andreas. I'm so grateful for all you've done for us—for me—since I arrived here," she said and gave Andreas a big hug.

Andreas placed a hand on her still slim stomach. "You're one of mine now. You're my sister-in-law and as Alpha of this Clan it brings me joy that you bring new life to us. As Laurent's best friend it makes me happy that you have brought so much love and life to him."

Laurent grinned at the three of them and the emotion in the room. "Okay, before we get too mushy let's make that call. Baby, sit here and don't say anything unless I motion for you to, okay?"

Rain nodded and sat, drinking from the giant glass of milk that Anna had given her in the kitchen. Phillip breezed in, put her feet up on the coffee table and winked at her before walking back out with a stack of papers.

Laurent went to his desk, dialed a series of numbers and waited for several rings until someone answered.

"Hello?"

Laurent looked at Rain to ask if it was her father answering and she shook her head no.

"I need to speak with Pietro Margoles."

"And who are you?"

"I'm Laurent Cole. I'm his new son-in-law."

"What? Are you talking about Julia?"

"Indeed I am." He growled. "Enough chitchat. I need to speak to Margoles."

"Is that so? And just who do you think you are?"

Laurent sighed. "I've told you who I am."

Rain handed Laurent a note. *He's an underling, no one of any real importance. Shall I say something? If not just dismiss him and demand my father.*

Laurent read it and nodded for her to speak.

"James, get my father and do it now, you're wasting our time," she ordered and both Laurent and Andreas looked at her with raised eyebrows. Rain smiled demurely and went back to her place on the couch.

"Julia? Okay, hang on."

A few moments passed until Pietro Margoles got on the line. "Julia? Get your stupid ass back home right now!"

"She is home," Laurent growled, low and threatening. Andreas growled in the background as well.

"And who the fuck are you?" Pietro spat out.

"I'm your daughter's husband. I've called to announce our marriage to you and to warn you to call off Anthony Vargas. Julia does not want to see or have a relationship with you. She wishes for you to cease attempting to contact her in any fashion."

"Oh she does? I don't give a fuck who you say you are. I own Julia and I gave her to Anthony Vargas. She's useful for a few things, one of them being a bride and sealing a rift between our families. She's caused enough grief by running away. She needs to get her ass on a plane and come back home before I have to come out there and drag her back myself."

"Pietro, you don't own Julia. Julia isn't property, no one owns her. She is however my wife, and as such it's my duty to protect her from scumbag woman beaters like Anthony Vargas and criminal riffraff like you. Now I'd like you to listen and listen very closely." Laurent took a sip of his coffee and leaned back in his chair.

"You *will* stop attempting to contact my wife. I won't have her living in fear."

"Who do you —"

"Ah, ah, ah! Shut the fuck up now, Pietro, I'm doing the talking. Now as I was saying, you'll call off this ridiculous hunt and you'll leave my wife alone. I know you think you're tough, many men do. I'm sure in your own element you are just that. However I *will* rip your throat out for ever speaking to Julia in a demeaning way again. I will eat your heart for dinner. I will eviscerate you and leave your body ripped open, empty of all internal organs and steaming, next to the road. Animals will be too afraid to pick your bones. Your organization may be old and powerful but it has nothing on mine.

"If fear of painful, violent death doesn't convince you, let me add that I've got quite a dossier of information about you and your *business* dealings, with names and dates even. This dossier will be mailed to the federal prosecutor's office and all major newspapers should any harm or threat of harm come our way. Now I don't want war with you, Pietro, I have no intention of turning you in. You're in your neck of the woods and I'm in mine. I think it's best if the two don't meet, don't you?"

"You bastard! You've messed up years of plans. Julia's marriage was necessary for business. What am I supposed to do now?"

"I don't give a crap, Pietro. Find another woman. Mine is taken. Now do I have your word that you will call Vargas back home or do I need to take care of him and then mail this information? Afterward I'll hunt you down and kill you slowly."

"Fine. I'll back off, but you'd better hope we never meet in a dark alley."

Laurent threw back his head and laughed, sharp white teeth gleaming. Rain had to join him. Her father had no idea. "No, Pietro, I don't think I'm the one who needs to be worried about such things. Now I'm going to hang up. My wife and I are going to live our life without interference or threat. I have friends who could and would take up my cause should I be harmed in any way. Don't let pride get in the way of continuing to breathe." Laurent hit the *off* button, cutting the other man off and terminating the call.

Andreas grinned and slapped him on the back. "Glad you're on my side! Well done, Laurent."

"My hero," Rain said, smiling, feeling the weight of worry lift from her shoulders. "Now I need to talk to Emma about setting up prenatal care and I need to call The Holt and arrange to have my other paintings that are at Drew's to be delivered to them for my show. I need to choose a postcard for the showing and...I need to vomit," she said, rushing out of the room.

Laurent bolted from behind his desk and followed her.

Coming out to see what the commotion was, Kari made him stop pounding on the bathroom door. "She's just got morning sickness, Laurent. Let her be for a few minutes."

As promised, Rain emerged after a few minutes, paler but smiling. "I'm okay."

"The hell you are. I'm taking you back home, you need to lie down. You can have the cordless in bed with you to make your calls. I want you off your feet." He crossed his arms over his chest and tried to look commanding and pretend fear hadn't just nearly knocked him to his knees.

Andreas came into the hallway. "You might want to sit down and hear this first. I just got a call from Grey Barton. You aren't going to believe this but vampires exist."

"What?" The room erupted with confused voices. Laurent picked Rain up and sat down on the couch in the living room with her in his lap. Anna appeared and brought her a cup of tea that Rain sipped slowly as she listened.

"They want to negotiate a treaty with all shifters. Apparently they've been here as long as we have. They have territories like we do, with an Alpha, only he or she is called a *Maître de Sang* or Master of Blood. French tradition as well, oddly enough. Anyway, they just got exposed and someone from the federal government has approached their grand council, which is in New Orleans."

"How very Anne Rice," Kari said, fascinated.

"Well, it gets worse. The same contacts from the federal government called on Grey this morning. There is now official knowledge of our existence."

"What does this all mean?" Rain asked.

"Well, it means that the world just got more dangerous for us. Humans are not always open and accepting to ideas that scare them. Different scares them. We are different. Grey is setting up a committee to deal with this. If we're outed we'll have to mount a public relations campaign, lobby for civil rights, that sort of thing. I'm not sure whether I'd advocate for Pack members to out themselves as Were. It might be better to live as humans still. At least for a few years."

"Wow. This puts having a child soon in a whole new light," Rain murmured sleepily.

"I need to meet with an architect and the same builders who built Jack's and Sean's homes. I want our house finished as soon as possible and I want it wired with high-tech security gear." Laurent stood, still holding Rain, and said to Andreas, "I'll be back in a few minutes, I just want to get Rain settled in."

"Put me down, Laurent. I can walk."

"No. You're sick and carrying my child. I'm going to take care of you and you're going to let me." He growled and walked out of the lodge and down the path to their cabin.

He settled her into their bed and brought her some water, a big glass of milk and some crackers and cheese. "Here's the phone, a notepad and pen. Call the lodge if you need me. I'll be back down to check on you in a while."

"Laurent, love, I'm fine. I'm better than fine actually. Why don't you come over here and let me show you just how fine I am?" she purred.

"Rain, stop that! I have work to do and you need to rest. If you take a nap I'll come back and see to my husbandly duty later on." He winked and blew her a kiss, knowing that if he got any closer to her, her scent would drive him back into her arms and he'd never get any work done.

Laurent locked the door behind him and went back up to the lodge. Anna promised to take by some food and check on Rain later.

Emma came by the cabin and checked Rain over an hour later. "You should only be sick for about a week or two, another plus of the werewolf pregnancy. I'll see you weekly to monitor blood pressure, which can be a problem for us. Eat when you feel like it. I've brought a prenatal vitamin for you that's been formulated just for us."

"Laurent is carrying me around and this morning when we were, um, having sex in the shower, he freaked out about hurting the baby and was gentle. Um, a little too gentle. Anyway, is sex okay?"

Emma laughed. "As you'll have noticed, werewolf males are dominant and protective of their Mates. Laurent will continue to act this way. Sean did it, drove me crazy! Devon did it, Andreas did it, Jack did it—it's who they are. But you're really healthy and sex is just fine. In fact, I think we talked about this the other night, your libido is going to go through the roof. Pregnancy for us is a major hormonal deal. Not only will you want sex all day and night but your mood swings, especially in the last two months, will be trying. And Laurent's will be too. It's going to threaten him because you're going to throw off a lot of hormones and it'll attract the other males. It'll be irrational and annoying but you'll have to deal with it. Kari was lucky, Andreas didn't really have much of a problem because he's the Alpha, but Sean was a snarling asshole who picked fights with every male who even looked my way in the last few weeks."

"Yeah, definitely dominant but really, really sexy. Can I do anything to ease my mood swings or stop his? I'm a little freaked, I have to admit, to think of him being angry and jealous. I did that, I don't want to ever deal with that kind of man again."

"Oh honey." Emma patted her hand. "Laurent isn't your ex. He's a werewolf. A very dominant, high-ranking werewolf, which makes his personality very strong. You two will spat a lot during the end of the pregnancy but he's not the type to lose it like that. He'll be pissy and the other males will give him space because it's what they all do. Hormones are hormones, not a lot you can do about that. And you've got a lot of them. You toss out a lot of sex and it already affects the males. No, don't apologize or feel bad, you're not doing it to provoke it's just who you are. I just wanted to warn you up front. Sometimes no one tells the converted wolves anything and we have to deal with this stuff blind. There's no need for that when we can share information. He'll get grumpy, you'll fuck." Emma shrugged. "You love each other, you'll make up and tomorrow is another day. Now I want you to rest up and try to get some fresh air later today, a walk around the lake, even a run. Your wolf will handle the sickness better than your human."

Chapter Ten

ॐ

The weeks passed quickly and the date of Rain's show came. Laurent, Rain, Emma, Sean, Kari and Andreas all came to Seattle a few days early, staying in the apartment and enjoying the city.

Rain had started to show and Drew made a dress just for her, for the show. It was a deep red with beautiful white hibiscus flowers silk-screened onto it. It had spaghetti straps and hugged her breasts but a high empire waist camouflaged her burgeoning belly. The hem had white beads hanging from it, lending a bit of fancy. Kari dressed Rain's hair into a chic bun at the base of her neck and Drew brought her a red hibiscus flower that they tucked into it. The finishing touch was the ruby and diamond earrings Laurent had given her as a congratulations gift for her first show.

"Rain, baby, you look beautiful," he murmured to her as she came into the living room where everyone else waited, ready to go.

"Thank you." She caressed the line of his jaw and kissed the cleft in his chin. She turned to Drew and smiled. "Drew, thank you for this dress. I feel so pretty in it and I barely show, which will be nice, as it would be hard to explain why I look so knocked up." She laughed and Drew kissed her cheek. "Shall we go then?"

They decided to walk over to The Holt as it was only a few blocks south. Rain caught sight of the group in a window as they all passed. Under the silvery light of the moon and stars each couple looked positively beautiful as they walked arm in arm.

When they got there Rain ducked off with Diane. She wanted to check the placement of each painting, make sure the height and distance between them was just right. Diane was an expert and of course Rain was pleased by the look of everything.

Half an hour later the doors opened up and the show began in earnest. Pretty much the entire Pack showed up at The Holt that night, touching Rain deeply with their show of support.

"Rain? My god, woman, you look beautiful. Marriage agrees with you!"

Rain turned to see Harrison standing there. Crying out happily, she rushed to him, enfolding him into a big hug. "Harrison! I'm so happy you came. I've sold four paintings already, isn't that amazing?"

"It's only what I expected. Your art is going to be in high demand. As for my being here, I wouldn't miss it for the world. In fact I just saw Laurent over there and he invited me up to the new house once it's finished. Something I'm definitely going to do because I've missed you," Harrison said, squeezing her hand.

"I've missed you too. Andreas has your photographs up in his office and I see them daily. Makes me miss you even more." She looked around excitedly. "I can't believe it. Our house is about halfway done already. Laurent wants it finished as quickly as possible so those guys are out there day and night and on weekends working on it."

"I can't wait to see it, cupcake. Oh look, I just saw Diane put a sold sign on two more paintings," Harrison said, motioning with his chin. He didn't say that he was the one who bought *Crazy Diamond*. "Oh I see some old friends just arrived. I'm off to tell them to buy your work now before it becomes too expensive." He grinned and she kissed his cheek.

"Thanks, Harrison. For believing in my work and being so supportive. It means a lot to me."

"Kid, I'm your number one fan," he quipped and headed off in the direction of a gaggle of professional-looking men.

Laurent approached and put his arm around Rain. "Are you all right? Not too tired?"

"I'm fine. Stop worrying. I even wore flat shoes for you," she said to him, touched as always that this man cared for her so much. Suddenly she stopped and stood motionless. Tears sprang into her eyes and she looked up at Laurent, amazed. "I just felt the baby move," she whispered to him.

He looked at her, wonder in his eyes. "Our baby." He put his hand on her stomach and kissed her nose. "Have I told you how proud I am of you?"

"Only about a hundred times but it never gets old," she said, eyes dancing.

"Rain, you've officially sold out! Only an hour into your first show. Congratulations. I know you're going to do the same in Portland too." Diane Holt hugged her.

Rain was floating on air by the time they were finished. She'd made more money in one night than she had in years. Not only that but she had the business cards of several people interested in commissioning her work *and* another show in four and a half months. Things were going so well. At long last she was living her dream and had a wonderful husband and family and a baby on the way. Life was beautiful.

With a laugh she stepped out onto the sidewalk, dancing ahead of the group of wolves who were on their way back to the apartment for a celebration. The night air felt alive on her skin.

Laurent approached and she smiled up into his handsome face. Suddenly things slowed. Laurent's smile crumpled into a mask of rage as he looked past her to the street. Rain began to turn to see what he was looking at when hands grabbed her, yanking her into a waiting car. The door slammed behind her, over her fear she felt a sharp pain in the back of her head and then nothingness.

217

* * * * *

Laurent Cole let out a howl of frustrated rage that raised the hair on the neck of every human within hearing distance as he took off running after the car that had Rain inside. Andreas sprinted at his side and he could hear Phillip on the phone calling 9-1-1, reporting a kidnapping. He felt like ripping trees up by their roots when the car got on the freeway onramp and sped away, out of his reach.

He crumpled right in the middle of the street, great wracking howls of fear and rage tearing out of his mouth. Ryan and Drew helped him up and back onto the sidewalk, rubbing his arms and back nervously, trying to calm him.

"I've called the police, Laurent. They're coming. See, that's the squad car parking. Come on, Laurent, let's go and talk to them. Skye and James have gone back with Archer and Bert to get some vehicles and make some calls," Phillip said, helping Laurent to his feet and toward the squad car. Andreas accompanied them, lending his strength to Laurent.

"Sir, I know this is hard but we need to get all of the information we can as quickly as we can." The officer was brisk and efficient and Laurent worked to keep it together and concentrate.

Laurent and Andreas gave a description of the car that took Rain and Laurent told them that she was pregnant. They asked if he knew why someone would do it and he debated with himself whether or not to say anything about her father because the information he had about Pietro Margoles was his only leverage. Carey approached and squeezed his arm, cautioning him. He said that she had an ex-fiancé who might be angry that she left him but that he didn't know much else.

When the police had gone Laurent got into the car that Skye was driving and pulled out his phone, punching a series of numbers.

"This is Laurent Cole, put him on now," he growled when Pietro's assistant answered.

"He's busy."

"He's going to be dead and you'll all be in jail if you don't put him on the phone right now," he screamed into the phone.

"Why are you bothering me? You said you'd leave me alone if I left you and Julia alone," Pietro barked, annoyed.

"You'd better tell your men to deliver Rain to me, unharmed, immediately. If not I'm mailing those envelopes and then I'm getting on a plane and I'm coming for you. You'll wish with your last ragged, painful dying breath, after I torture you for a week, that you had done it," he said in an eerily calm voice, in shocking contrast to his scream of moments before.

"What are you talking about?"

"Don't fuck me around, Margoles. Rain, Julia, was just kidnapped less than fifteen minutes ago, outside of her first gallery showing. She's carrying your grandchild, old man. If anything happens to my wife you'll beg for mercy and get none."

"Someone kidnapped Julia? I'm telling you, Cole, I had nothing to do with it. I told the Vargases that Julia had gotten married and that we'd find another wife for Anthony. I was in the process of working out a deal for Julia's cousin Andrea."

"Listen, asshole, there's no one other than you or your people who would have reason to hurt her. She was a waitress who painted. She has no enemies other than the ones attached to you."

Pietro Margoles was scared. He'd been in charge for a very long time and he had no plans to give that up. This information could not only end his leadership but could land him in prison. Or worse. He'd heard a lot of death threats over his life, faced down a lot of tough guys and guys who thought they were tough. But he knew, deep in his gut, that the man on the other end of the phone was capable of every threat he'd uttered.

"Listen, let me get some of my West Coast men on it to help find her. Give me your mobile number and I'll get back to you. I swear I had nothing to do with this. Julia may not be my favorite person but I don't want her dead and I don't want my grandchild to be harmed."

He jotted a note to his assistant, whose eyes widened before she got on another line, dialing furiously.

Laurent could hear the truth in the other man's words. He grunted and gave him the phone number and hung up. Sighing, he put his head in his hands and tried to concentrate.

"Laurent, let's go back to the gallery. I saw an alley. We'll change and see what we can sniff out. We'll find her. I promise. But we can't drive around aimlessly, it's not going to help. We need to see what we can find back at the scene, all right?" Skye said gently.

Laurent took a deep breath and pulled himself back together. He needed to be strong and thinking clearly to save Rain. "You're right."

They went back and changed, trotting out to the sidewalk where Rain had been taken. As they sniffed around Laurent smelled Rain, her fear, the rich scent of her fertility. He smelled two men, one very, very angry. After a few minutes they changed back in the alley and walked back to the car.

"I think it's Vargas. I need to know if he's back in New York or not and I want to see if we can find something he's touched to get his scent," Laurent said as he knocked on the door of The Holt.

Diane saw him and rushed to open the door. "Have you found Rain? Is she all right?" she asked, worried.

"Not yet. Listen, Diane, do you remember a little over a month back, a guy came here looking for Rain? Anthony Vargas?"

Diane shuddered. "Yes, one of those guys who looks nice and well-mannered but after a few minutes you begin to feel his greasiness. Why?"

"Did he give you a card or anything? Something with his phone number on it? Did he touch anything special? We have special scent dogs that I'd like to use if we could just get Vargas' scent somehow."

"Yes! I have his business card. I meant to send it to Andreas but I forgot. Hang on a sec, I'll get it from my office." She ran into the back and came out a few moments later, holding the card.

Laurent took it. "Thank you, Diane. We'll call you if we hear anything, you do that too, okay?"

"Of course. You'll find her, Laurent. She'll be all right," Diane said, hugging him and watching as he and Skye drove away.

Laurent took a deep whiff of the card, eyes closed. "It's him. I can smell him on the card. It's the same as the scent at the scene."

"Let's go back to the apartment. You can call Margoles from there and see what we can do for the next step."

When Skye and Laurent walked through the door Laurent went straight for his and Rain's room to call Margoles. Andreas joined him with Phillip, Ryan and Skye.

"Margoles, it's Laurent. Vargas did it. He's the one who took Rain."

"Yes, I'd just come to that conclusion. I did some checking and apparently he's been...upset that Julia had made other choices."

"Where is he?"

"I don't know. We're looking for him. He's not answering his mobile. I have people in Seattle who are looking for him now. Trust me on this, Cole, he can't exist without me finding him."

"I want him. When you find him don't kill him unless it has to be done to save Rain. He's mine."

"Okay. I'll be in touch." Margoles hung up.

221

Laurent leaned back and put his face into Rain's pillow, breathing in her scent. Andreas sat on the bed next to him, massaging his arm.

"We'll find her, Laurent. She's going to be fine."

•

Chapter Eleven

ॐ

Rain came to with a terrible headache. She opened her eyes slowly and the memory of what happened rushed back.

"She's awake," a voice said.

"Good, get out," another voice answered. One she recognized, and fear slithered down her spine. Anthony Vargas.

Her heart beat wildly in her chest. She saw spots in her vision as she was hauled into an upright position.

"So the little whore is awake now. That's good, I want you to be awake when I take back what's mine," he spat out.

She recognized the signs. He sweated profusely, his eyes were glossy and red-rimmed. He was high, and by the looks of him had been for days. He'd be very dangerous at that point and she had to think carefully on her next steps to keep herself and the baby alive.

"Did you think I'd just let you do whatever you wanted? Did you think I'd just let you humiliate me in front of my family?" He shook her then, so hard her teeth chattered.

She kept quiet. She knew from past experience that when he'd been doing meth he was irrational and easily angered. She had no desire to have any more bones fractured. More importantly, she had her baby to protect. She had to stay calm so she could change and escape. But the other man had a gun and she wanted to be sure she could take Anthony down first before the other man could get off a shot.

"I see he's knocked you up," Anthony said through gritted teeth. "You should be carrying *my* kid!" he shouted and slapped her face hard. She thanked her new physiology, it hurt but not nearly as much as it would have if she had been human. Still she tasted blood.

Before he could strike her again the other man came back into the room. "Tony, Pietro is looking for you. He's been calling your mobile and has his guys out on the streets. I just got a call from Paulie and he says that Margoles has a do-not-kill order on you. Maybe he'll spare your life if you let her go."

Anthony stood, hauling Rain up with him. "She's coming back with me! There's no letting her go. She's my property," he screamed and punched her hard in the stomach.

The air rushed out of her as she crumpled to the ground and he kicked her over and over, right in the stomach. Through the haze of pain she knew she didn't have the luxury of waiting. She changed and leapt up, knocking the second man over and ripping out his throat, silencing his screams for mercy.

Rain spun around and yelped as a bullet slammed into her shoulder but she charged Anthony anyway, knocking him down and tearing into his flesh. She didn't stop, she just kept ripping into him, making sure he'd never terrorize her again.

Finally, after she didn't know how many minutes, she stopped, collapsing and changing back. Her stomach cramped and she crawled out to the main room. Taking in her surroundings, she realized they were in a hotel room and she continued her crawl to the phone. Pulling it down to the floor, she noted the information panel as she dialed Laurent's cell.

"Laurent," she gasped out, the cramps becoming more and more consistent.

"Rain, where are you? Are you all right?"

"No. I don't think so, no. I'm at the Embassy Suites, room four fifteen. On the water. Oh god, the baby. I'm bleeding," she cried out when she looked down and saw the blood, the same color as the dress she'd been wearing earlier, on her thighs. "I've been shot too."

"Shot?" Panic tinged his voice. "Baby, hold on. I'm running to get into the car now, Emma is coming with me. Can you call the police?"

"There are two bodies here, I don't know if I could explain," she moaned out, holding her stomach and rocking back and forth.

Laurent was losing it. He had to put his head against the dashboard for a few moments to get back in control. Sean looked at him as they took off. "Why don't I keep on the line with her?"

"NO! I'll do it. I've failed her enough."

Andreas drove hell-bent for leather through the streets of downtown Seattle.

"We're almost there, baby, another five minutes. Hold on, all right? Keep on the line with me. Rain?" *Silence.* "Rain? Baby?"

Laurent continued to call her name until Andreas pulled into the circular drive at the hotel and skidded to a halt. Emma and Laurent jumped out, followed by Sean and Skye. Andreas went to park and would meet them.

Laurent ran up the stairs three at a time up to the fourth floor. He pounded on the door of room four fifteen. "Rain?" he called into the phone and at the door. "Baby, I'm here, I need to you open the door. Come on, baby, wake up and get to the door."

He was just about to kick the door down when the lock clicked open and he slowly pushed inside. And nearly lost his mind when he saw what lay there. Rain was lying on the floor at the door, naked, covered head-to-toe in blood. There was a trail of blood on the carpet from the bedroom to the phone table and from the phone table to the door. An inarticulate sound of grief came from deep inside him.

He rushed to her and Emma stepped around him. "Wait, Laurent. Don't move her just yet. Let me see what's going on." She gave him eye contact. "I need you to go grab me some wet towels. Can you do that? I need to see if this is her blood or not." Sean and Skye busily swept the suite to see if there were any threats and came back out to the living room. Sean laid out a blanket to put over Rain, who'd begun to shiver violently as she lapsed in and out of consciousness.

Andreas came into the room followed by Phillip, Ryan, Devon and Kari, who'd just pulled into the hotel as Andreas had raced inside. Kari fell to her knees and began to speak softly to Rain. She looked down at the blood on Rain's thighs and held back tears as she caught sight of Laurent coming back with warm, wet towels.

He and Kari helped Emma by cleansing Rain's body of the blood she had all over her. The bullet had gone straight through her shoulder and the resultant wound had already begun to heal.

The movement woke Rain up and she looked to Emma, panic in her eyes. "Anthony kicked me, he punched me. The baby, is it all right? I'm losing it, aren't I? He killed my baby, didn't he?" Rain whispered to Emma, who nodded solemnly. Rain began to cry. "I should have changed sooner. I thought to wait until the gun guy was out of the picture but I waited too long. It's my fault. Oh Laurent, I killed our baby."

Laurent pulled her into the shelter of his body, trying to feel absolutely nothing so he could be there for her right then. "No, Rain. Oh baby, Anthony killed our child and you killed him and his thug friend. I should have been watching you closer, had you next to me. It's not your fault. I failed you," he said with an anguished voice. Kari squeezed his hand and Phillip held his shoulders.

"We need to get her to the hospital. Let me call Elaine and set it up," Emma said, sadness thick in her voice.

As she turned to make the call, Skye knelt at Rain's side. "You killed them both, babe, you're so strong. You and Laurent will have more children, not that this one wasn't special and already loved but this won't end your happiness forever." He stroked her hand and looked into Laurent's eyes.

Andreas paced like a madman, barking instructions into his cell phone for others to come and take care of the scene.

Rain passed out again. "She's lost a lot of blood, Laurent. We need to take her to the hospital now, all right? Elaine will be waiting in the ER for us. We need to make sure Rain's not hemorrhaging. It's bad enough that the baby is gone, we don't want to lose her too."

Laurent stood and picked up Rain, holding her tight to him. He felt nothing. A great, white void in his chest. Nothing but Rain existed at that moment.

Sean tucked the blanket around her snugly. Kari opened the door for her and they all went out the back stairs and loaded into the SUV for the trip to the hospital.

Elaine was waiting for them and took Rain immediately in for an ultrasound. The baby was dead. Laurent was on autopilot, he had to get them both through this mess. He'd deal with the grief later.

"I'm going to do a D&C to be sure that her uterus is all clear, Laurent. Archer and Emma will be in the room with me. We'll take her into a room shortly. Why don't you rest for a bit?" Elaine said gently.

Andreas nodded at her and helped Laurent sit down in between himself and Phillip. Sean paced and Ryan looked sullen and furious. Kari was silent except for the tears tracking down her cheeks as she sat on the floor between Laurent's knees, resting her head on his calves.

"I failed her," Laurent whispered.

"No you didn't, Laurent. You did your best for her and she knows it. You two love each other, you'll get through this. There'll be other children, which means exactly nothing right now but later it will," Phillip said quietly and Andreas nodded, squeezing Laurent's shoulder.

By the time they wheeled Rain into her own room to recover the entire Pack had gathered, solemn and supportive.

"Laurent, she'll be all right. Her gunshot wound is almost completely healed. The D&C will have cleaned out her uterus. Your baby, it was a boy. I'm sorry." She paused for a moment, swallowing hard. "But her reproductive system is still healthy. If she'd been human she would have sustained major kidney and liver damage. From the bruises it appears she was kicked repeatedly. Her shoulder was out of joint and she's got some torn tendons in her shoulder and neck. They're already healing."

"Can I see her?"

"Yes, she'll be regaining consciousness shortly. We gave her some blood, she lost quite a bit. I'm sorry, Laurent," Elaine said softly.

Laurent let her hug him and he walked past her and up the stairs to the room where they'd moved Rain. He went in and lay beside her on the narrow bed, where he enfolded her into his body, needing to know she was alive.

* * * * *

The morning sun streamed through the slits in the blinds when Laurent awoke, Rain still in the curve of his body. Sitting up, he looked around and saw that Andreas, Kari, Alek and Phillip were in the room with them. Andreas met his eye.

Rain awoke then, inhaling in a panic and sitting bolt upright. Laurent cupped her cheeks in his hands. "It's okay, baby, you're all right. I'm here," he whispered against her skin and she collapsed into him.

"The baby. Our baby. Gone?"

"Yes, Rain, I'm so sorry," he whispered.

"Oh god. How could this have happened? I was so happy, you were there, my paintings sold, I was dancing on air and then everything that was good ceased to exist."

"Everything?"

"Well, not everything. You're still here. Do you hate me?"

"Why would I hate you, Rain? My god, how is it that you don't hate me? I failed to protect you. Did that bastard Vargas hurt you?"

Rain looked down at her battered but healing body and blinked back at him, uncomprehending.

Laurent shook his head. "No, I mean did he rape you, Rain?"

"No, although that was next I'm sure of it. He kept ranting about taking back what was his. I killed him, Laurent, and I don't feel bad. God, I'm a killer. I should have changed earlier. If I had our baby would be alive."

Sean walked over and put his forehead to hers. "No, don't what-if yourself, Rain. You did what you had to to survive and you tried to save your baby. You said the other man had a gun and obviously, given the gunshot wound you sustained, Vargas had one too. You were right to think it out and hold back until you thought you were safer. You're alive and you have no idea how happy that makes me, how happy it makes all of us."

"Don't waste guilt on Vargas or his accomplice. They got what they deserved. You were so strong, Rain. Vargas was the coward for kicking you like that. He's the one who killed the baby. You saved yourself and I'm sorry we weren't there in time to save your pregnancy but there will be other pregnancies. I promise you," Kari said.

"I wish everyone would stop talking about it like the child I lost can be replaced like a light bulb!" Rain yelled out, fists balled up. Laurent pulled her to him tightly, tears streaming down his face at her anguish.

Kari reached out to caress Rain's face. "I'm sorry. I can't even begin to understand the pain you're feeling. My babies are home, alive and well. It was insensitive of us to keep on telling you there would be more children. We didn't mean to hurt you or to make it seem like it wasn't a big deal, of course it is. I'm your friend and your Alpha, I love you like a sister and I'm here for you," she said and kissed her cheek and Rain rubbed her face along Kari's jawline and then allowed Kari to hug her.

"Am I going to prison?"

Andreas laughed, a rueful sound, and stepped forward, taking her hand. "No, love. The scene is cleaned up. No one will miss human trash like them. Carey handled the police and your father's people dealt with the details. He's asked you to call your mother, at home, when you feel up to it. In the meantime you will come back home where you belong and let us, your family by choice, take care of you and Laurent. Let us love you, Rain." He dropped a kiss on her nose and stood back.

"We'd like to be alone for a while please," Laurent whispered, not taking his eyes from Rain's.

"Of course. Elaine said Rain can go home today and Emma will take care of her until she's better. I'm pretty good at grief counseling so please come to me when you're ready," Sean said and, together with the others, left the room.

Rain sank back down to the bed, lying within the shelter of Laurent's arms, staring up at the ceiling tiles. Feeling dead. Laurent lay on his side, propped up on his arm, looking at her. She sighed. "I can't believe it's gone. Our baby. Do you know, was it a boy or a girl?"

"Elaine said he was a boy."

"I was thinking of Sebastian, after your father, if it was a boy," she said, feeling like she was wrapped in cotton.

"That would have been nice," Laurent murmured. "Rain, I thought I'd lost you."

"Never, Laurent. I'd never leave you without a fight. You're stuck with me forever."

"Oh thank god." He chuckled and sat up. "Let's go home, baby. We'll get you back and in bed and I'll pamper you until you are better."

"When will that be? Laurent, when will it feel better? Twenty-four hours ago I was full of life, last night I felt him moving inside of me and now I am so empty. When will I feel okay again?"

"I don't know, Rain. Let's help each other through this, okay?"

"Laurent, you know, you don't have to be superman every moment of the day. You're hurting too. I can see it. Let it go. Let me be strong for you for a change," she whispered.

He looked into her face and the weight of his terror, grief and relief bore down on him until he collapsed against her body, sobbing.

Emma knocked softly on the door and when she walked in, Laurent was lying, his head on Rain's lap, Rain's hands slowly stroking up and down his back. The sobs had stopped and they both felt a little better.

"Hi, honey. We brought you some clothes. Let's get you changed and into the car, all right? It'll be a long trip so I want you warm and comfortable." Emma had some clothes in her hands and put them on the bed.

Rain nodded numbly and Andreas took Laurent off to the side and held him, arm around his shoulder. He refused to let Rain out of his sight. Emma, Kari and Perri helped Rain change and Laurent gasped when he saw that she was still bleeding.

Elaine saw it and moved to him. "She'll be bleeding for a while longer. Not as long as if we hadn't done a D&C and as a werewolf she'll already have begun healing but still, it'll be at least another day or two," Elaine said to Laurent softly.

When they started to help Rain down Laurent came over and picked her up himself. "I'll do it," he said and Rain put her face in the hollow of his neck, sighing softly.

Elaine signed her out and they loaded Rain gently into the car, Laurent settling in beside her. Elaine kissed Laurent's cheek and Rain's forehead. "Call me if you need anything. I had a miscarriage three years ago, I know where you are right now," she said quietly and Rain gave her a small nod.

The ride back to the lodge was quiet. When at last they pulled into the drive Kari turned around and looked at them both. "Why don't you stay in the lodge for a few days? You'll be closer so that we can help more. I had Anna make up a room downstairs."

Rain looked dully out of the window. Laurent looked at her and then back to Kari. "Thank you, *reine,* but I think we'll stay in the cabin for now. The time to ourselves will be good," he said before picking Rain up and walking with her down to the path that led to the cabins.

When Laurent walked through the door he saw that Anna had brought them food and fresh flowers and had opened the windows a bit to let the place air out. "Baby, why don't I put you in bed so you can rest?"

"Because I've rested enough. I can't rest this away," she said. "I need to work, Laurent. I'm going to sit here on this couch, facing the lake, and I'm going to sketch."

He brought her an afghan to put over her legs, her sketch book and charcoal. "Can I stay here?" he asked, kneeling beside her.

She turned to him and lunged into his arms. "Don't leave me, Laurent. Please," she whispered into the warm skin of his neck. "I thought that I was going to die, either that or he'd get away with it and drag me back to New York and I'd never see you again."

He sighed. "Oh Rain, you have to know that I'd brave the fires of hell for you. When I opened that door and saw the blood, saw you lying on the floor, pale, lips blue, I thought that I was going to lose you and I knew that I couldn't have survived it. I knew right then that there would have been no life for me if you weren't in the world." He kissed her softly and it built into an all-consuming kiss of passion. He couldn't get enough of the way she smelled, the way she tasted. He kissed her eyelids, her ears, her temples, her forehead, he kissed each lip, her chin and her jawline. Each one a kiss of devotion and possession.

He broke off and sank down onto the floor next to the couch, his head resting against her thigh, eyes closed. He stayed there against her as she sketched until the sun sank low.

"Laurent?" Rain whispered, touching him gently and he awoke. "I need to take a shower. Can you help me please?"

He stood up and helped her to her feet. "Of course. Come on, let me get the water running and some towels. How about your flannel pajamas, the purple ones?"

"Oh that would be lovely," she said as he sat her down in the bathroom and bustled around, turning on the water and going to grab towels and her clothes. The floors of the cabin were heated and a pleasant warmth stole over Rain as she watched Laurent at work.

At last he helped her out of her clothes and undressed himself, easing her into the shower. She stood under the nearly scalding-hot spray and let the water wash over her skin. There were no tears left as Laurent tenderly shampooed her hair and used a washcloth to get rid of the blood and grime that the cursory sponge bath at the hospital hadn't gotten. She refused to leave when it was his turn to wash off, instead she leaned against the wall and held onto his arm while he showered. Her eyes hungrily feasted on the long muscular lines of his body.

After they returned to the living room he turned on the television. "Rain, I'm going to see if someone can't bring us down some dinner. I know that Anna will have made us something special."

Before he could grab the phone though, Jade knocked on the door, carrying a large basket and an ice chest. "I brought you down some dinner. Anna…we didn't want to intrude but we wanted to make sure you ate," she said, holding out the things she'd brought for Laurent to take. "Anna made a beef stew. There's homemade bread, a salad, some strawberry shortcake. Oh and she told me to remind you she'd put milk in your fridge."

"Thank you, Jade. It's very thoughtful. I was just about to call up there to see if we could scrounge some dinner."

Jade hugged him tightly. "I'm so sorry. I love you both so much." She kissed his cheeks and turned to Rain. "Sweetheart, I know you don't have your *maman* near but I want to tell you that I'm here for you. Please think of me as your substitute *maman*, yes? There isn't a thing I can say to make this hurt less so I won't even try. Just know that each and every one of us loves you both and is here for you."

"Thank you, Jade. That means so much to me," Rain said, her voice cracking.

"Oh sweetie. Come here." Jade sat and enveloped her into a hug.

Chapter Twelve

ဆာ

Two weeks later Rain finally began to feel again. Not just the numbness and emptiness of her womb, not just aching loss, but small moments of happiness. She'd finished three paintings in that time, all very dark and haunting.

She and Emma, who'd come by to visit, drank tea out on the deck, watching her house being built across the lake. The builder told Laurent that morning that if everything went according to plan it'd be done in just under three weeks.

"Emma?"

"Hmm?"

"Um, when can I—can Laurent and I—that is, uh, when can we have sex again? I haven't asked until now because I haven't felt the slightest bit sexual. But this morning I was watching Laurent get dressed in our room. The sun glowed off his skin and he looked so handsome, so beautiful and strong. He saw me watching him in the mirror and turned back, our gazes connected. And, um, yeah." Rain smiled as a shiver worked through her at the memory of it. That old surge of lust, of total sexual heat, had returned and singed them both. Laurent's lips had parted slightly, his pupils had dilated and his breathing shallowed.

Emma smiled, taking Rain's hand and squeezing it tightly. "This is good news. I examined you last week, you're fine. Healed up and ready to go. It was all about your hearts at this point anyway."

"Um, about birth control. I can't wrap my head around being pregnant again just now. I need some time. You said there was birth control made for us?"

Emma looked at Rain seriously. "Listen to your inner voice on this. I'm glad you're waiting until you feel ready. I have a month's supply of the pills at home, let me call Sean and have him bring them over. Obviously you can't run down to the pharmacy and get them, we have them specially made. I'll get you several months' more supply in a few days." She went inside and called Sean, who was home with the kids and agreed to bring the pills over.

"Another thing, Rain," Emma told her as she hung up. "We've got a very highly developed sense of smell. An ovulating wolf smells a certain way. The only way I can describe it is we smell like maple syrup."

Rain burst out laughing. "No way!"

"Way," Emma replied, grinning. "So you can do a bit of backup. Just either smell yourself or have Laurent smell you."

"And when I smell like a pancake breakfast use a barrier method?"

"Precisely. The pills won't be effective for two weeks so be careful." She leaned in and took a deep sniff. "You aren't ovulating now but it may happen any time so be vigilant. Even if you wanted to get pregnant again right away I'd caution you to let at least two months pass. You may be a werewolf with healing ability far greater than humans' but your body needs to build strength back up. And your heart needs to recover too."

"I think I'll pop up to the lodge to say hello."

Emma grinned. "It's been so long, everyone will be so happy to see you." She put her hand through Rain's arm and they walked slowly up the path toward the big house, meeting up with Sean on the way.

Sean gave the pills to Rain, kissing her cheek. "The instructions are on a card in the bag."

"Thanks, Sean."

He hugged her. "It's really good to see you. It's been a while since you've been up here."

"Yeah, well, it was time," she said with a shrug. "I'm going to pop in and see if Laurent is around. I'll see you at dinner?"

"If you're going to be here, you bet," Emma said.

Rain walked to the office and knocked on the door. "Yeah," Andreas grunted distractedly.

She poked her head inside. "Am I interrupting?"

Andreas looked up and smiled when he saw it was her. Getting up quickly, he moved around the desk and gave her a hug and a stroke over her jawline. "You interrupt? Never! Now if it were anyone else it'd be interrupting." He winked, indicating the couch near the desks. "Sit down. You know Anna will be here any minute with iced tea and something to eat. I'm sure news that you're visiting has spread to the kitchen by now. Laurent had to run into town to the post office, he'll be back shortly."

Anna indeed did come in with a tray of iced tea and what looked to be turnovers a few moments later.

"Hey there, honey. It's so good to see you up here. It hasn't been the same without you. You should eat though, you look a bit peaky. Here, try one, they're empañadas. I saw the recipe in a magazine. Beef with green olives, garlic and onion. Try one and tell me what you think."

Rain took a bite. "Heaven. Anna, these are really scrumptious. They're my new favorite food."

Andreas nodded in agreement and Anna beamed at the compliment.

"I'm glad you like them. I made them to entice you up to the house for dinner tonight but you beat me to it. We've missed you. I hope you two will stay."

"Anna, you're the best. Yes, Laurent and I will be at dinner tonight."

"Well, that's good to hear," Skye drawled, flopping down onto the couch beside her and perching his head on her shoulder. "I've missed you, Snow White."

"I've missed you too but it's not like you haven't all made ten thousand excuses to come by the cabin four times a day," she said, arching an eyebrow at the chief offender of drop-in visits.

"That's different. And anyway, god knows you needed to look at a truly handsome face to help you through your day. Laurent's ugly mug just can't cut the mustard," Skye said, looking very earnest and Rain burst out laughing.

"What's this? Skye, get your paws off my wife." Laurent growled in jest as he came into the room. His heart lightened to see Rain laughing and teasing with Skye, to see her back and visiting the rest of the Pack at the lodge. She'd been at the cabin since she'd gotten back from the hospital.

Shoving Skye out of the way, he sat down next to her, burying his face in her hair and breathing her in deeply. She sighed in contentment, relaxing back into him.

"I told Anna we'd be here for dinner. Is that all right?"

"Of course."

"Are you finished for the day or do you still have work to do?" she asked, her voice going down an octave. Her hand had worked its way under his shirt and stroked up and down his spine.

He looked at her and time stopped for a moment. He'd been waiting for this to happen between them again. That morning he'd seen her watching him and they'd shared the first heated moment since she'd lost the baby. He reached down and traced her bottom lip with his thumb. A sound of pleasure so raw it shot straight to his cock broke from her lips.

"Um, you two need to get home," Andreas said, his voice a bit shaky. Laurent and Rain threw out so much sex it filled the room, their combined power touching and caressing.

Laurent leaned in and touched Rain's lips with his own, his body lying across half of hers. Her back rested against the arm of the couch as she reached up to stroke her palms over his shoulders and up his neck, stopping when she'd gotten wrist-deep in his hair. She sighed into his mouth and he swallowed the sound eagerly, his body tightening in response.

The lights flickered. "Jesus," Skye whispered.

The flickering lights shook Rain back to awareness. "Laurent, let's go home for a while or we might end up sharing more of our personal life with these boys than they'd prefer. We'll come back for dinner." She pushed him back a bit and blinked slowly and he nodded, helping her to her feet.

"Don't leave on our account. We like to know all about you. Every detail."

Snorting, Andreas smacked Skye as they watched Laurent and Rain leave the room.

They walked slowly back to the cabin and Rain felt as if she were wading through warm honey. He traced circles with his thumb on the hand he held in his. The sensation spread outward, echoing through her like ripples in a pond.

He opened the door for her. "Are you sure?"

Tears sprang from her eyes and she nodded, drawing him to the bedroom. "I am. I need you so much, Laurent. Make it better."

He pulled her hair loose of its clip and slowly unbuttoned her shirt. Drawn to him as always, she gazed up into his face as she pulled the tie holding his hair loose, threading her fingers through the dark softness. His scent filled her nostrils and she inhaled deeply, closing her eyes. His body heated as his desire for her rose, his pheromones working overtime, melting her from the inside out.

He growled low and sexy as he pushed the shirt off her arms. Without pausing he popped the front closure on her bra, freeing her breasts. "So beautiful," he whispered and reverently bent to kiss each nipple. His large hands skimmed over them and she arched into his touch as his lips traveled down over each rib and the flesh of her belly.

On his knees, he yanked her skirt down before standing and picking her up and carefully laying her on their bed. She shivered at the feel of his hands sliding up her calves, up the insides of her thighs, fingertips skimming over her pussy through the panties she still wore until he pulled those off too.

The sight of him there above her, fully clothed as she lay naked before him, brought a rush of honey to her pussy. "You look very much in charge up there, Laurent Cole. I like that a lot. Still, you have entirely too many clothes on."

A wicked grin of promise lit his face and in moments he'd stripped off, his clothes tossed behind him as he crept over the bed toward her.

"Hey! I like a slow unveiling!" she protested and he shook his head, moving to crouch above her.

"Next time," he said as he leaned his mouth to hers. "I don't have the control for slow just now."

Their combined heat flared into an inferno. Hot flames of desire and reconnection licked at their flesh as Laurent slid his body along hers, trailing scorching kisses down her throat, swirling his tongue at the hollow, feasting on her pulse. His hair felt like a living thing, caressing her as it trailed behind his wicked lips and tongue.

She attempted to reach him but he shook his head. "No. If you touch me, I'll lose it. Let me do this. Let me feast on your body. I've missed your fire."

He nibbled just this side of painfully on her nipples, flicking his tongue over them again and again, moving from one breast to the other over and over until she thought she'd die from it. Continuing to kiss down her body, he paused to draw his lips over the curves beneath each breast. She could manage little more than to lie beneath him, writhing from the pleasure of his touch.

He paused to dip his tongue in the well of her navel, bringing a ripple of shivers and a gasp from her. He settled himself between her thighs, put his hands under her ass and brought her pussy to his mouth, serving himself of her body as he nudged her labia open with his tongue.

"Laurent," Rain whispered. It was an entreaty, one that he was happy to answer. Her taste slid into his senses like triumph. She roared through him as her scent wrapped around his cock and squeezed. Long slow licks, pausing to dip into her gate and gather her honey, brought his mouth over the entire map of her cunt over and over. He wanted to roll in her, coat himself with her scent, feed on her desire for hours and hours until she was utterly spent.

But he couldn't because he had to have her. It had been two long weeks since he'd been inside her body. Two weeks that he'd wanted to connect with her in this way, watching her grieve and ache at their loss. And now he was where he wanted to be most in the world.

He relearned every bump, every fold of flesh, every dip and ridge of her. Her clit bloomed under his ministrations until her thighs trembled and her head thrashed on the pillow. Her fingers tunneled through his hair, clutching strongly enough to bring tears to his eyes. When she came it was with a cry from deep within her, a cry of love and pleasure but also the residual of anguish and sadness.

He licked her slowly, gently as she relaxed, still panting, muscles jumping from the aftershocks of his loving.

Sitting up slowly, Rain pushed him on his back, smiling down at him all the while. After kissing his lips and tasting herself there she moved the kisses down the warm column of his neck, stopping at the place where it met his shoulder and breathing in deep. A growl trickled from her lips and his hands on her hips convulsed and tightened in response.

She ran her tongue over and over his pebbled nipples and he arched into her mouth. "I've missed you, I've missed this," he whispered.

A smile curved her mouth before she continued kissing him, licking over each rib and each band of muscle in his belly. Her fingernails traced the path of dark, silky hair from his navel to his cock and down to his balls. She lowered her head and took him into her mouth and he groaned.

241

There was nothing else in the universe except for the warm wet cavern of her lips and mouth over him, the cool tickle of her hair trailing along his stomach and thighs, the fingers she stroked up and down the inside of his thighs and over his stomach.

"Rain," he said with clenched teeth as he pulled her gently away. "I need to be inside you. Shall I get a condom?" He knew she wasn't ready to be pregnant again. Neither one of them was ready yet.

"No. Emma says I'm not ovulating right now. We can talk more about that later. Right now I have an itch that you need to scratch," she said as she pulled her knees up, feet flat on the mattress, looking up at him with carnal invitation as the glistening flesh of her pussy opened to his view.

"You don't have to tell me twice," he said, settling himself between her thighs. She reached down between them and helped guide his cock to her as he leaned forward, bracing his weight on his elbow.

He nearly lost his mind as he pressed into her. He wanted to be gentle but it was a challenge as her warm wet body enfolded him, rippling around his cock. He felt an unbelievable sense of rightness in that moment. Rain must have felt it too because she sighed long and low as he slid home.

His gaze never left hers as he slowly slid in and out of her. They shared so much more than physical lovemaking in those moments. Yes, they were bound by the ceremony and shared a connected link but as he looked down into her eyes just at that moment it was as if tiny filaments had come from her body and wrapped around his heart and soul. It was the most intimate moment he'd ever shared with her and he knew that it would be all right. They'd make it past this low point and move on to much happier times.

"It's going to be okay, Laurent," she murmured thickly, as if she'd read his mind, and he nodded solemnly.

"Rain, I love you, *mon coeur.*"

"I love you too, Laurent, always and forever."

* * * * *

"They made the lights flicker?" Ryan asked incredulously.

"No kidding! Ask Andreas. When she touched his skin it was as if we were in a jungle. I swear, their sexual energy made the room hot and humid. You could literally feel it. And when he touched her lips and she made this *sound* of arousal the lights flickered."

"Wow. Too bad I missed that," Ryan said, looking a bit awed.

"Ah, here they come now and wow, is that a postcoital glow or what?" Skye grinned as he approached them. "Hey, hot stuff. Come to trade up?" he asked, kissing her cheek and rubbing his face along her jawline.

"You wish," Laurent growled and Skye waggled his eyebrows in agreement with that assessment.

When Laurent and Rain went to the dining room everyone had come to give hugs and nuzzles. Hellie squealed in delight to see Rain and insisted on sitting next to her at the big table.

"Uncle Skye, I need your chair because Rain needs me to sit next to her in case she wants a hug," Hellie said seriously and Skye nodded solemnly and moved down a seat. Rain smiled down at Hellie and kissed the top of her head.

"Thank you so much, Hellie, you knew just what I needed," Rain said to her, winking at Skye when Helene turned her head.

Dinner was normal. And that was just what Rain needed. After dinner though, they put the kids down and went to gather in the great room to talk.

"Rain, did I tell you that a business associate of mine saw one of your paintings hanging in Devon and Perri's firm and went crazy? He wants to talk to you about commissioning something. He's been raving about you. I have his card in my office, I'll give it to you after a while," Andreas said, breaking the silence.

"Really? Wow. I had no idea that Devon and Perri even bought one of my paintings. In fact, I don't know who bought any of them at all. I need to talk with Diane, I've done three new paintings and she wanted to see them."

"I don't think anyone who hadn't seen your work before the show had the slightest idea of just how talented you truly are. Kari and I bought *King's Men*, it's in our bedroom. I had to pull rank and go behind everyone's back to snap it up because three other people wanted it. The brawl ensued when all of the paintings got sold and the Pack wanted more." Andreas laughed. "Bert tried to get Devon and Perri to draw straws for it but Perri told him no way. I know some of us are going to be at the Portland show early to snap up paintings before anyone else."

"Everyone has been so good to me. I don't know that I can ever repay your kindness." She looked around the room and realized that these people who'd been total strangers just months ago were her family. It touched her deeply to know that they bought her work.

"You don't repay family, Rain. We love you and you've got an amazing talent." Laurent said softly, taking her hand in his own and running his thumb over her knuckles.

"Thank you, Laurent. Thank you, everyone," she said, putting his hand to her lips and kissing him.

Skye patted the couch next to him. "Have a heart, you two. Come sit by me, Rain, because I can't deal with another one of the sex power spillovers that you and Laurent create every time you touch each other. Andreas can go upstairs to Kari but Phillip, Ryan and I are all sleeping alone tonight." He grinned.

"So I take it it's rare," Rain said, sitting next to Skye, putting her head on his shoulder.

"Well, Kari spills power when she's challenging someone or showing a dominance display. It's electric, like static electricity. I've met another mated pair who has a similar spill to yours and Laurent's but nowhere near the range and level of energy that you two put out," Andreas said, sipping a brandy. He shrugged. "It's certainly something to behold and it says a lot about the power of your bond. I notice that it really began to happen after the bonding ceremony. Your wolves recognize each other to be sure."

"Yeah, recognize and want to hump," Ryan added with a laugh.

"Rain, can you come taste this for me?" Anna called from the kitchen. "I've made that pineapple upside-down cake you like so much but I tried a new recipe."

Rain lit up, nearly clapping with joy as she hopped off the couch and headed into the kitchen.

"It's good to have her back." Phillip laughed at her excitement.

"I agree," Laurent said softly. He knew everyone had been hurting for them both, feeling helpless in the face of the pain they both endured.

"When are you going to try to have another baby?" Ryan asked, now that Rain had left.

"I don't know. I'm leaving it up to her. She's going to use birth control for the time being. I don't want to rush her. It's her body and she's the one who had to bear the physical loss of the baby. You know, she felt him move just before we left the gallery that night."

"I didn't know that. God, Laurent, how awful for both of you," Skye said.

"I'd like to try again within the next six months but I don't even want to broach the subject right now. She's healing but I don't want to pressure her or set her back."

"Good idea," Andreas said.

Chapter Thirteen

ഇ

Rain stood in front of the mirror in the bedroom she and Laurent shared in Portland. It was twenty minutes until she needed to be at the gallery for her show. She wore a forest green velvet blouse and a short black skirt. Pretty boots rode her legs to her knees. Her hair was twisted into a French braid and she wore the ruby and diamond earrings Laurent had given her.

Laurent sat on the bed, putting on his watch and looking at his mate's black hair gleaming in the lamplight. He smiled then, she looked so amazing, so confident and self-assured. He got up and walked to her, wrapping his arms around her waist and looking at her in the mirror. "You look beautiful, Rain," he said in her ear, nipping the lobe slightly but enough to make her shiver.

She gave him a sexy smile. "Thank you, love. You look good as always. I told you that shirt would look perfect with those pants."

He rolled his eyes. "You were right. We should get going. Skye went to grab the car and pull it around." They stayed in the Pack-owned apartment not too very far from the gallery in Portland's Pearl District.

She grabbed the black velvet wrap that Drew had made for her and Laurent helped her put it across her shoulders. "This is pretty. Drew has an eye for pretty things." He raised a brow and Rain laughed at the suggestive comment.

After one last look in the mirror they walked hand in hand into the living room where everyone waited.

The small gallery was already packed when Rain arrived. She'd already been by earlier in the day to look over everything and check in with Diane. It was still ten minutes before the official opening and already her friends from Seattle were there as well as the entire Cherchez Clan. Laurent stayed glued to her side, memories of the last show still burned into his brain.

Twenty minutes later, as Rain sipped a glass of champagne, Diane saw her and came over. "Rain, darling, you're a hit again! The doors have only been open a short while and you've just sold out again! Didn't I tell you that you had a promising career ahead of you? Congratulations, my dear. I'd like to do another show for you in about six months, what do you say?"

"How about eight months and I think that it's only fair to renegotiate our commission split," Rain said, grinning, and Diane threw back her head and laughed.

"Eight months it is and I'll have our lawyer call you about the commission split later on in the month."

Laurent hugged her tightly.

"I think you and I need to go on our honeymoon. I can afford to treat you now. Somewhere warm and tropical sounds good," Rain murmured into his ear.

"Hmmm. You in a bikini? Sun, sand, tropical drinks? Sounds good. Although you know, we still haven't had a more elaborate wedding ceremony."

"Laurent, we don't need that. We had our own little ceremony and that was enough. A honeymoon though, yes, I think that's a necessity. Jamaica? Virgin Islands? The Bahamas?"

"One of the Pack members is a travel agent, we should talk to him and see what's out there right now," he said, lips against her ear enticingly.

Suddenly Rain froze and a panicked sound came from her throat. Laurent went on alert and, seeing that, Ryan and Skye surrounded Rain. Instantly Phillip and Alek pushed Kari and

Andreas back. More males began to surround Rain until she wasn't visible at all.

"Julia? Are you there? You don't have to be afraid. I didn't bring your father with me."

Rain pushed her way through the circle of males, gently reassuring them that she was fine. Laurent wasn't convinced and he stood in front of her such that she sighed in annoyance and looked around him. "Mom? What are you doing here?"

"You said you had a show for your paintings. I've missed so much of your life, I just wanted to be here. Your father isn't here but he does know I am." The petite overly done woman looked around Laurent's massive frame to try to talk to Rain.

"Laurent, for god's sake it's just my mother. Nothing's going to happen. There are thirty of you here protecting me. Please let me go to her," she said calmly in his ear and he looked annoyed but stepped aside, staying right at her side.

Rain enveloped her mother in a hug. "Mom. I've missed you so much."

"Me too, sweetheart."

Rain turned and looked at Laurent. "Mom, this is my husband, Laurent Cole. Laurent, this is my mother, Patrice Margoles."

"I'm so happy to meet you. From what I understand you're very good to my daughter and you've protected her. Thank you for that. I'm ashamed I didn't do more."

"And what, Mom? Risk your life? You did enough to get me the money and help me get out."

"Are you telling me you wouldn't risk your life for your child? Didn't you? Didn't you nearly die to try to save your baby from Anthony?" Patrice said quietly.

Rain looked stricken at the memory and Laurent growled, raising the hairs on Patrice's arms. "I'm sorry, can we not discuss this right now? It upsets Rain deeply." Laurent put his arm around Rain's waist and dropped a kiss on the top of her head.

"I'm sorry. I-I didn't come here to upset you. I just wanted to see you, it's been so long and I've missed you so much. It upset me too, you know? I'm sorry."

Rain smiled. "I've missed you too. I'm glad to see you. How long are you here for? I'd love for you to see our house."

"I can't. I have to leave in an hour. Your father, well, he's your father, you know how he is." Patrice looked down at the ground.

"Let's go and grab a coffee then," Rain said, grabbing her mother's hand. "Visit a bit before you have to go back. I'll even take you to the airport."

"Your show. You can't just leave."

"I've been here half an hour. I've sold out the show. I haven't seen you in a year and a half. I'd love to talk to you, to see how Suzanne is."

"If you're sure."

"*We'll* take you to coffee then," Laurent said, still not trusting his mother-in-law.

"Oh good, I'd like to get to know you." Patrice smiled hopefully.

Laurent leaned over and told Skye that he and Rain were taking her mother to coffee and then to the airport. Andreas came forward and insisted Skye come with them. Rain bristled but she knew it wasn't an argument she could win.

At Peet's near the airport, Rain and her mother visited. Her mother cried as Rain described the miscarriage and Anthony's crazy behavior. Her mother told her Pietro had refused to allow any mention of Julia's name in his presence but that she'd stood up to him and he'd allowed her to come to Portland but only for the day.

"Mom, why do you stay? He's such an asshole. Come and live with us. Or don't if you don't want to. We'll get you a place nearby if you don't want to live with us."

"He's my husband, Julia. We've been together for thirty years. I have no skills, I've never lived alone. What would I do?"

"You could be a grandma to my children. There will be children, Mom. I hate that you're on the other side of the country."

Patrice sighed. "Honey, he's my husband and he's not all bad. He treats me decently enough. I can't walk away from my life like you did. You're brave and young and you have passion and talent and drive. I'm old."

Rain laughed. "You're fifty-six! That isn't old by a long shot."

"You always were my favorite," Patrice said with a small laugh. "I'll come back out when you have a baby, I promise." She dug a large expandable folder out of her bag, handing it across the table to Rain. "In the meantime, you're owed this. Even your father agrees."

Rain opened the thick package and saw that there was a stack of money inside. "What is this?"

"It's thirty thousand dollars. It was part of your dowry for your marriage to Anthony. Take it, put a down payment on a house, go on vacation, start a college fund for my future grandbabies." Patrice looked at her watch. "I have to go, my plane is leaving in an hour and they won't let me check in if I don't get there soon."

They went to the airport and walked Patrice to the security checkpoint. Rain hugged her mother tightly and kissed both cheeks. "I am so glad you came, Mom. Fly safe. I love you."

"I love you too, Julia, or rather, Rain," Patrice said and in minutes was gone from sight.

Laurent got one side and Skye got the other and each of them put arms around shoulders and waist respectively and they headed back to the car.

"Only my mother would get on a damned plane with thirty grand in cash," Rain murmured and Skye laughed. "Thank you for coming tonight, Skye. You've been so wonderful to me and Laurent through all of this. I'm glad you're in our life."

Skye smiled, winking at her and then at Laurent, who looked at him appraisingly. "It's my pleasure, cupcake."

By the time they returned to the apartment Kari and Andreas had already gone to their room and everyone else was out or asleep.

Skye kissed Rain's lips quickly and hugged Laurent before heading into the kitchen. He turned, standing in the doorway. "You two up for a glass or three of wine?"

Rain laughed. "After all the craziness of tonight? Yes, that sounds good."

Laurent kissed her forehead, chuckling. "I'd wager you're hungry too?"

"Are you volunteering to forage for me?"

"Well if by forage you mean get some grapes and cheese, perhaps some crackers, yes."

"Mmm. Forage away. I'll totally have sex with you if you bring me chocolate."

His eyes deepened in color as he followed Skye into the kitchen. After she'd looked her fill at both very fine behinds she went into their room and changed from her dressy clothes into a pair of loose-fitting yoga pants and a tank top.

When they returned, arms filled with food and wine, she was in the process of shaking her hair loose of its braid, massaging her scalp.

She bounded over and hopped on the bed, tossing out pillows for Skye and Laurent to prop on.

Wine was poured and Rain fluttered her lashes at Laurent when she noted the dark chocolate on the plate with the grapes and cheese. "My, someone's getting lucky later."

"Really? The chocolate was my choice." Skye winked at her and a shiver ran up her spine.

Laurent chuckled. "What do you think, baby? Is Skye going to get lucky tonight?"

She blushed but couldn't deny the idea made her wet. "I don't know. I mean, he's here with us so..." Her words trailed off as she shrugged, taking a huge gulp of wine.

They sat there, drinking wine and snacking, the tension growing, heady and tantalizing. Skye rested his head on Rain's legs as Rain idly played with his hair. Laurent sat behind her, kneading her shoulders, absently kissing her neck.

Skye's normally flirtatious manner had mellowed. Because it was real. The attraction hung in the air and stroked over Laurent's skin like a caress. Laurent loved the way Skye looked at Rain, like she was a precious thing. Not in an adoring fashion, it would have been too close, too uncomfortable in that way. But Skye saw the things under the surface that made Rain so appealing. And that appealed to Laurent. In a sense Laurent wanted to share that with Skye. Wanted to unite with his friend, a man who saw his woman for the special person she was, to bring her pleasure. And in doing so to comfort her as well.

Laurent watched Rain closely, scenting her honey. His eyes met Skye's, which had gone dark and glossy. Laurent knew those eyes like he knew the scent of his woman when she was turned on.

Skye had been on the outside as his friends had found their Mates one after the other. He'd watched as they started families and built lives together. Laurent knew what that loneliness felt like, he'd been there not even a year ago.

And Rain had been through the wringer in the last eighteen months. On the run from her father, being kidnapped and assaulted, losing their child. The appearance of her mother had shaken her deeply. Her laughter that night had been edgy, he could feel her tension through their link.

He wanted to comfort her and comfort his friend and he couldn't deny the allure of the idea of the three of them together.

"Rain, are you attracted to Skye?" he murmured in her ear as he leaned over her shoulder.

Startled, she laughed. "He's a beautiful, smart and funny man and a powerful wolf. What's not to be attracted to?" Getting to her knees, she went to him and put her arms around his neck. "But there's a problem. He's not you. I seem to have a terrible attraction to this big bad wolf who talks dirty in French."

"Would you like his mouth on your pussy?"

Her breath caught and Skye moaned softly. Laurent caught his friend's gaze and knew Skye had been thinking the same way he had.

"Why?" Rain's voice was breathy as she sat back to look at him.

"Why?"

"Yes, why? Are you asking me if I'd betray you? If I want another male sexually instead of you? Or are you asking if I find him sexy in a general sense and fuckable in an entirely fantasy-type way? Because the answer is different depending on just what you're asking and why."

He nodded as he mulled over what she'd said. "Okay, I see your point. Not only that but I like your point." He turned his gaze to Skye. "And what about you?"

"I don't think you fully answered Rain's question."

"Fair enough. Rain, under some well-defined circumstances, would you like Skye in our bed tonight?"

"Um." She blinked quickly.

Laurent laughed. "I know he's attracted to you. I see you're attracted to him. He's hurting and lonely without a Mate and he wants to reach out and comfort you as well. Comfort us. And I want to comfort both of you."

Skye nodded. "Very succinct. And correct. I am attracted to Rain. Yes, I'd be honored to share your bed tonight. If that's what she wants as well. She's a very sexual being, she's beautiful, strong and creative." He ran a tentative hand up Rain's spine and her eyes slid halfway closed a moment before she cleared her throat. "And yours. I understand that and have a deep desire to find it for myself with my own Mate."

Laurent felt better at that.

"How…what?" Rain stumbled over her thoughts in the rush of endorphins and testosterone these two males poured off.

"No penetration of anything but your mouth. I don't want him to come inside you. Is that all right with you? I want to see you on fire between me and my dear friend. I want to let him glimpse a small part of your beauty, to share that with him. But not if you're uncomfortable. And I want to keep the boundaries here very clear. You're my Mate. My woman. No other man's seed inside your body, ever."

She shivered at the way he wanted to give her pleasure but still was possessive. "I'd be lying if I said the idea didn't turn me on. I just want to be sure you're going to be okay with me afterward. With him. We see each other every day. And um, will you two be, er, you know?"

Laurent laughed as he looked around her to Skye for a moment. "As I told you, this isn't unheard of, especially with unmated males and mated couples. You take up my entire libido, Rain. I don't know how to explain it. I like to look at Skye naked, he's very nice to look at in general. And if cocks or mouths touch that's icing. I don't plan to fuck him. Or anyone but you for that matter. As for the other? Skye knows what you and I are, you heard it just now. And tomorrow you'll be the same woman you are to me tonight. We'll just have another memory to add to a lifetime."

Skye watched them, his hands gently stroking over Rain's legs and back. "Rain, this is up to you. I'm your friend, first and foremost. That's not going to change tomorrow. It'll be special, this sharing. This will be what it is and nothing more." He smiled, quieting to let the two of them work it out, and Rain appreciated that.

Desire, heady and sweet, stole over Rain's senses. As a human woman this scenario, while nice wank material, would have freaked her out. She wouldn't have believed it would work. But as a werewolf she knew the power of the Pack. The feel of the stroke of another of her family. The way it resonated, the need to touch and be touched. Certainly she'd seen a lot of public sexual expression and affection since she'd transformed and it hadn't shocked her. It did indeed seem natural. And she'd be a damned liar if she denied her curiosity and the heat building between the three of them at that very moment.

Taking a leap that wasn't so big after all, Rain leaned into Laurent's body to kiss him. Softly at first but then passionately, a melding of lips and tongues. A new scent joined the one Rain had grown familiar with. *Skye.*

He moved to his knees behind her, pressing against her back. She felt her hair being drawn to the side and his lips met her skin. Laurent swallowed her gasp of surprised pleasure eagerly as he nipped her bottom lip.

Her hands yanked at the front of Laurent's shirt and he helped her get the buttons loose and the cufflinks off. She shoved his shirt off and a blast of heat from his upper body bathed her.

Her hands slid over those familiar and yet still so very sexy muscles and Skye's tongue, warm and slick, flicked out and teased the hollow just beneath her ear.

"Naked. Both of you," she gasped and moved to stand.

Laurent, looking confident and very much in charge, got off the bed and disposed of socks, pants and boxers and moved behind her.

Skye stood and went to stand before her. "I think I need your help."

Rain's hands moved to his waist and under the hem of his shirt, finding the skin warm and so very hard. Each button showed more of his body. A body she'd tried not to look at overlong but now had the chance. Where Laurent was bulked, Skye's muscles were flat and whip-hard. Rain moved to kiss his chest over his heart.

In a flash Skye's pants were off and Laurent had tossed her to the bed. Wearing a smile, she looked up at them, side by side. "My, grandmother, you look so very big."

"Oh Snow White, you're mixing your fairy tales. But I like it." Skye winked.

"Take your hair down, both of you."

Laurent reached up with one hand to remove the tie while the other hand grasped her pant leg and yanked. When his hair was free, he used the other hand to get rid of the pants, leaving her in a scrap of barely there lace. "The shirt now, Rain. I want to see your breasts."

Wriggling, Rain took off the tank and got rid of the bra, lying back against the bed in nothing but a pair of pink panties and a smile.

"I think you said something about a mouth on a pussy?" Skye asked Laurent.

Bowing, and making his cock bob with the movement, Laurent gracefully waved his arm toward Rain. "Be my guest."

Rain's eyes widened as Skye got on the bed and crawled toward her. His hair wasn't quite as long as Laurent's and was more blue-black than Laurent's dark chocolate. Still it was soft as it whispered against her legs as he moved between them.

Not taking his gaze from her own, he bent one knee up and kissed the back, drawing the flat of his tongue over the sensitive skin. A trail of openmouthed kisses burned her as he moved up toward her pussy.

Laurent moved to her side, lazily stroking a tongue over one of her nipples as he watched Skye.

Slowly Skye drew her panties off, tossing them over his shoulder before turning back and widening her thighs.

A bolt of heat spread through her when Skye's tongue slid through the folds of her pussy. Laurent gave long slow licks but Skye's tongue was quick and agile, much like he was. Funny how that worked. She'd never had oral sex in her life before Laurent and she'd come to enjoy it very much. And the man currently at work on her cunt knew what he was about, liked it.

Her back arched as Laurent's teeth grazed her nipple. Sweet heaven, the sheer abundance of pleasure was overwhelming. She reached down around the arm Laurent leaned on and found his cock hard and weeping at the slit. Her thumb slid over that wetness, spreading it in big circles.

"Laurent, I want your cock in my mouth," she murmured before gasping as Skye dipped his tongue deep into her and found his way back up to her clit.

"Later. I promise later. I want to fuck you and then you can suck my cock. First though, come." Strain edged his voice.

She didn't have long to wait. Laurent's mouth on her nipples, Skye's on her pussy, hands stroking over her skin, two men so very virile and masculine that she fairly drowned in the testosterone—it all built up until she was ready to overflow. When Skye's fingers dipped into her gate and his mouth suctioned over her clit as his tongue relentlessly flicked against it she came so hard she brought blood when she clamped onto her lip to keep from screaming loud enough to wake everyone. As it was, the heat from her orgasm and the combined pheromones she and Laurent threw off hung heavy in the air and the candles they'd lit when they'd returned to the apartment flickered.

Laurent flipped her over to her hands and knees as she straddled Skye.

"Something tells me you two have done this before." She looked back over her shoulder at Laurent, whose face showed strain as he pressed his cock into her still-fluttering pussy.

"Hmpf. There's no one but you in the world. Who can remember what life was like before that?"

Rain laughed as she turned back to Skye, her breasts moving forward as Laurent hilted inside her completely. She drew her hands slowly up the muscles of his legs and thighs. A smile curved one corner of her mouth as she beckoned him to her with a crook of her finger.

He leaned up and kissed her and she tasted herself on his lips. It was different, the way she tasted there instead of how she tasted on Laurent's and yet he was Pack. He was hers in a sense and it was all okay, the way he raced through her blood.

She kissed down his chin and neck and he flopped back on the bed as she adjusted herself to grab his cock in one hand, looking closely at him. It wasn't like she hadn't seen him naked, she had many times when they ran. But this was different so she looked her fill. Long and lean and a hitch to the left. A dark shock of hair at the root contrasted with the pale skin.

She wanted to take him in her mouth but she didn't know what was all right with Laurent.

He flexed his hips, driving himself into her cunt hard and deep, moving his lips to her ear. "Do you want to suck his cock, Rain?"

Her back arched, curving to take more of him as she turned into his face. "Do *you* want me to?"

He grabbed her hair, wrapping it around his hand. "Yes. Don't swallow," he murmured, his lips cruising down her neck as he let his grip loosen enough so she could turn back and face Skye, who looked up at her, eyes glossy, smiling at her.

"Give it to me, Snow White."

Bending down, she caressed the thick length of his cock with her cheek, breathing in his scent before angling him with her hand so she could take him into her mouth, her tongue swirling down as lowered herself onto him.

Laurent watched her, catching glimpses of her mouth and Skye's cock as her hair parted around her movements. Her pussy was an inferno and he teetered on the verge of coming but he wasn't ready to let go just then. He wanted to hold out as long as he could.

Watching her was the sexiest thing he'd ever seen and the way she'd looked to him before going down on Skye had renewed his confidence in his bond with her. They could share this moment and enjoy it for what it was and know it had nothing on the connection he shared with her.

His eyes met with Skye's and his friend smiled up at him. Laurent wanted to throw back his head and howl with joy. This beautiful creature was his. He'd wake up every day for the rest of his life as hers and she his.

"Fuck," he murmured as he lost the battle and fell deeply into climax as he pressed into her, his fingers gripping the muscles of her hips.

"Rain, honey, I'm so close," Skye gasped out. Rain let go of him with her mouth and Laurent pulled out. She lay down, putting her head on his thigh, and used the wetness from her mouth to continue stroking his cock. Skye's hand joined hers, his fingers threading with hers.

Laurent licked up her spine and moved his eyes to Skye's face as he came.

After a quick cleanup Laurent bounded back into bed, followed by Skye. Both men looked at Rain, who laughed a deep, throaty laugh laced with promise.

Chapter Fourteen

ဩ

Several nights later, back at home as they lay in their bed in the new house, watching the night sky through the large windows, Laurent asked, "You said there would be more babies?"

Rain smiled. She'd been wondering when he'd ask. She'd mentioned it to her mother at the coffee shop and he'd tensed and leaned into her so she knew he'd bring it up when he was ready. "Yes. It's been four months. It's not like it still doesn't hurt but I think it's time to move on. Move forward. That is, if you want to. I know you've been letting me decide the pace for this and I appreciate it so much. Having the luxury to deal with losing our son and letting go without pressure has been wonderful."

"Do I want to have a child with you? Hell yes, Rain. I want to have ten children with you. I want to fill up every room in our house with them. And I gave you time because we both needed it."

"Um, let me just state up front that there is no way I'm having ten children. That being said, I think we should try again when we go on our vacation. Sun, sand, lots of hot monkey love."

"Sounds like the perfect vacation to me. I suppose I can live without ten children, but we should negotiate backward from there. I think we can think of some incentives that might get me lower than five." He arched an eyebrow invitingly and she laughed.

* * * * *

261

The phone cradled in her neck, Rain multitasked as she tossed her newly purchased vacation clothes into their suitcase. A black bikini with a green metallic fleck through it, a powder blue tank suit, a few new pieces of lingerie—all to help with the whole baby-making plan. Not that they needed any help in the romance department, she and Laurent were still making the lights flicker on a regular basis, but it never hurt to show a bit of special interest for a special occasion. And she was due to ovulate sometime within the next three or four days.

On hold with the hotel in Maui—she wanted to arrange to have chilled champagne in the room when they got there—she rolled her eyes, pushing away any feelings of annoyance because after all, they'd be on their way in a few hours. One of her new clients who'd just commissioned a massive painting from her had sweetened the deal and put himself at the head of the line by picking them up in his helicopter and flying them to SeaTac Airport, saving them several hours of driving.

The hotel finally got on the line and agreed to have the champagne for her and Laurent, and in apology for making her wait so long on hold they threw in an appetizer platter as well. *Score.*

Rain finished packing and zipped everything up, grabbed the plane tickets, the itinerary, the traveler's checks and the carry-on that had the books, magazines and Laurent's snacks in it and dragged them all to the foyer. She put Laurent's laptop bag back in the bedroom with a snort.

The house had turned out so beautifully. Instead of the more rustic architecture of the other houses on the lake and the lodge, Laurent and Rain's home was modern. Lots of glass and angles and Rain loved it. Her attached studio had skylights and opened to the shoreline of the lake. When she returned from the trip Rain would start to plant a wildflower garden along the back of the house.

The master suite looked out the rear of the lot into the forest and off to the side that didn't have any houses. It was on the first level and had large glass-panel doors that slid into pockets in the wall so essentially the entire wall opened up to the outside. Rain wanted to take wildflowers and natural plants and fill their view with them. She'd chosen the stones to make the walk to the path on the north of the house that led to the main trail back to the other houses and the lodge—a blue gray octagon-shaped stone—and it was in their garden shed waiting for the rain to let up so she could lay it.

There was another bedroom downstairs adjoining the master suite that would be the nursery. There were four more bedrooms upstairs and an office for Laurent next to Rain's studio. It was home and Rain loved it more each day as they filled it up with memories.

Pulling the last suitcase into foyer, Rain straightened to watch Laurent walk up the path to their front door, smiling at her. He looked so relaxed and handsome, better than he had in months.

"Ready, baby?"

"Yep. The suitcases are here along with the carry-on and my purse. I have your magazines and book and that trail mix that Anna makes that you like so much. Oh and some Goldfish and Doritos too." The man couldn't live an hour without eating so she had lots of snacks to take on the long flight.

He grabbed the suitcase and locked the door behind her. There were no roads on their side of the lake so Laurent brought the golf cart to carry their stuff in. The helicopter would land in the field abutting the lodge.

"Our fancy ride should be here in a few minutes. Ryan will pick us up from the airport. I'll email him from Maui."

"No you won't. Your laptop is back at home. You promised that you wouldn't do any work while we were gone. I made a copy of our itinerary for Andreas so Ryan can get all the info he needs from that."

"You left my laptop at home?"

Rain looked at him, eyebrow raised. "And what would you use it for? I mean, we both *know* you'd never break your promise to me by working secretly and of course, you've got a lot of work to do with me. So what would you do with it?"

Laurent sighed, he knew he couldn't win this argument. He pulled the cart into the shed and took their bags to the clearing and joined Rain, where she kissed the kids and their gathered friends goodbye.

"So?" Skye asked as Laurent approached.

Laurent pulled out his wallet and gave Skye a ten and another to Ryan. Ryan burst out laughing. "I knew it!"

"What's going on, Laurent?" Rain asked.

"We bet him that you'd make him leave his laptop home. He said you'd buy his lame line about using it for fun and sending me the flight information," Ryan said.

Rain raised an eyebrow at him. "Hmmm, betting on me were you? You can make it up to me later," she purred and turned back to her conversation with Emma.

Laurent felt his insides melt and he smiled at the thought of just how he would make it up to her.

"I hear the helicopter approaching, let's get out there," Rain said, hugging Emma and Kari one last time.

The flight to Maui was long. Rain slept, resting her head in the hollow of Laurent's shoulder while he read his book and gobbled her lunch, his lunch and the snacks she'd brought.

The resort was secluded and they had a private beach cabin with a hot tub and outdoor shower on their lanai. Once they got settled Rain shrugged off her clothes and sauntered outside with a look over her shoulder at him. He growled and the fine hairs all over Rain's body stood at attention. He tossed off his clothes and stalked toward her, his wolf showing in his eyes. She trembled with recognition of his feral nature, of their elemental desire for each other, as her pussy grew wet and her nipples hardened.

"Very daring, Rain," he said in a husky whisper as he backed her against the side of the hot tub.

"The feel of the breeze on my skin is very enticing. You and me, naked and outside, it's always a combination that does it for me," she said slowly as her hands moved over the muscles on his chest.

He dropped to his knees and rubbed his face along her calves and thighs. Her hands twined through his hair. "I want you, Rain. Right here and right now."

"Oh yes." She moaned and he stood up and turned her so that she faced the hot tub. Deftly, he spread her legs apart and slid inside her and she gasped and arched her back, her head resting on his shoulder. He bent his knees and thrust into her and her body welcomed him home. Their combined energy whipped around them like a mini-tornado. "Laurent, Laurent, Laurent," she whispered over and over again as her flesh took his in an embrace as old as humanity.

"Oh baby, you feel so good. I love you so damned much." He growled and they both exploded and slowly sank to the ground in a heap of sweaty tangled limbs.

"This is the best vacation I've ever been on," she joked and he chuckled.

* * * * *

Six days later a very nauseated Rain came back into the lodge, Laurent right behind her, looking concerned. Emma saw them and chuckled. "Welcome back, you two. I'll go get my medical bag but I'm guessing you know the source of the nausea already."

Laurent sighed. "She's been sick for the last two days."

Sean brought Rain some crackers and Anna bustled off to get her some tea. Emma took the blood test and beamed at them both. "Congratulations, you two!"

Laurent knelt before Rain and put his head in her lap. "Thank you, baby, you do me such a great honor."

Rain caressed his face and then shoved him out of the way and ran to the bathroom.

* * * * *

Over the next months Laurent proceeded to treat Rain as if she was made of glass and she chafed at it. Her hormones flared, just as the other females had promised her, and Laurent wore a grin all day long.

Rain sauntered into the lodge one afternoon and saw Laurent sitting with Skye and Andreas, drinking lemonade and playing cards. Her body tightened and the clarion call of her need rang through her.

"Laurent," she said and he looked up and the others just sat back as the wash of sexual energy flowed over them. Rain projected even stronger now that she was pregnant.

Laurent stood and walked toward her, already hard. Her voice—her presence—made him want to take her every single time he thought of her or she came into view. Rain emanated such an earthy sexuality that his wolf rose each time she came near him. He could feel the waves of the consciousness separating his two halves vibrate. "Yes, baby?" he answered, reaching out and running his cheek along hers, the air shimmering with heat.

"I need you. Now."

"We need to use the office," Laurent murmured and they walked in the door and he kicked it closed.

Inside the office Laurent sat in his chair, foot braced so that it wouldn't move. Skirt hiked up to her thighs, Rain lowered herself onto him and they both gasped. They'd already made love three times that day and Rain had shown no signs of being sated. He remembered Andreas whining about being sexed out when Kari was pregnant but so far Laurent was very happy with the situation. He woke her up each day by bringing her to pleasure at least twice and then making love to her. He went home at ten for a nice midmorning lovemaking session and then again at lunch, at three and then before dinner, after dinner and at bedtime.

After their climax he helped her to stand and cleaned up before putting his cock away. He grinned at her and caressed her stomach. She was three months along, only a month to go to her due date. They'd decided not to find out the gender of the baby but when Rain saw the ultrasound she *was* relieved she wasn't carrying twins.

"Feeling better, baby? Can you hold off for another hour or so?" He chuckled and she arched a brow.

"We'll see," she said and they went back out into the other room where Andreas and Skye still played cards.

"Hey, Snow White, feeling better now? I don't think I've ever seen Laurent smile so much." Skye chuckled and ran his face along Rain's rounded belly. Things hadn't changed between Rain and Skye after their night in Portland. There was a bit more teasing but she never felt uncomfortable with him and the vivid image of her mouth touching Skye's as they both kissed Laurent's cock would never leave her brain. In fact, it brought a new round of shivers and she had to look back at her man, wanting him all over again.

Laurent smiled even more broadly at that. "I seem to recall Andreas whining about Kari wanting sex so much when she got to this stage. I must have the stamina he lacked because I'm quite happy to take care of my beautiful Mate as many times a day as she wishes."

"Well it's hell on the electricity flow here at the lodge when you two go off to a closet or the bathroom or wherever. I had to buy new surge protectors for the computers," Ryan said, coming into the room and giving Rain's belly a caress. "It's too bad you don't need us to bring in a relief pitcher, Laurent, I'd gladly volunteer for the job," he said, winking at Rain.

Laurent growled but this time it seemed real and they all stilled and looked at him. Ryan put his hands up. "I apologize, Laurent, I was only joking."

Laurent shook his head as if to clear it. "No, I apologize. I realize you were joking. The level of hormones Rain is putting out is very hard on my wolf, it's got me feeling very predatory."

"Oh goodness, I should go home. I'm causing trouble. I'm sorry," Rain said, standing, and Skye gently pulled her back down. She'd noticed the little dust-ups and dominance displays when she was around and all the women had explained it was normal behavior and the males all seemed to work around it but it made her feel bad that she was the cause.

"No, lamb, don't. Andreas was the same, actually worse I think, when Kari was pregnant the last time. Even calm and collected Sean was a snarling fool when Emma was pregnant. It comes with the territory." He stroked his hands up and down her arms to calm her and it worked.

Laurent hugged Ryan then and reached out to touch Rain to comfort and reassure her but their fire flared and Andreas groaned.

"Enough! Kari won't be home for hours."

Rain, laughing, got up and took her leave before she jumped on Laurent again.

Still, as the weeks wore on Laurent became worse and Rain got hornier and grumpier, especially as her due date came and went without any sign that the baby was ready to be born.

The quarterly Gathering arrived and the lodge filled to bursting with celebrating wolves. The moon was full and high and the air was festive. Rain was on the couch, sitting with Emma, who had grown into her dearest friend. Perri and Skye sat across from them and Phillip, the dearest wolf ever, massaged Rain's sore and swollen feet. Emma stroked through Rain's hair rhythmically with a brush and Skye and Perri told stories to amuse her and to try to keep her mind off her discomfort.

Laurent came into the room from outside and saw the group. Growling, he stalked toward them, his wolf shimmering toward the surface. Skye and Phillip backed off, both being lesser males and also knowing that showing any dominance in the face of how Laurent was reacting would only cause a fight.

Rain, feeling grumpy and annoyed, got to her feet and into Laurent's face. "Knock it off for god's sake, Laurent! This is ridiculous."

"Their hands were all over you!" he growled more than shouted.

"On my *feet*! My swollen feet. This isn't *Pulp Fiction*, Laurent. A man can massage a woman's feet without fucking her on the side. Perri had been massaging the muscles of my lower abdomen where *your* baby is pushing against and causing me pain a few minutes ago, are you going to rumble with her too? In case you hadn't noticed there are at least twenty people in the room, Laurent. What did you think was going to happen?"

"I could have done that," he responded, trying to get himself under control.

"But you didn't. You were out on a run instead while I was stuck here. Did you have a nice time, Laurent? Running free and easy while I was beached in here, sore and *huge* as I gestated for you? How dare you come in here after that, looking relaxed and give me shit about getting a foot rub!"

"Rain, you're spilling sex all over the place!" Laurent took her hands, kissing them.

"Oh for goodness' sake! It's not the first time a pregnant female has done it, it's a common thing. Generations of wolves have dealt with it just fine. So just stuff a sock in ...OUCH!" She bent over, yanking her hands away and grabbing her stomach.

"Baby? What's wrong?" Spat forgotten immediately, Laurent grabbed her arm and helped her back down to the couch.

"Damn it! This hurts!" she said, gasping.

Emma smiled and put her hands on Rain's stomach. "A contraction. Let's watch and see what happens. It might be time to have that baby. I know it was time to end that stupid fight."

Laurent grinned and then looked sheepishly at Skye and Phillip who shrugged and smiled at him. He knelt in front of Rain and held her hand, stroking a thumb across her knuckles to calm her.

She was breathing normally again and had relaxed. Kari rushed in with Andreas. "Is it time?"

"It seems to have stopped. Oh. My. God!" Rain yelled and doubled over again. "Laurent," she gasped out. "I want to go and lie down."

"Emma?" Laurent asked.

"Let's get her to your house. The room we've prepared to deliver in is all ready, if it's time we can deliver, if not she can get some rest."

Andreas went out to grab the cart. Laurent helped Rain to stand and then she doubled over again. He picked her up and Emma nodded to Kari, "It's time I think. Can you run and get Elaine or if she's not around, Ellen? Bring them to the house." Kari nodded and went out the back door.

They quickly went back to their house and Laurent carried Rain to the second floor bedroom that they'd prepared for the home birth. Anna and Jade came in and helped get Rain into a front-opening gown for the labor and delivery. Emma scrubbed her hands and felt Rain's abdomen. "Head down it feels like. Good. Now I need to check you and see how dilated you are. I won't lie, it's going to hurt but I'll be as quick as I can. Just try to relax as much as you can and try to remember to breathe." Emma put on gloves and checked Rain, who moaned in pain.

"Honey, you're at six centimeters. You have a ways to go. Let's get you walking, all right? It will help with the pain and keep the labor progressing."

"Fuck that! I want drugs," she screamed as another contraction hit and her water broke. "Gah, what the hell *is* that? Gross."

"Good, Rain! Your bag of waters just ruptured. You should move along faster now," Emma said, ignoring the request for painkillers, their metabolisms rendered them useless anyway.

Elaine and Ellen came into the room and got scrubbed and prepared. Laurent walked with Rain all around the second floor. Rain labored on for another six hours and she was still only at seven centimeters.

"What? Six hours for one centimeter? At this rate I won't have this child for months!"

Laurent rubbed the small of her back by rolling a tennis ball over it. Ryan, Andreas, Skye, Phillip, Alek, Sean and Devon had all arrived as well and everyone took turns walking, massaging and soothing Rain.

Exhausted and at the end of her rope, Rain slumped back on the bed, refusing to walk another step. "Laurent, I can't do this. Honestly. Take me to a hospital and do a C-Section. Cut this baby out of me. Please," she begged him.

"*Mon coeur*, you'll be all right. You're at nine centimeters, you'll be pushing soon and then we'll have Grace or Philippe in our arms. You can do this, baby, you have to. You survived a bullet, you can do this," he urged her.

"Which one of us has a baby pressing down on her pelvic floor?" Rain snarled. "I can do it? *You* do it! Your heart my ass. You made me this way, Laurent." She continued to mutter and Emma tried not to laugh.

"Into the shower with you, Rain. It'll help, I promise." Emma shooed Rain and Laurent into the bathroom.

After standing in the shower under the hot spray until the water cooled over and over, Rain walked back toward the bedroom and suddenly an agonizing pressure brought a gasp from her lips as she bore down to relieve it. *Only, was that the head?* "Oh my goodness, Laurent, the baby, it's coming out!"

Laurent picked her up and ran into the room, waking up everyone in the process.

Ellen ordered Anna and Jade to prop pillows up behind her back. "Oh yeah, that's the head all right. Okay, Laurent, you get this leg, Skye, you get the other, push back and give her a counterpoint to push against. Rain, sweetheart, you're not only ready but the head's crowning right this second. On the next contraction I want you to take a deep breath in and bear down, count to ten, suck in a breath and push again. All right?"

Rain nodded. Andreas, Phillip, Ryan, Alek, Perri, Devon and Sean were all in the room, sharing the moment. The contraction came and Rain did as she was told and in one push the baby was out and the pain evaporated.

"After twenty hours of labor you push twice and the baby is born," Kari said with a huge grin.

"A baby girl. Here, sweetheart, nuzzle up to your momma," Emma said, smiling. She placed the wrapped-up bundle on Rain's chest and Rain felt the shock of recognition rush through her. Her daughter. She and Laurent made this tiny, precious gift.

Pursed pink lips rooted as big, wide blue eyes stared up into Rain's. She brought the baby to her breast and she latched on the second try and both Rain and the baby relaxed.

"Grace Karin Cole, welcome to the world," Rain crooned. Laurent beamed at his women and stroked a finger over the shock of black troll-doll hair on that sweet-smelling head. "Ah,

Rain, baby, you've given me the best gift. She's perfect," he whispered, kissing Grace and then Rain.

Skye kissed them both as well. "This is the fourth birth I've been lucky enough to witness. Thank you both so much for sharing it with me."

"Ah, another life come to the Cherchez Clan. Rain and Laurent, you've honored Kari and me. Grace, your Alphas welcome you to this world," Andreas said in a gentle rumble and stroked the tiny back of the bundle at Rain's breast. "Almost makes me wish for another baby," he said wistfully.

"Almost," cracked Kari who shoved the big men aside and kissed Rain's forehead and then baby Grace.

"Another reason to change Pack culture," Rain said to Kari and Emma.

Laurent groaned and gave a wry grin in Andreas' direction. "Only you, my love, would start talking revolution less than five minutes after giving birth. I love you."

"It's my job, Laurent. Our daughter deserves as much of a chance as a son would have. And I love you too but I'm not going to do this again for a while."

Laurent chuckled and Emma shooed everyone out of the room so Rain, Grace and Laurent could be alone.

Laurent carried Rain, who held Grace, downstairs to their room and they settled into the big bed with Grace between them, tiny and sleeping. Laurent's hair was loose around his shoulders as he gazed down at his daughter and back up into his Mate's face. He caressed the line of her jaw. "We've got quite a future ahead of us, *mon amour*. I for one can't wait."

Rain smiled and looked down at the tiny bundle, the combination of their genes, of their love. She ran a finger over the clasped fist, the skin as smooth as velvet. "Me either."

Also by Lauren Dane

ॐ

eBooks:
Ascension
Cascadia Wolves 1: Enforcer
Cascadia Wolves 2: Tri Mates
Fire and Rain
Reluctant
Sudden Desire
Sword and Crown
Witches Knot: Threat of Darkness
Witches Knot 1: Triad
Witches Knot 2: A Touch of Fae
Witches Knot 3: Vengeance Due
Witches Knot 4: Thrice United
Witches Knot 5: Celebration for the Dead

Print Books:
Cascadia Wolves 1: Enforcer
Cascadua Wolves 2: Tri Mates
Crown and Blade *(anthology)*
Feral Fascination *(anthology)*
Sexy Summer Fun *(anthology)*
Witches Knot 1: Triad
Witches Knot 2: A Touch of Fae
Witches Knot 3: Vengeance Due
Witches Knot 4: Thrice United

About the Author

∞

Lauren Dane has been writing stories since she was able to use a pencil, and before that she used to tell them to people. Of course, she still talks nonstop, and through wonderful fate and good fortune, she's now able to share what she writes with others. It's a wonderful life!

The basics: Lauren is a mom, a partner, a best friend and a daughter. Living in the rainy but beautiful Pacific Northwest, she spends her late evenings writing like a fiend when she finally wrestles all of her kids to bed.

∞

The author welcomes comments from readers. You can find her website and email address on her author bio page at www.ellorascave.com.

Tell Us What You Think

We appreciate hearing reader opinions about our books. You can email us at Comments@EllorasCave.com.

Why an electronic book?

We live in the Information Age—an exciting time in the history of human civilization, in which technology rules supreme and continues to progress in leaps and bounds every minute of every day. For a multitude of reasons, more and more avid literary fans are opting to purchase e-books instead of paper books. The question from those not yet initiated into the world of electronic reading is simply: *Why?*

1. ***Price.*** An electronic title at Ellora's Cave Publishing runs anywhere from 40% to 75% less than the cover price of the exact same title in paperback format. Why? Basic mathematics and cost. It is less expensive to publish an e-book (no paper and printing, no warehousing and shipping) than it is to publish a paperback, so the savings are passed along to the consumer.

2. ***Space.*** Running out of room in your house for your books? That is one worry you will never have with electronic books. For a low one-time cost, you can purchase a handheld device specifically designed for e-reading. Many e-readers have large, convenient screens for viewing. Better yet, hundreds of titles can be stored within your new library—on a single microchip. There are a variety of e-readers from different manufacturers. You can also read e-books on your PC or laptop computer. (Please note that Ellora's Cave does not endorse any specific brands.

You can check our website at www.ellorascave.com for information we make available to new consumers.)

3. *Mobility.* Because your new e-library consists of only a microchip within a small, easily transportable e-reader, your entire cache of books can be taken with you wherever you go.

4. *Personal Viewing Preferences.* Are the words you are currently reading too small? Too large? Too... ANNOYING? Paperback books cannot be modified according to personal preferences, but e-books can.

5. *Instant Gratification.* Is it the middle of the night and all the bookstores near you are closed? Are you tired of waiting days, sometimes weeks, for bookstores to ship the novels you bought? Ellora's Cave Publishing sells instantaneous downloads twenty-four hours a day, seven days a week, every day of the year. Our webstore is never closed. Our e-book delivery system is 100% automated, meaning your order is filled as soon as you pay for it.

Those are a few of the top reasons why electronic books are replacing paperbacks for many avid readers.

As always, Ellora's Cave welcomes your questions and comments. We invite you to email us at Comments@ellorascave.com or write to us directly at Ellora's Cave Publishing Inc., 1056 Home Avenue, Akron, OH 44310-3502.

MAKE EACH DAY MORE *EXCITING* WITH OUR

ELLORA'S
CAVEMEN
CALENDAR

WWW.ELLORASCAVE.COM

ELLORA'S CAVE
Romanticon

Annual convention
for women who
refuse to behave

Discover for yourself why readers can't get enough
of the multiple award-winning publisher

Ellora's Cave.

Whether you prefer e-books or paperbacks,

be sure to visit EC on the web at
www.ellorascave.com

for an erotic reading experience that will leave you
breathless.

CPSIA information can be obtained at www.ICGtesting.com
Printed in the USA
LVOW100725111011

249996LV00001B/6/P